A BETTER MAN

Audrey Lynn

ISBN: 0615449689
ISBN-13: 9780615449685
Library of Congress Control Number: 2011928166

Iskra: (ee' · skra) Russian, meaning spark.

From a spark, a fire will flare up.

Vladimir Odoevsky
Russian Philosopher

For Zoe Markell and Roman Arthur.
May you always have an Iskra.

Tchaikovsky Conservatory

MOSCOW, RUSSIA, SOVIET UNION

February 1980

Konstantin Verstakov tucked his prized Stradivarius violin into his ribs and bowed to the packed audience. Another performance of Tchaikovsky's Concerto in D, done, without fail. He smiled, waved to the audience, and took another bow. As he did so, the Makarov pistol in his left pocket brushed against his thigh. *This will be perfect*, he thought, standing up to full height.

To much applause, the entire orchestra stood up, bowed, and exited stage left. Konstantin went right. As if it were the tiniest of babies, he gently handed over the Stradivarius to Ivan, the scruffy stage manager. "After tonight, I want my nephew, Vladimir, to have this," Konstantin said over the bubbling crowd. "He's sixteen. Lives in Sverdlovsk."

Ivan looked at him quizzically, but the cheering audience stole his attention away. "This place is about to erupt, Verstakov, all because of you," he said, shaking his head. "Shit, I'd give my right nut to be you right now!"

Konstantin turned, headed to the front of the stage where a lone microphone awaited on its stand. He brushed the outside of his pocket as he walked, felt the pistol one more time. *This will be perfect.*

The lights went dark as he stepped up to the mic. A single spotlight clicked overhead, surrounding him in a cone of warm, yellow light. A hushed, yet vibrant silence swept over the audience. From it, a female voice called out, "I love you Konstantin!"

Konstantin's lips lightly brushed against the microphone. In his signature voice, *gritty yet soulful*, as one music critic wrote, *Deep, rich, and robust, much like a fine red wine,* wrote another, Konstantin began the Soviet national anthem a capella. Just as he had done countless times before.

> *"Unbreakable union of freeborn Republics*
> *Great Rus has welded forever to stand.*
> *Created in struggle by will of the people,*
> *United and mighty, our Soviet land."*

Normally this would be the time to launch into the powerful chorus in which everyone would take part and wave their hands overhead in a show of Soviet pride. But Konstantin stopped, leaving an uneasy silence in his wake. He took a heavy breath and said into the mic, "Been doing this nineteen years. Sorry, I can't do this anymore."

Like the theatrical showman he'd always wanted to be, Konstantin paused to light a cigarette, allowing the tension to simmer.

"I wanted to play the guitar," he said calmly into the mic. "But the Commie bastards didn't approve." He took a drag off the cigarette. "Even threatened to kick me out of the symphony if I didn't cut my hair."

Amidst the silence, he took another drag. "Well, I got just one thing to say to that."

He cupped the mic with both hands. The cigarette smoldered between his fingers, smoke hovered around his eyes as he bluntly stated, "Rock and roll ain't no crime." With that, he picked up the microphone stand and hurled it stage right. It crash-landed on the steps.

At once, worried men in suits stood up out of their assigned seats. But the bubbling crowd became uncorked. Young people, both crazed by Konstantin's declaration and fed up with the men in suits, pumped their fists and chanted in unison. "Rock and roll ain't no crime! Rock and roll ain't no crime!" They filled the aisles, rushing against the suits, pushing their way to the stage.

Konstantin laughed heartily at the all-out spectacle he'd created. *This will be perfect.* He looked to the left and nodded to the young, extremely eager, sound technician. They'd planned this, the first part anyway, a week ago, and now this kid was no doubt having the single best moment of his Communist-weary life.

The kid ran out with a left-handed, cherry red, Fender electric guitar. As he ran, he tossed the guitar to Konstantin, who slung it low around his hips. Konstantin exhaled a plume of smoke and threw the cigarette to the floor. "I thought we'd do things differently tonight!" he shouted to the cheering crowd at his feet.

The sound technician scurried about, unveiling a wall of amplifiers at stage right. He plugged in the Fender. Smiling, he gave Konstantin two thumbs up.

Konstantin hit a blaring C chord, followed it with a fist in the air to get everyone's attention. Not that he needed it. A single G note on the fifth string, followed by B, C, A, G, G, B, C, A, G, G in rapid fire.

From the final, long, lingering G, he whipped his unruly hair back and launched right into the chorus of the Soviet national anthem. The notes flowed like water. For the first time in years, he was focused, in control, fully content. No amount of vodka could do that anymore; the pills he had been taking for years had never brought about this kind of euphoria.

He closed his eyes and let the music wash over him. *Perfect.*

Wailing on the guitar, he slid down on his knees, feeling soft hands on his face, in his hair. He opened his eyes to see a raven-haired girl with deep red lips blow him a kiss. He smiled at her. As he hit the final notes, he stood up, and walked backwards to stand at center stage.

The sound technician was at the amps, wildly clapping. "Hell, yeah, man. Hell, yeah!"

The men in suits pushed through the crowd at the stage, elbowing past screaming fans. Konstantin unslung the Fender, held it overhead by the neck, and slammed the body to the floor at his feet. Red splinters shattered across the stage to hyper applause. He hurled the neck across the stage.

Konstantin scanned the audience. Half wanted a piece of him; the other half was frantic, trying to put an end to his antics. He held his arms out. *This is perfect.* He threw his head back, drinking in his final moments of life. *Bloody perfect.*

The overhead lights boomed on. Auditorium workers were scrambling at stage right, yanking cords out of the amps. Two security guards were coming up the steps. Konstantin reached into his left pocket, pulled out the Makarov. Just last night, he had traded his amped-up motorcycle for it. He thrust the gun beneath his chin and closed his eyes.

"*Nyet*!" a male voice called out. A frantic young woman, maybe the one with raven hair, called out as well, "Konstantin! No!"

Konstantin pulled the trigger. He fell on his back, seizing, choking on a gush of his own warm blood. Kneeling above him, the security guards blurred together. He flopped his butchered head to the right. The young sound technician had fallen to his knees, his mouth open, his face as white as fallen snow.

As life drained from his body, Konstantin smiled as best he could. *Perfect*.

ELEVEN YEARS LATER

1.

SVERDLOVSK, RUSSIA. SOVIET UNION

I am running like hell.

Hyperventilating, heart pounding, sweat pouring, I am sprinting uphill leaving a trail of gray dust, slipping over shale and skidding around craggy switchbacks; staying low, quick and small despite my size. It's over now; the whole convoy is dead. But I still hear the two blasts. I still hear the gunfire. I still hear the commands. I am running, skidding, darting around, trying to avoid the bodies, both Afghan and Soviet. Mostly Soviet.

The Afghan sun beats down upon my shaved head. Pulsating, severe, relentless is that damn sun. My face feels like leather, the back of my neck is fried. But I don't even feel the heat anymore, nor do I feel panic because I'm beyond that now. Now I am running, trying to survive this minute. Maybe live to see the next. Got my dead captain's AK-47 slung over my left shoulder. No bullets left, but I could bash the butt of this rifle into a mujahid's skull if I had to.

I've already done that once today. So, bring it on. Bring it on.

Around another craggy switchback, I dart left. To my right, splayed out at my feet is Mikhail Astafurov. His legs are blown off, but not cleanly. Ragged flaps of flesh and a mangled mix of tendon and dull muscle hang limply from his hips. His temple is caved in on the right side, a broken bone jets out where his jaw used to be. His hazel eyes are wide open, looking at the sky. I know this is Mikhail Astafurov only because of the gold wedding band hanging around his neck among his dog tags. Otherwise, I would not recognize this contorted man. Earlier today, he casually bummed a cigarette off me while he changed a flat tire. Was that him? Was that today? Yes, that was him. That was today.

Finally, a concrete arch. The Salang Tunnel up ahead. No vehicles in sight; no obvious mujahideen activity. I come to a clumsy halt inside the tunnel, barely remaining upright. The air inside is stagnant, smells like diesel; but thankfully, it's cool and dark. I lean back against the wall, let my head drop back, trying to catch my breath. I pat my chest pocket, pull out a cigarette, then a lighter.

My lips are sunburned; they sting as I stick the cigarette between them. I flick the lighter with my left hand. After one drag my breathing slows, my heart rate steadies. After the second drag, I feel calm. Finally, it is quiet. In an eerie way, there is much peace in the darkness. No more blast. No more gunfire. No more commands.

A distant sound in the sky gets my attention, the familiar whir of a helicopter. It's getting closer. Most likely, it's the Black Tulip coming to remove the Soviet dead. The Black Tulip is working hard these days. It makes a few passes. It lands.

My wife's sparkling voice resonates in my head even louder than the helicopter. "I want to live life." She said that to me on the evening we met. I can't stay in this tunnel because Zhanna is at home, in Russia, waiting for me, and she is everything. She is not giving up. Neither will I.

I hustle out of the tunnel. "Hey! Hey!" I yell, but my voice is gravel. The helicopter is down below, hovering off the ground. I think the pilot sees me, but I'm not sure. I wave my arms overhead. "My name is Vladimir Stepanovich Verstakov!" I run down the hill, coughing, frantically waving. "Hey! Hey! I'm alive! I'm alive! Hey, I'm alive!"

2.

Startled by the harsh memory, Vladimir Verstakov snapped back to reality. His eyes shot open. His body jerked so hard that his head slammed back against the bathroom tile. No longer running for his life along the Salang Pass in Afghanistan, but trying to end his life here, at home in Sverdlovsk, Russia. Must have been four, maybe four-thirty in the morning. The usual time. In the dimly lit bathroom, wedged between the toilet and sink. The usual place. Naked, shivering, knees to chest, thrusting his father's clunky old Makarov beneath his chin. The usual way.

"Why," Vlad whispered between short, labored breaths. He put the gun down on the floor near his hip, dropped his forehead to his knees. "Why did I survive?"

***

"There was a survivor? Wow," says the doctor outside the tent. "That's refreshing, given the goddamn slaughter that's come through here today. Shame about Yurchenko. Good man. Knew him back in officers' training. You have the survivor's file?" A few seconds go by, and then he says, "Verstakov, Vladimir. All right, I'll take a look."

The army doctor walks in through the canvas opening. He looks so smart; file in hand, wearing glasses. He smiles and nods, even takes his beret off. He's trying to make me feel at ease, but the guy looks utterly spent. I can only imagine the bloody mess he has seen today, and what I must look like sitting here on this table. Beat to hell, an ankle swollen to the size of a balloon. Can't hear much but blast, gunfire, commands. Can hardly talk over the noise. He's asking me questions but I barely respond. Too much noise.

The doctor checks my eyes with a little light that looks like a pen, takes my blood pressure, asks me to take several deep breaths as he listens to my lungs. He wraps a bandage around my ankle. Tells me to stay off it. Another bandage above my eye, a few stitches. Afterwards, he slaps me on the back and says I must be the strongest soldier he's ever seen. It's amazing how I survived such a brutal attack. The sole survivor. A real hero.

I shrug it off by saying, "Nah, I'm no hero. I just ran like hell, man. Like bloody hell!" We chuckle as men do, but I start coughing. It hurts to cough. Hurts to do anything. Everything hurts.

He gives me a bottle of pills for the pain. Little white pills. Tells me I can get more if I need them. Even when I get back to Russia, just go to the pharmacy and show my military ID. I thank him. I know I'm talking too loud, but the noise, it's too much.

***

Vladimir again shook the memory away, hating himself and this mess he'd become. The turmoil inside his head had started out benign, a little crankiness here and there during the first few months home. Zhanna fully understood and catered to his every need so as to make the smoothest transition possible from battlefield to home. Everything was fine, a delicate balance at times, yet fine. But six months ago, the noise returned out of nowhere. *Blast. Gunfire. Commands. Blast. Gunfire. Commands.* The vivid flashbacks came along for the ride.

Now, every minute detail played out clearer, more vivid with each passing day. Afghanistan and Russia meshing together; present and past, all one eternal loop. Discerning the past from real time was perhaps the most difficult, and getting more confusing every day. Loading the supply truck, or helping Zhanna put away the laundry? An AK-47 violently shoved in his face, or a screwdriver handed over at work on the construction site? The light whistle of a teakettle, or the sound of an exploding land mine? As each day passed, it was getting harder to know the difference.

The graphic memories were one thing; somewhat manageable by themselves. But the chaotic noise was something else entirely. First came a high-pitched whine followed by a deafening blast, another whine layered on top, and then the second deafening blast: two land mines detonating in quick succession, ripping apart a fine soldier. Soon after the blasts came the syncopated *rat-tat-tat* of AK-47 gunfire from all around, and through it all, the succinct commands of Captain Yurchenko, *"Return fire! Repeat, return fire! Go! Go! Go!"*

The noise never stopped. *Blast. Gunfire. Commands. Blast. Gunfire. Commands.* That one day in Afghanistan played like a record forever broken. *Blast. Gunfire.*

Commands...during morning tea. *Blast. Gunfire. Commands*...at work. *Blast. Gunfire. Commands*...while making love to Zhanna. *Blast. Gunfire. Commands*...here, with a gun, on the bathroom floor.

Vladimir picked up the gun. Turned it over and studied it. A twelve-year-old Makarov, once belonging to his father. Nothing fancy. Heavy and horribly inaccurate at a distance, but it would get the job done. One shot and there would be no more memories. One shot and there would be no more guilt. One shot and there would finally be rest. One shot would make it right, the way it was supposed to be. A warm sense of relief swept over him knowing the noise could be turned off and the images shut down permanently with one pull of the trigger, the gun gave him hope. The hope being there wouldn't be a future; that this hell would end.

Just then, loud knocking on the door followed by frantic turns of the knob. "Viva?" came a hurried but sleepy voice. It was Zhanna. Most likely, she was standing there shivering in her thigh-length, red T-shirt and nothing else, because in all her worry, she jumped out of bed, forgetting to grab her bathrobe or slippers. She probably had her forehead to the door, looking down to her pink-painted toes. "Viva. Baby, are you okay?" she asked, knocking again.

Vlad clumsily dropped the pistol. The barrel made a heavy, dull sound as it hit the linoleum floor, so loud that he had to cover his ears. *Blast*.

Zhanna knocked again, three frantic times in a row. "Viva?" *Gunfire*.

"Please, Viva, just unlock the door. Let me help you." *Commands*.

Enemy approaching, time for battle. Vlad swiped the pistol off the floor and screamed, "Get the hell away from me!" He hurled the pistol toward the door where it hit with a solid thud before it crashed to the floor. The thud exploded inside his head. He sat there on the linoleum struggling to take a breath while his body shook from the noise.

Zhanna stayed silent. For months, they'd been through countless nights just like this one. Her fingernails tapped lightly against the door, her voice remained stable. "I love you, Vladimir. You know that, don't you? I love you and I need you." She slid down to the floor and leaned her strawberry-blonde head against the door, a sound he'd heard many times. "There are a lot of people who love you." She said, stifling tears. "Oleg calls a lot. Guess he got tired of waiting for you to call him back, so he came by the beauty shop the other day for a haircut."

She gave a fragile laugh and started rambling as she always did when nervous.

"You should have seen him, that big brute of a hockey player sitting in the waiting area with all those little old ladies. He had an appointment, but once he sat down in my chair, he said he didn't want his hair cut, just wanted to ask if you were okay. He says you barely make eye contact with him at work anymore. Baby, I've never known Oleg to have much emotional depth, but he was upset. He wants to know why you no longer play darts with the guys on Wednesdays. You two used to have such a good time at Wednesday night darts, remember?"

Another nervous laugh, then she said, "I cut his hair anyway. Gave him a good conditioning treatment, too. He really needed it; he looks much better."

She went quiet for a moment, then went on. "Your mother and Stepan have been calling, too. Your mother has a poetry reading next week. Stepan thought it would be nice to get together beforehand, have a light supper. He's worried because he hasn't talked to you for a while. I can't keep making excuses. He knows exactly what I'm doing."

A long pause. Zhanna sniffed and exhaled. "Viva, I need you, too. Please come out and talk to me. Don't give up, baby, because I'm trying real hard not to. Please. I don't know how much more of this I can ta—" She couldn't finish, her voice halted by tears.

Vlad said nothing in return. Couldn't, really. Hot tears choked his throat, filled his eyes. Wednesday night darts with Oleg and the guys; that was a lot of fun, but so long ago. Mother and her poetry, Stepan and his desire to make everything copasetic. But there was no going back, not after Afghanistan. One by one, fat tears trickled down his face. He heard Zhanna finally stand up and pad back to the bedroom.

He quickly wiped away the tears because Vladimir, whose very name means "the ruling one," reflected his given name perfectly. Standing just over one hundred and ninety centimeters, weighing in at a solid one hundred kilograms, a cool twenty-seven years of age. Dark mahogany hair coupled with bright, Slavic green eyes and highly defined cheekbones; he easily commanded attention everywhere he went. Vlad worked hard, played hard; he kept his friends close and his wife satisfied. Men such as Vladimir are born with the heartiest of Russian souls. They do not need help, and they sure as hell do not cry.

He managed to stand up. At the sink, he leaned forward on his open palms to see a tired reflection staring back. His eyes, once so bright that his mother had described them as "two fields of grass, kissed by the morning dew, sparkling like mighty emeralds under the brilliant Slavic sun," now looked dull. There was no sign of the energetic young man he had been only two years ago.

Ever since the army shaved it all off, his hair had grown back more of a rich, warm, brown as opposed to the light, airy chestnut color it had been prior to deployment. Thick and full of volume, if it grew past his earlobes, his hair became an unruly mess. Zhanna usually kept it clipped short, but lately she hadn't broached the subject of Vlad's unruly locks. Couldn't blame her. Given his erratic behavior, it was best not to push too hard.

Three days' worth of dark stubble sprinkled with gray heavily dotted his chin, spreading up his ruddy cheeks. Zhanna positively detested stubble, but again, lately she had not bothered reminding him to shave.

Vladimir pulled open the left drawer and watched as the plastic bottle of painkillers rolled to a stop. The usual five pills no longer brought on sleep, so he spilled seven into his palm. A bottle of vodka stood beneath the sink where he'd stashed it. He popped the pills into his mouth and took a good swig from the bottle. Fistfuls of pills combined with hefty swigs of vodka now the therapeutic routine.

A square hand towel lay folded by his side, a dull white, but embellished with a yellow satin flower at the edge. Yellow satin flowers sewn onto the dull, state-made towels—just one of Zhanna's many efforts to make the standard Soviet-issue apartment a real home. Yellow was all over the apartment because it was her favorite color. She was perfect. The last thing he wanted to do was hurt his wife. He patted his brow with the towel.

With a head of fog and a chest made of concrete, Vlad shuffled back to the bedroom, where he stopped at the dresser and placed the pistol back in the top drawer under a stack of folded shirts. A pair of eyeglasses lay there, too. He brought out the glasses and held them up to the window, where a three-quarters moon illuminated them. The frame was bent; a faded smudge of blood marred the right lens. The left lens had a distinct crack in it. He stared at the damaged glasses as the noise crept in. *Blast. Gunfire. Commands. Blast. Gunfire. Commands.*

Vlad placed the glasses back in the drawer and slid it closed. He turned around, lifted the covers of the double bed. At first, Zhanna denied his presence, pushing against his chest, but soon her entire body relaxed in his arms as she nuzzled into his chest and said, "I can feel your heart."

Vlad rested his chin atop Zhanna's head and stroked her hair. Long ribbons, like warm vanilla. "I hate this, Zha-Zha. I hate this," he whispered with gravel in his voice. Zhanna reached up, placed her hand on his cheek. He kissed the top of her head and closed his eyes only to be greeted by an endless barrage of noise and bloody images.

***

I am running like hell.

Hyperventilating, heart pounding, sweat pouring. Trying to avoid the bodies, both Afghan and Soviet. Mostly Soviet.

***

Vladimir thrashed around, falling in and out of a noisy sleep.

***

Got my dead captain's AK-47.

"Hey, I'm alive, I'm alive!"

I am running like hell. I am running like hell. I am running like hell.

***

The noise became too loud for sleep. He rolled over, lit a cigarette, lay back down, and stared at the ceiling. *This is hell.*

3.

19 January

One by one, the eight floodlights out in the courtyard boomed on, filling the dark January morning with streams of harsh, yellow light. Vladimir jerked and opened his eyes. The booms sounded like land mines.

Their bedroom was a square, barely three meters by three meters, covered in pale golden wallpaper with a dizzying white-and-green floral design. Their double bed, flanked by two pine tables Vladimir had built himself, made a T against one wall. A sixties-era lamp with a short, bulbous base of amber-colored glass stood on each bedside table. A flimsy, four-drawer dresser stood across Vlad's side of the bed. The dresser and squeaky metal bed came standard with their state-issued apartment, as did the gas stove in the kitchen and the old brown couch in the alcove off the kitchen. A very nice, modern, full-length mirror framed in wrought iron hung on the wall alongside the dresser. The mirror was payment from their neighbors, Sergei and Maria for building them a sturdy bookshelf.

Across the foot of the bed, a small, open closet housed Vladimir's one pair of nice slacks and two dress shirts. The rest was jammed packed with Zhanna's clothes. On the floor of the closet lay at least eight pairs of her shoes, all high heels, all ridiculously expensive, and all bought off the black market.

This morning, shadows danced along the ceiling and walls as the dim sun filtered through the curtain. The light somehow seemed brighter this morning, more harsh than usual. Vlad closed his eyes, trying to avoid the uncomfortable light, but there was no getting away from it.

***

The sun is not yet high, but already stifling hot as I step outside the mess hall. I have to squint. August in Afghanistan and it's hotter than hell.

At our morning briefing, Captain Yurchenko warned the temperature will most likely reach fifty degrees today, so be sure to drink our entire water ration and keep our berets on. And he told us to wear our sunglasses too, those of us lucky enough to have them.

Fifty degrees. Did he say that right? Fifty degrees. Is that Celsius? Of course it is. Fahrenheit would make it sound even worse. Bloody hell, it is going to be a ridiculous fifty goddamn degrees today. How can anyone live like this? Maybe that's why these Muslims are so temperamental; they're all crazy from the heat.

As I walk along base, immediately my feet sweat inside my bulky, black leather combat boots. These camouflage pants are heavy. I pull my camouflage jacket on and button it up over my white T-shirt so the sun doesn't burn my arms. My name is sewn in black onto the left chest pocket, V. S. Verstakov. I stick a cigarette between my lips, stop to light it.

My entire company is out here, busy, getting ready to move out. The air is a mixture of motor oil and sweat. I hear a wrench clanging against metal; men are shouting, some are cursing. Music is playing somewhere. It's the Scorpions' "Rock You Like a Hurricane," I can see the platoon so clearly. These are my guys. They are alive. Right here, right now, everyone is alive.

***

"Everyone's dead. Everyone's dead," Vladimir mumbled as he recoiled from the memory. But it wouldn't go away. With a gasp, he jerked into a sitting position. "Everyone's dead!" Chest heaving, heart pounding, noise ripping through his head like a freight train. *Blast. Gunfire. Commands. Blast. Gunfire. Commands.*

Vlad turned toward the bedside table where he kept an extra supply of the little white pills. Perhaps another two pills would take the edge off, quiet the noise. He rifled around in the dim light. A bottle of vodka, with just a splash left, lay near the bed. He finished off the vodka, but the pills were gone. "Bloody hell!" He threw the plastic bottle across the room where it hit the wall. Instantly, the memory struck again, even more vividly than before.

***

My men. They are alive. Right here, right now, everyone is alive.

***

"They're all dead!" He yelled, the noise growing louder. *Blast. Gunfire. Commands. Blast. Gunfire. Commands.* He swung both legs over the edge of the bed and sat, shivering, foggy head in hands.

4.

A soft, graceful hand with long, glossy, pink fingernails snaked up around Vlad's shoulder. "It's just another nightmare," Zhanna said, attempting to catch her breath. Her voice softened a bit, as did her grip. "Baby, come back to bed. It's okay now. You're okay."

Vladimir looked at his right shoulder, placed his hand over hers. Zhanna could not physically keep him from standing up, nor could she keep him from getting more pills and vodka, but he wished she could, so he allowed her to keep him in place. She was a distant mooring, he the buoy, bobbing along, slowly cutting away.

Zhanna scooted forward, rose to her knees, and clutched Vlad's chest. Her fleshy thighs warm on either side of his back. her half-naked body forming a safe barrier from the *Blast. Gunfire. Commands. Blast. Gunfire. Commands.* She nestled her lips close to his temple and whispered, "Please, baby, just come back to bed. You need to rest."

Vlad muttered a weak, "Yeah, okay," before collapsing into Zhanna's soft, curvy body. She fell sideways, struggling under Vlad's weight and sheer length to gather his legs and bring them around. But she never took her eyes away from his, never let him go. She kept her hand behind his head until it came to rest on the pillow. "Try to relax, baby. Breathe. Just breathe," she said.

Vladimir nodded, still unable to stop his heaving chest.

Long shiny ribbons of strawberry blonde hair brushed against Vlad's chin as Zhanna moved her hand up to his forehead. "Viva, you're burning up. I'll go get you some water." But she hesitated, looking around the room, most likely hoping a glass of water was already close. Leaving Vladimir alone was not a good idea; she had learned that lesson months ago. She could come back to find him gone, locked in the bathroom again.

Feeling Zhanna's burden and hating himself for it, Vlad took her hand and said, "No, Zha-Zha, don't get up. I'm fine."

Zhanna sat up against the wooden headboard. Small tears leaked from her chocolate eyes. "I miss you, Viva. I miss us."

Vladimir slowly propped himself up on his right side, rubbed the inside of her thigh. "Please don't talk like that, Zha-Zha." Immediately, he felt like a child pulling at the hem of his mother's apron. At exactly what point along the way had he become such a needy mess? And at exactly what point along the way had Zhanna decided to give over all of herself to care for such a pathetic excuse for a man?

Zhanna's tears grew bigger. "But we can't keep living like this. You need help." Trembling, pinching the inside corners of her eyes, her voice weak, this was Zhanna as Vladimir had never seen her, truly and utterly defeated. He put his head down, resting his cheek against her satin thigh.

After a lifetime of dead silence, Zhanna ran her fingers through Vlad's hair. "It's getting shaggy again," she said. "I can probably trim it this evening."

Vladimir nodded, his check rubbing against her thigh. "Yeah, I could use a trim."

She took a breath and rambled. "I have to work for most of the day today. I've canceled so many appointments lately that my regulars were starting to balk, so I opened the books for Saturday. They all jumped on it. Oy, you'd think I was the only hairstylist in town. The nice thing about those old ladies is they always pay in American dollars. Most shops won't even take rubles anymore." She let out a timid laugh. "You should hear my dad go on about Gorbachev's reforms. *Perestroika* will bring great economic prosperity to Russia, he says, except, of course, we will starve to death. He doesn't think much of Yeltsin's plans, either." She again laughed nervously. "But do you think you'll be okay here by yourself?" she finally asked. That, of course, was her real concern, the real reason for the rambling.

Vlad nodded. "Yeah, don't worry. I'll be fine."

Zhanna inhaled and kept talking. "I was hoping you could go to the butcher shop today. See if they have any calf's feet so I can make *kholodets*. We can't be too picky. Buy whatever you can. We have some American dollars; make sure the clerk sees that. I'll pack you a snack because I know the line will be long. If there is any money left, try to find some fruit. Tangerines, maybe. Sergei said there weren't any in the stores but Maria bought some from a street vendor; you'll have to ask, though."

She took another breath. "There I go again. I'm talking too much, aren't I?" Another nervous laugh.

Vladimir lifted his head off Zhanna's thigh and smiled in an attempt to make her feel more at ease. "I'll be fine, Zha-Zha. Really, just standing in line should take hours. And I'll find tangerines, too. Go to work, don't worry." He reached up, touched his wife's face. "And you know I love your voice. You should talk as much as you wish."

Zhanna allowed Vlad's hand to rest on her cheek, even laid her own hand over his.

He pressed his lips to hers. Her tears transferred to his cheeks as he released slightly and whispered, "It's going to be all right. Don't give up. Please, don't give up." He kissed her lips until her tears dried. Her breath gradually deepened. With each kiss, her body relaxed a little bit more. Eventually she wrapped her arms around his neck. "I really hate you sometimes," she said, bringing one bare leg over his hip.

Vlad firmly held her hips and rolled over onto his back. "I know, Zha-Zha. I hate myself, too." Zhanna rode him deeply, deliberately, all the while keeping her chocolate eyes locked onto his. With quiet intent, they went on, sweating, breathing hard under the covers until she melted into his body. Her hair a wild, sexy, mess, Zhanna gingerly pushed herself up. "What is it about you, Viva? Every part of my brain tells me to get out of this, but I can't. You've got a pull on me that I can't resist. Scary thing is, I don't even want to resist."

Zhanna sat on the edge of the bed, gathered her hair. She abruptly covered her mouth as her body jerked forward. "Whoa, I feel woozy," she said, steadying herself. She shook it off, stood up, and reached for her robe. "Anyway, would you like some tea?" she asked, looking over her bare shoulder.

Vlad sat up and brought his legs over the edge of the bed. "I'll make the tea. Come back to bed and rest."

Zhanna secured the belt of her robe while padding across the room. "No, no. I'm fine." She said, crossing the hall to the kitchen, a distance of less than two meters, to prepare the morning tea. On her way, she paused to flip on the light, which immediately turned into an Afghan sun.

***

I stop, reach into my left chest pocket to fetch my new sunglasses. At last, no more squinting. They are a cool black with silver, reflective lenses. Won them last night after a game of poker with Captain Yurchenko and a few others. Cleaned everyone out, even the great captain himself. Got plenty of cigs now, a stack of cash, and oh, how I love these shades. Hell, I might as well be a rock star.

To the right, I nod to First Officer Mikhail Astafurov. He's in the middle of changing a tire but he stands up, walks toward me with a greasy pry bar in his hand. He asks if he can bum a cigarette off me. "Sure, man," I say and dig into my chest pocket. Pretty sure these cigs used to be his anyway before I laid down that royal flush. Mikhail is average height for a man, a bit on the chunky side. He's maybe twenty-seven or twenty-eight. His eyes are dark, very big, with bushy eyebrows that are black. His hair is black, too; what's left of it. He's got his gold wedding band mixed in with his dog tags around his neck. I've done the same thing with my wedding band.

Over the past eight months, I've learned that Mikhail grew up in Kirov and Georgia. Parents are divorced; both are remar-

ried with more children. Altogether, he's got eight sisters. Says he plans to have a career with the army, been in since the day after high school graduation. God, I'd run off and join the army too if I had eight sisters.

I hand him a cig then I light it for him. Mikhail takes a drag; he looks up and nods. "Spasiba," he says. He turns around, goes back to the changing the tire.

I approach my assigned vehicle, a black pickup. There are about fifteen wooden crates stacked up next to it. I reach down to pick one up. The aluminum cans inside make a tinny, jingling sound when they hit against each other. I push the crate way back into the bed of the pickup truck. Another wooden crate, this one filled with first-aid supplies, goes in next. One last drag off my cigarette, and I snuff it out under my dusty, black boot. I reach for another crate.

***

Immediately Vladimir opened his eyes, jolted, his heart racing, jumping out of his throat. A heavy chest made breathing difficult, couldn't swallow. Nervous as hell, he wiped the sweat from his brow and shook his head, but the noise remained. *Blast. Gunfire. Commands. Blast. Gunfire. Commands.*

5.

Just as a fresh, spring rain washes out all the dust and grime of the day, Zhanna's voice gradually rose above the noise. "Viva, what would like on your *khlyeb?* We have a little butter left, oh, and I think there is some more of that jam my mother made, or you could have both."

Vladimir snapped back to reality. This was home, not Afghanistan, something he had to keep reminding himself of. "Uh...yeah...babe...Just butter," he replied, trying to sound as if his head had not been back in that godforsaken desert for the past five minutes.

Vladimir stepped to the dresser where he pulled out a pair of Levi's. Size thirty-four by thirty-six with the English word "long" printed after the size. Light, swirled denim, one knee faded, but a good fit. Zhanna had bought the Levi's months ago off a street vendor. He pulled on the jeans and opened the top drawer to take out his favorite hooded sweatshirt. Red, with one wide pocket on the bottom front and the letters CCCP in gold embossed across the chest. As he pulled out the sweatshirt, the damaged eyeglasses fell to the bottom of the drawer. The pistol rattled. Better get rid of it. Later, he thought, and shut the drawer.

A pair of Nike high-tops, technically illegal to have in one's possession, but thanks to the reforms, no longer a punishable offense, sat neatly to the side of the dresser, just below the mirror. He crouched down on his right knee and pulled on the left sneaker. As his heel touched down, the noise returned. *Blast.* Vlad stopped, shook his head. That was loud, louder than before. *Gunfire.* Came out of nowhere. He looked up. The air slowly grew stagnant, restricting. The commands of captain Yurchenko came out of nowhere, "*Get down! Go, go, go! Run like hell!*"

He turned around to look. The light fixture on the ceiling was not a light fixture anymore, but a huge, orange-and-red sun. An Afghan sun. Pulsating. Severe. Relentless. Sweltering heat set in all around. He looked back down to his shoe, but it was not a shoe anymore. Instead it was a bulky, black, army-issue combat boot.

***

We haven't even left yet, five more crates to pack, but already my feet are drenched in sweat within these leather boots. My feet are itchy, burning up. We are supposed to be the greatest superpower the world has ever known, the mighty USSR, the all-powerful Soviet Union, inferior to no other nation. So then, why the hell don't we have socks? A mighty superpower at the very least ought to have socks for its soldiers.

***

Vladimir quickly looked up to his reflection. The sun faded away, leaving just a plain, glass light fixture. He looked back down, just a sneaker, no combat boot. But that short memory was as real as this single moment. The noise grew by the second. *Blast. Gunfire. Commands. Blast. Gunfire. Commands.*

He tried to focus on the normal household sounds, mostly Zhanna's sparkling voice—but to no avail. Now even her voice could not penetrate the noise or the images.

***

I am almost finished loading the crates, two more to go. As I go to pick up another one, I see Captain Yurchenko walking toward me with a clipboard in hand. I promptly put the crate down and salute; he nods back. He's dressed in camouflage, like the rest of us. A few wisps of platinum blond hair poke out from underneath his red beret.

Captain Yurchenko is fit and lean, clean-shaven, thirty-seven years old, not very tall. He's quiet and always serious; I've never seen the guy laugh—he barely even smiles—but he carries with him a calming influence that we all need around here. I heard that back in his younger days, Yurchenko won Russia's National Judo Championship three years in a row. Looking at him now, I believe it.

He looks up and asks if I will have the truck loaded and ready to head out by nine o'clock. I reply with a decisive, "Yes sir." He jots something on his clipboard and says, "Got seven in our convoy. We'll drive up the Salang Pass to Baghlan, drop off the supplies, and stay the night. We'll return in the morning."

Again, I reply with a "Yes sir."

"I want you behind me. Got it?"

I respond, "Yes sir."

Again, he looks down at his clipboard and starts to leave. But he turns around, points to my chest. "And I want a chance to win back my sunglasses, you bastard." He smiles as much as he can smile, which isn't much.

I salute, but I can't help breaking out in a goofy grin even though he is still here in front of me. I am trying so hard not to laugh right now. I cleaned out Captain Yurchenko in poker last night; a great man folded to a lowly foot soldier. Man, it doesn't get any better than that.

***

The teakettle whistled from the kitchen, producing a high-pitched whine. Vlad startled, frantically looking around for the land mine. "Zhanna! Get out of there. Now! It's gonna blow!"

But the whistle stopped. Silence. No explosion. Zhanna called out, "Viva, did you say something?"

Vladimir couldn't respond because the noise was too loud. *Blast. Gunfire. Commands. Blast. Gunfire. Commands.*

6.

"Please, Viva, take these. The smell is making me nauseous." Zhanna came to the door balancing two white saucers, each with a plain white teacup wobbling around on top. On one saucer was a slice of rye toast coated with butter, cut in two so each half rested on either side of the cup. She held both saucers out in front of her body as she walked into the room. "Baby, take these, please."

Vlad couldn't hear through the *Blast. Gunfire. Commands. Blast. Gunfire. Commands.*

Still reeling, he looked up. "What did you say?"

"I'm going to throw up!" she shrieked. The cups wobbled atop their saucers as Zhanna turned her head away from the steam. Liquid spilled down the sides of the cups. "Oy!" she yelled again. "I can't stand the smell. Take these!"

Vlad quickly stood and reached out, ready to grab the two saucers.

But Zhanna stumbled. Toast fell to the floor as the saucer tilted forward. "Oh, no!" she said frantically. Vlad lurched and grabbed the tilting saucer with his left hand, straightening it out. But the other cup fell, spilling tea onto the dingy, white carpet.

A single ordinary moment: a nauseous wife, a stumble, spilled tea. Could happen any day. But everything within that ordinary moment slowed down. To. A. Dead. Stop. Tea landing on carpet. *Blast.* Tiny drops ricocheting off his shoes. *Gunfire*. Zhanna's distant voice. "Oh, no!" *Commands.*

***

Blood is everywhere, splattered on our faces, pooling in the sand. Blood is on my chest, soaking through my shirt. I try to stop the bleeding, but can't. Can't save anyone. Blood is everywhere. Blood is everywhere. All I see is blood.

***

It took a half-second, maybe less, for Vladimir to react. "There's too much blood! I can't save anyone!"

Zhanna went blank, stepped backwards. "Vlad, what are you talking about?" But slowly she turned into a rebel fighter. He wasn't about to let this one get away.

In one swift motion, Vlad heaved the saucer upwards, smashing it hard into Zhanna's face. "Get the hell away from me, terrorist!" The cup broke into three ceramic shards, cutting her forehead, cheek, and upper lip.

With her hands covering her face, she stumbled backwards. Steaming tea mixed with blood dripped down her nose and chin, down along the front of her robe. "Burning! It's burning!" she cried. Frantically she wiped her face with the sleeve of her robe. In full battle mode, he grabbed her left forearm, gave it a twist, and yanked her forward like a rag doll. "Vlad!" she cried, "Baby, please, no!" But Vladimir had already made a fist, plowed it directly into his wife's right eye socket. Her head snapped backwards, hitting the edge of the dresser. She slumped to the floor shrieking, covering her face, trying to protect her head. "Viva! Baby, don't do this!" Zhanna was nothing but blood, tea, and tears.

Blast. Gunfire. Commands. Blast. Gunfire. Commands. No time to think; only react. He whipped around, grabbed the glass lamp off the bedside table, and ripped it out of the outlet. "They're dead! All of 'em!" In one powerful motion, he crashed the lamp into the full-length mirror. Shards of glass rained down on Zhanna, who sat hunkered into a ball, screaming. A few stray shards of glass flew back, gouging his face, but that only intensified the noise.

"Vladimir!" Zhanna cried, clambering up to her knees while guarding her belly. Glass chunks fell out of her hair to the floor. Vladimir shot forward, grabbing a handful of Zhanna's hair, yanked it backward. "We were sent to keep you safe! This is how you thank us? Huh? By waging war on us?" He cried.

Zhanna shrieked, "Nyet!" She tried to break free but to no avail. All she could manage was a weak swipe with her long nails.

Vladimir roughly let go. Her head flopped forward and her body fell onto the pile of broken glass. Zhanna frantically rose up to her hands and knees, crawled toward the door. Not about to let the enemy go, he grabbed her shoulder and flipped her around. "Where do you think you're going?" he yelled. She immediately curled into a fetal position, crying with all the energy she had left. "Viva!"

"Shut up!" he barked, taking a swift kick to her abdomen. Blood immediately spewed forth from her mouth, splattering onto the carpet. She was clutching her belly and crying, "No!"

There came pounding on the front door. Maybe it had been going on for a while, maybe it just started, Vlad had no idea; but it was just another noise that needed to be stopped.

"Vladimir! Zhanna! What's going on in there?" came a distant voice. Sergei the neighbor, or maybe an enemy. "Vladimir!" Sergei yelled. "Vladimir, I've called the police. The police are coming!" More pounding on the door. "The police are on their way! Vladimir! Zhanna! Are you all right? Open up!" Outside, sirens approached, making the noise all the more intense.

"The fuckin' noise!" Vladimir yelled with his hands over his ears. "The noise has to stop!" He turned and yanked open the top dresser drawer so forcefully that it pulled out completely. A pile of shirts flew to the floor, followed by socks. Without haste, he grabbed the pistol, held it up to his temple, and promptly cocked it with his left hand.

Wide-eyed, Zhanna tried to push herself up from the glass, but only flopped back down in a puddle of her own vomit. She held out one hand. "Nyet! Vlad, no!" She turned her battered head around and yelled, "Sergei, quit pounding!" But the physical exertion proved too much; she slumped down again.

The cold steel barrel slipped down his sweaty cheek but he slid it back up again. This time he would do it; he would pull the trigger.

"Baby, don't listen to the noise," Zhanna pleaded, as she pushed up to one hip. "Don't listen to it. Just me. Just listen to me. I'm here. I'm here." She clumsily extended one arm out, focusing on his eyes. "Please Viva, drop the gun. Come here. Drop the gun."

Vladimir let the pistol slide all the way down his face. Hot tears filled his eyes at the sight of Zhanna, bruised and bleeding.

Zhanna kept her eyes on him. "It will be okay, it will be okay, just put the gun down."

The gun shook in his wet grasp. It slipped down to his thumb and forefinger. He kneeled down to her and mumbled, "They came out of nowhere. I'm the only one alive."

Zhanna grew whiter by the second, but she nodded. "I know. Keep talking. It will be okay." Her right eye was already swelling; streaks of blood matted her hair down. The gun slid out of Vlad's grasp to the floor. Zhanna exhaled. "Don't listen to the noise. It's just you and me. Talk to me."

Tears fell from Vlad's eyes as he spoke. "Just a supply mission, that's all. But—"

Within seconds, the front door burst open. Heavy boots stomped down the hallway, the thunder quickly spreading throughout the apartment. Gruff male voices barked, "Police! This is the police!"

The noise returned in an instant, with a harsh vengeance. *Blast. Gunfire. Commands. Blast. Gunfire. Commands.* Vladimir swiped the pistol off the floor and thrust it firmly into the center of Zhanna's forehead.

Zhanna shrieked, "Nyet!"

Blast. Gunfire. Commands. Blast. Gunfire. Commands. Without hesitating one additional second, Vlad pulled the trigger.

7.

The walk to the patrol car was a battle. Flanked by two officers, one middle-aged and burly, the other young, tall and skinny, Vladimir fought hard against the handcuffs. "I killed the rag head!" he screamed. "Just like I was trained, I killed the rag head!" Doors opened a crack. Neighbors emerged from their tiny apartments to see what was happening. Some pointed. Some looked away. Mothers quickly brushed curious children back inside.

Neighbor Sergei, still in his bathrobe, stood next to a police vehicle, gesturing wildly, talking to a uniformed officer who was nodding, jotting notes on a pocket-sized spiral notepad.

An ambulance pulled up, doors flew open, and two compact medics in blue uniforms jumped out, sprinting up the stairs.

"No!" Vlad yelled to the medics, fiercely struggling to free himself. "It's gonna blow! Another land mine! Get out of there now! Get out!" With his head, he bashed the young skinny officer in the ear, easily breaking free of his grasp. But the burly officer kept a solid hold on the other arm, repeatedly jerking him back. Ultimately, Vladimir broke free into a sprint, screaming across the courtyard, "Get away from there! Another mine! There's another mine!"

With both hands restrained, he didn't make it far, only to the first step. He stumbled, landing face-first. "They are all dying," he cried, turning his head to spit out blood and bits of gravel. "They're all dying."

With strained breath, the burly, middle-aged officer was right behind him. He roughly grabbed Vladimir by the hood and yanked him up. The skinny officer, so young he still had a face full of acne, finally made it over, and said, "Land mine? There are no land mines here, you freak."

Vladimir froze, looked around. No desert. No sweltering heat. No land mines. Home. Housing unit number thirty-four. Sverdlovsk. Russia. Soviet Union. Not Afghanistan.

In a flood of chaos, the whole morning came rushing back. Zhanna. Zhanna. Beautiful Zhanna. Beautiful Zhanna bringing in the morning tea, a smile on her face. Beautiful Zhanna in tears, trying to shield her face. Beautiful Zhanna, pleading for her life, her face bruised and bloodied. Beautiful Zhanna, her battered face turned to the side, no longer moving, a bullet in her head.

"Oh God, Zhanna! Zhanna!" Vladimir cried, shaking his head. The burly officer moved to situate himself between his skinny partner and Vladimir, but too late. Vlad slammed half his body into the young officer, who fell hard to the concrete. Vlad fell too, skidding down to his knees. "Zhan–!" Vomit traveling up his throat cut off his voice.

The burly officer grabbed him from behind. "Goddammit," he muttered, and hefted Vlad up under the armpits. Vlad barely made it to standing before throwing up all over the young officer.

8.

Vladimir bounced along as the police vehicle headed toward the station, his wrists cuffed behind his back, his head resting against the frosty window. Zhanna was gone forever, at the hands of the one she loved. Her last moments on earth filled with pain and fear, all because he could not control the noise.

Vladimir had been twenty-three the night he met Zhanna. He, his friend, Oleg Maksimev, and a few other guys from Revolustia Construction were throwing darts at the Red Torch Pub one summer night. Must have been on a Wednesday, because that was the night the guys got together to play darts. Between throws, Vlad and his friends slung back vodka, talked *futbol* scores, and traded construction misadventures. Later in the evening, in a wild flurry of shiny hair, flowery perfume, lip gloss, and laughter, Zhanna walked in with a trio of her friends, celebrating, they so loudly exclaimed, their recent graduation from hair-cutting and styling school.

Dressed in a light denim miniskirt, high-heeled white sandals with laces that wrapped around her ankles, and a denim jacket over a white tank top, she turned and blew Vlad a kiss after she strode past. She was not overly large, but certainly not petite. Plenty of cleavage squeezed up through that tank top; full hips swung side to side within the skirt.

With a cigarette hanging from his mouth, Vlad threw a five, a bull's-eye, and a twenty in quick succession. He finished his turn with a shot of vodka and a quick glance over to Zhanna, who sat in the nearby booth.

The table became hushed, the girls smiling and looking at each other. Slowly, Zhanna scooted herself out and confidently walked over to where Vlad stood. She smiled and wrapped one arm around his neck. Her chin cleared his shoulder only because of the high heels.

With the other hand, she slowly pulled the cigarette from between his lips. "These will give you premature wrinkles, you know," she said with a flirty little smile. She placed the cigarette between her own glossy pink lips and took a long drag. "But hey, what the hell? We only live once, right?"

She ran her hand through his hair, but suddenly scowled, almost offended. "Oy, your hair. It's downright unruly!" She stifled her laughter. "You really need some conditioner!" Vladimir had not a clue what conditioner was, but he would do anything those shiny lips told him to do, so he shook the hair from his face and said, "I installed an air conditioner the other day, will that help?"

She let out a hearty laugh, cupping the side of his face with her hands. "You are adorable!" All through the night, she had a puddle of vodka in her glass, but had no interest in finishing it. Instead, she talked happily about her friends, her family, and the new job she would be starting at the October Woman beauty shop later in the month. Amidst her rambling chatter, she stopped and tapped Vladimir on the nose. "Oy," she said, "I don't like straight vodka, I'm a happy person, and I talk a lot. Not a very good Russian, now am I? I just don't understand all these miseries of life we Russians are supposed to silently suffer through. I want to live life!"

The sound of metal locking against metal jolted Vlad back to reality. That night he met Zhanna seemed a lifetime away now, standing in the cold prison cell with nothing on but a pair of orange, prison-issue pants. He turned around. The burly cop stood on the other side of the bars, looping his key ring around his belt. Fresh blood dripped from his left ear onto his white uniform shirt. He took a drag off the cigarette hanging from his mouth, tossed it to the cement floor, and promptly snuffed it out beneath his boot. Pointing one meaty finger, he barked, "You need to cool off, son," and walked away.

Vladimir looked around. Metal toilet in the corner, concrete slab for a bed, a thin mattress with a green wool blanket thrown on top. Just this morning he was snuggled next to Zhanna in their bed, so warm, and Zhanna, too, had been safe. Now she was gone forever. He slid down the cold gray wall to the equally cold gray floor and brought his forehead to his knees, whispering, "I should have died. I should have died." The noise slowly crept in. *Blast. Gunfire. Commands. Blast. Gunfire. Commands.*

9.

The jail cell was freezing. Naked but for the bright orange drawstring pants, Vlad shivered with the cold but his mind remained numb, laden with regret for what he had done. Dinner came and went, as did the supper tray loaded with a slippery pile of boiled beets. He sat against the gray concrete wall. Everything gray, dull, and dingy, except the orange drawstring pants, which were abrasive, tight around the waist, and too short, hitting at mid-calf. Zhanna would most certainly hate these pants, he thought.

"Zhanna!" Vlad shuddered. Immediately, he straightened up. Up on his feet, he bolted to the vertical steel bars that held him captive. "What have I done to Zhanna?" he yelled, grabbing the bars.

A bellowing voice, the burly cop's voice, shouted from somewhere down the corridor, "Shut the fuck up!"

Vlad released the bars, slammed his open palm against them. "Hey! I need to know! What have I done?"

But the burly cop shouted back, "Excuse me, Mr. Verstakov, but I don't think the phrase 'shut the fuck up' needs any further explanation. Now, I've dealt with enough of your shit today, so, Shut. The. Fuck. Up. I'm busy!"

But the sound of water came down the corridor. Water pouring into a cup, hitting the sides, filling it up. "You're not busy. You're making tea!" Vlad yelled. "I hear it. I can hear everything you know!" The cop did not respond. Like the sounds of war, the sound of water filled the tiny cell.

***

I step out of the shower and walk over to the row of sinks, turn on the faucet. Captain Yurchenko and I stand next to each other. His faucet is running, too. He has a clean, white towel wrapped around his waist; I have on nothing. I stand head and shoulders above him. He's in the process of shaving; I am about to brush my teeth.

We nod to each other's foggy reflections. As he applies shaving cream, he asks me how my new bride is getting by back home all by herself. I tell him she stays busy at the beauty shop, plus she's so damned independent she probably doesn't even know I'm gone. He smirks, says his wife is the same way.

I squeeze a stripe of toothpaste onto my toothbrush. Doing so, I try not to jab his head with my elbow. Being a lefty, that's always something I have to think about, accidently jabbing someone with my elbow.

Yurchenko makes one diagonal swipe down his right cheek, then rinses his razor, taps it on the edge of the sink. "Aw, hell, Verstakov, this is my fifth tour of Afghanistan. My wife doesn't even know who I am anymore."

I chuckle and begin to brush my teeth.

He leans into the mirror to get every last bit of sparse blond stubble. "And to tell you the truth, this life of mine, the five deployments, has really taken a toll on my son, Luka. He's a serious kid, real sensitive. I wish I could make things better for him. Wish I could take his pain away, put it all on myself. It's not right. My son's just a kid, but he's suffered from this war far more than I have."

I stop brushing and spit. I have never heard Yurchenko say anything personal before. Maybe the poker game last night loosened him up, or maybe it's the nakedness. Yurchenko was the first man I met when I got off the plane in this hellhole. He barked a few orders at us, tossed us each a rifle, and off we went. For the past five months, I have seen him as a kind of mythical slayer of dragons, silent and stoic, a true warrior. If Saint Ilya Muromets ever existed, I bet he would have been just like Captain Yurchenko, only taller. I'm actually surprised to hear Yurchenko has a family. Just figured his home was right here on the battlefield.

He makes another swipe with his razor and goes on. His latest deployment notice arrived, "on an ordinary Tuesday, as my wife was preparing supper," he says. Later in that same week, eleven year-old Luka began stuttering. It started out fairly benign, occasionally getting stuck on common words. He repeated them over and over until he could move on. But six weeks later, as Yurchenko finished packing his duffel bag before leaving for the airport, Luka stood in the doorway. It took the kid over a minute to stammer out his words: "Dad, I don't want you to leave again."

Captain Yurchenko is now taking short downward strokes to shave the stubble off his chin. "That broke my heart into a million pieces, Verstakov, I tell you. I couldn't stand to leave him. It kills me to be away."

I lean down to scoop some water from the faucet then look at his reflection. "Captain, you care about your son. That's the important thing. Luka knows he is loved and wanted. No kid can ask for more." Those are my exact words. Sounds silly coming from a beast like me, a big, bulky, naked guy without kids of my own, but I am being honest. I know a thing or two about family drama. More than that, I understand the importance of having a good father.

I put my toothbrush down. "Maybe you should write him a letter, tell him what you told me, that you hate being away from him. I bet that would go a long way to making him feel better."

Yurchenko tosses his hand towel in the sink. He runs his hands down his smooth face. Now he turns to me, looks up. Maybe he will write that letter, he says, now, before we head out. He gives me two hearty slaps on the shoulder and walks away.

I see the towel wrapped around his waist. It's perfectly crisp, clean and white, makes a swishing sound. It hits him below the back of the knees.

***

Vladimir released the bars and leaned his forehead against the cool metal mumbling, "Five tours is too much. Bloody hell."

10.

Heavy-soled boots stomped down the corridor accompanied by horribly strained smoker's breath. The stomping stopped, and then came a raspy voice. "Five tours of duty? Man, that's brutal. You don't look old enough, son, so who are you talkin' about? Who was called to duty five times?"

Vlad lifted his head to see the burly officer standing there. Dressed in his blue and white uniform, a round blue hat atop his trim, reddish-brown hair. The name Rogusskii, P. typed neatly across the silver badge.

"Doesn't matter. He's dead now. They're all dead. So is my wife." Vlad snapped. He turned away, sat down on the concrete slab that served as a bed and wrapped the flimsy green blanket around his shoulders.

"Well, excuse me, Mr. I Can Hear Everything!" barked Rogusskii. "I hear things, too, ya know. You spent the morning in an all-out rage, beating that poor wife of yours, yelling, and screaming about land mines. You wasted away the afternoon slumped against the wall. Now you're crying about someone who was called up five times. You, sir, are a sorry-ass, pathetic mess. Now, I have finally had my tea, had a chance to breathe. You now have my full and complete attention, so you might as well tell me what the hell happened over there in that desert to make you so damn crazy?" Rogusskii stuck a cigarette in his mouth, utterly annoyed.

Vlad shivered under the flimsy blanket and glanced at Rogusskii. He looked to be somewhere in his fifties. Just as tall as himself, but beefier, a pudgy stomach hanging over his belt. His left ear, which had been bleeding earlier, was scabbed over now and some droplets of dried blood marked his stiff white collar. Vlad turned back to stare at the concrete wall. "Why don't you tell me what happened to your ear, first?"

Rogusskii let out a deep sigh. "Son, I've just about had it with you today. You can't remember? Shit, you're even worse off than I thought." He patted his chest pocket and brought out a pack of cigarettes. "Smoke?" he offered.

Vlad sat staring at the wall.

Rogusskii took a long drag on his own cigarette and leaned one shoulder into the bars. "Ya know, son, I quit smoking thirteen months ago after my third daughter was born. She was born a month early and her lungs weren't developed all the way. At first, I went outside to smoke, but that's a bunch of half-assed bullshit. I need to dive into things, can't stand to do anything half way, so I quit altogether. One of the hardest things I've ever done, but I did it." He took another drag, let out a long trail of smoke.

"See son, I really messed up family life the first time around, so, in order to be a good husband this time, and be a real father to my little Katya, I quit smoking." He patted his belly. "Put on fifteen kilograms in the process, and I panic if I have less than four packs of gum in my possession at any given time, but the point is, I quit smoking." He leaned into the bars. "Did you hear me, son? I quit smoking!" He stood up straight, tossed the cigarette on the floor, and promptly lit another one.

After a short drag on that one, Rogusskii tapped his ash. "Was doing fine, too, without one single smoke. Been breathing better, not coughing so much. Little Katya and I, we walk to the park. We get ice cream at October Square. My wife turned thirty-five this year and I remembered her birthday. I'm a good husband and a real father this time around. It's been great, truly, truly great, and all because of what? Because. I. Quit. Smoking!" He immediately placed the cigarette between his lips, took a hefty drag.

Vladimir pinched the space between his eyes. "Excuse me, sir, but where is all this going? Because I can't help but see you are smoking, and in case you haven't noticed, I have destroyed everything worth living for. I'm still trying to remember what exactly happe—"

"Eh, eh. Stop talking, son. Just shut up. Look who has the badge, okay? It's me. And look who's behind bars, it's you and your pathetic ass. Now I've put up with your crazy shit all morning, even lost an earlobe over it, so you can at least hear me out."

Rogusskii took another drag. "This morning rolls around and I start my regular beat downtown, rounding up last night's heroin addicts and prostitutes the government says do not exist, bring them in to sober up. Two hours into it, I get dispatched to housing complex number thirty-four, over in the Koni district. I pull up along the sidewalk in the squad car and some frantic man in a bathrobe comes running towards me. The poor guy could barely put two words together, but he eventually tells me that his next-door neighbor is going crazy and his wife is screaming." Rogusskii inhaled, tapped the ash.

"I called the station for back up. But headquarters sent me some skinny kid just out of training. First day on the job, he tells me. First day on the job, well, isn't that fucking beautiful! The kid's uniform was impeccable. He even gave me a salute. Can you believe that, a salute?" Rogusskii rolled his eyes, tapped the quaking ash from his cigarette.

He pointed one beefy finger. "Son, you were completely out of control, going on about the noise inside your head, pistol jammed to your wife's head, yelling how everyone was dead. She was already a bloody mess, that poor girl."

Blast. Gunfire. Commands. Blast. Gunfire. Commands. The noise crept in. Vlad stumbled in his stance, brought his chin down to his chest, and covered his ears. "I remember now. Zhanna. She wasn't feeling well. She spilled some tea. But I saw blood. I saw blood and soldiers dying in front of me. I went into battle." He looked at Rogusskii. "It's the blast, and then the gunfire. All the commands. It gets so loud sometimes; I don't even know where I am or what's happening. And Zhanna, oh god, Zhanna."

Rogusskii shifted his weight, snuffed out his cigarette beneath the toe of one boot. He leaned into the bars, grabbed with one hand, and said, "Son, you didn't shoot your wife."

11.

Vlad stood perfectly still and quiet, waiting for the words *you didn't shoot your wife*, to register.

"You heard me son," Rogusskii said. "You didn't shoot your wife. She was taken to the hospital. As of yet she is not pressing charges, so I can only hold you for twenty-four hours."

Rogusskii lit another cigarette. "We busted into your apartment. Heard you yelling. We ran down the hall to the bedroom. You had a pistol jammed into your wife's forehead. I feared she was dead already, so I immediately ran in. Kicked you in the forehead just as you pulled the trigger. Man, one tenth of a second later, and her brain would have been splattered all over that room and you'd be on your way to *Kopeisk* with a life sentence, I'm sure." Another pull on the cigarette.

Rogusskii shifted his weight and chuckled. "I have to give you credit, son. You're a damn good shot with that clunky old pistol. You had the entire room. But oh no, you can't shoot into the wall or anything like that. You shot off my earlobe, goddamn it! Look, it's gone!"

He turned his cheek and pointed to a scabbed earlobe. "The bullet kept flying, right where my proper little deputy was standing. I managed to throw myself over him. Just in time, too, otherwise his first day on the job would have been his last one on earth." He shook his head, took another drag. "Son, thanks to you, I've been smoking all damn day! I can't stop!" He took another drag.

"To top it all off, you fought all the way to the patrol car," Rogusskii gingerly straightened up. "My back may never be the same. You even vomited all over Deputy Skinny-Ass. Should have seen the look on his face. The kid was so shaken up; I had to send him back home to mommy."

Rogusskii paused, then laughed. "Oh, man, I play cards with the guys on Tuesday. This is going to be a great story. Shit, son, all these years of the job, it never gets boring, I'll tell you that much." Another chuckle, another drag.

"You saved her life," Vlad said, finally able to breathe. "Because of you, Zhanna is alive. You kept me from killing her. I don't even know what to say." He leaned his sweaty forehead into the cold bars in a pure mixture of relief and exhaustion. "I owe you everything."

"Damn straight you do, son!" piped up Rogusskii, his cheeks hot, the veins in his necks looking as if they would explode. But he closed his eyes and took a breath, then calmly leaned his shoulder against the bars.

"Son, listen to me. I know this hell you are living in," he said. "Your eyes are stone dead. You can barely keep your own soul intact. Basically, you're an asshole to everyone, especially to those who love you the most. You can't distinguish reality from the past. Can't sleep worth a damn. Your stomach is a mess. Have you tried killing yourself yet? Bet you're in the planning stages by now. You'll figure it out eventually, believe me."

He shifted his weight. "And the flashbacks, they're getting worse, aren't they? Just one little trigger? Comes out of nowhere? Let me tell you something, son, the flashbacks ain't ever going away. The noise will never leave your head. They are yours forever, compliments of that godforsaken desert, and will only get worse unless you do something about it."

He took another drag. "Believe me, son, when I say I know you. I know you because I used to be you. Now, you say you owe me? Hell yeah, you do. Hear what I have to say. You owe me that much."

12.

Rogusskii flicked his head upwards, tapped a column of ash to the floor, and began his story. "Like you, I'm a member of a reserve unit. Was working as a prison guard when my unit was called up in '82 to serve in Afghanistan. Kandahar Province."

He took another drag. "I was forty-one, had a wife, two daughters, aged eight and thirteen. My unit worked reconnaissance, which is really just a glorified cleanup crew. We arrived on the scene after the battle, or after the accident, or after the land mine exploded. The medics swept through first and took the injured soldiers away; it was up to us to identify and clear away the dead that remained."

He looked down. "Can't tell you how many nineteen-year-old boys I picked up and carried over the sand." He paused to tap the ash off his cigarette.

"And the land mines, they went off all the time. Killed an awful lot of children, Afghan children, from the countryside. They suffered horrible burns, their legs blown off, or their arms. The mines weren't buried, but sticking up out of the ground and painted bright colors. Russian candy and toys were strewn about. One of the engineers told me the mines were meant to maim the children, not actually kill them, because the top brass in

Moscow thought a crippled child would keep fathers at home, so they were less likely to join up with the mujahideen resistance."

Rogusskii took another long pull off his cigarette and exhaled. "Guess that logic didn't exactly pan out, huh? Ten years at war and we got nothing but a good ass-kicking to show for it." Another drag.

"But I still hear those land mines go off as if it were yesterday. A car backfiring, thick smoke wafting out of a chimney, it's enough to take me back. Images of children writhing in pain, all alone, with bloody stumps for limbs. Each plume of smoke means an adventurous little Afghan boy chasing after his ball just lost both of his legs; each blast means a shy little girl on her way to collect water had her face blown to bits."

He looked away, then back again. "It tore me up to think about those kids. Still does. Nothing would drown out the images, not pills, not booze. Couldn't sleep for years."

Rogusskii sighed and snuffed out his cigarette. "Son, I'm not telling you this for sympathy. I'm telling because I see you heading down the same path I went down. Let me tell you where that path leads." He shook his head.

"First, you drink yourself into oblivion every night, get hooked on pain killers, lose your job, alienate your friends. Snap at your wife. Your daughters can't do anything right, so you berate them until they cry.

"After a few years, your older daughter stops eating. When she does manage a bite, she forces herself to throw up. She exercises constantly. Your daughter slowly starves herself before your eyes, but you hardly notice. You overhear your younger daughter on the phone; she says she wishes you had died in the war. It hurts, mostly because you know she's right, but you keep popping painkillers and slinging back the vodka to drown it all out.

"Finally, after four years of abuse, your wife gathers the girls and tells you she has found someone else, someone who treats her well. She should have left long ago, she says. That really sends you into a tailspin. And there you are, all alone with pills and vodka and your horrible, pathetic self.

"A few years go by. Your children's stepdad attends the recitals, the doctor's appointments, and the high school graduations while you've been drinking. One day, you reach the point where you are so damn sick of yourself that you decide that you are done. So you call your oldest daughter to say how sorry you are for everything and you wish her all the best. Then you load up on booze and pills and lock yourself inside your apartment to finally put an end to it all."

Rogusskii looked Vlad dead in the eye. "That's how far I got. Made some pretty good headway, too, until my daughter's boyfriend and his two friends busted down my door, grabbed me, and threw me in the back of a car. Behind the wheel was my eldest daughter. I was yelling obscenities at her, out of my mind, even tried to grab the wheel. But she said nothing, drove me straight to the hospital. Bless her heart." He took another slow drag, exhaled.

"Been clean and sober ever since. In fact, I met my second wife in the hospital while I was drying out. See, I was going through withdrawal, couldn't stop shaking,

I would have killed for a drink. Irina was my counselor, and my angel."

Rogusskii tossed his cigarette. "Son, I love my second wife and baby daughter dearly. I just wish I hadn't made such a mess of it the first time around. My two daughters wrote me letters while I was away at war. I received more letters than any other soldier in my unit. When I landed at the airport, they ran down the tarmac to throw their arms around me. But I was nothing but a brute for years." He looked away, and back again.

"I guarantee you my story is not unique. It's a scenario playing out all over Russia and will continue to play out for years to come. Our government shipped a lot of boys to Afghanistan; they went through hell and came home to a country in ruins."

He patted his chest pocket. "Don't head down the same road I did, son. You have a chance to do it right."

Vladimir stepped back "How?" he asked. "How do I get rid of this?"

Rogusskii chuckled, shook his head. "You don't, son."

Vladimir closed his eyes. *Blast. Gunfire. Commands. Blast. Gunfire. Commands.* This would never go away. Fuck. Get the Makarov. End this now.

Rogusskii looked down, pulled out a pack of gum from his chest pocket. "You don't get rid of it. You learn to live with it." He took out a stick of gum, looked up. "You want to manage this?" He folded the gum into his mouth. "I got one word for you."

13.

Vlad leaned into the bars. "What is it? How do I manage this?"

Rogusskii chewed his gum twice. "*Iskra*," he said, as if that made perfect sense.

Not at all impressed, Vlad released the bars. "Huh?" "Iskra. What the hell is that supposed to mean?"

Rogusskii pointed a finger. "You gotta find yourself some hope. Something to believe in. Something that'll get you up in the morning, and help you through the dark days. That's an Iskra. A spark in your life. It doesn't have to be a big thing and you don't need to share it with anyone. In fact, it's best if it's something that is only for you and you alone."

Vlad rolled his eyes. "Iskra. Whatever."

Rogusskii put up his hands. "Just hear me out, son. An Iskra is important and not very complicated. Could be a passage in a book, or a song. Maybe take up a sport, religion. Cooking. Writing. Pottery. Hell, start knitting wool sweaters with little matching hats and mittens if that's what makes you feel good! I don't care what it is, but you need to find some hope. You need an Iskra."

Rogusskii went on. "Once you hear the awful noise, when the violent images creep into your head, try to focus on your Iskra. Keep the focus even while you feel the agitation coming on. Just focus, and the anger will clear, the images will fade away. They will never leave entirely, but you will be able to go on with life. It takes time and it sure as hell ain't easy, but in the long run, the demons will become more manageable."

Annoyed, Vladimir sighed, "All right. So what's yours?"

"I discovered photography a few years back. I go for long hikes out in the mountains, just me and the dogs. I take all kinds of photographs. Black and white is the most dramatic, but now that we can buy color film, I have been experimenting with that. I look for shots of tranquil landscapes—mountains, lakes, streams, anything that portrays a sense of calm, beauty, and serenity."

"Whenever I hear that thundering boom of the land mines in my head I have to stop and deliberately replace it with the sound of my shutter closing and opening again. I replace the boom with a click. I replace the images of crippled kids and mangled soldiers with images of sweeping mountains and streams. Eventually, I feel calm, better able to handle my life. It takes a lot of effort, but everyday gets a little easier. Even dropped by to see my oldest daughter the other day at her work. She's training to be a nurse over at People's Hospital Four. We took a walk and had an actual conversation. I take that to mean my Iskra is working."

Vladimir exhaled, then looked back to Rogusskii and nodded. "Guess I can try. Can't hurt."

Rogusskii shook his head and pointed a big meaty finger directly in Vlad's face and barked, "Don't just try, son. Find an Iskra or you're dead!"

14.

Vladimir leaned sideways into the bars with his eyes on the concrete wall across the cell. *Blast. Gunfire. Commands. Blast. Gunfire. Commands* still echoed beneath the folds of his brain. A simple Iskra could manage this hell? A thought? A stupid hobby? Didn't seem possible. Nevertheless, Vlad closed his eyes and tried to think of something to bring about hope. Nothing came to mind. Zhanna would never take him back. There was nothing. Finally surrendering to weak legs and a heavy head, he slumped down to the floor and leaned against the wall. The wall across the cell grew more dull and dingy with each passing second. He kept staring at the grayness before him.

***

It's gray. Made of strong canvas, this Russian-made tarpaulin. I pull on it, the last corner is difficult, but I finally secure it around the bed of my truck. I then signal to Captain Yurchenko that I am ready to move out. There is an armored vehicle at the front; it looks like a small tank. Mikhail Astafurov is standing next to it along with three other men. He, too, signals his readiness. Second in the convoy is a pickup with a machine gun mounted on top. Two soldiers are seated in the back. They wear black, fingerless gloves and helmets with the straps unsecured. They must be ready to go, too, because they snuff out their cigarettes and latch their helmets tightly under their chins. Yurchenko's vehicle is next; a pickup like mine.

Then it's my truck. Fourth in the convoy. Three more trucks packed full of supplies just like mine are behind me. Two well-armed Russian soldiers flank each truck. Lastly, another truck with a machine gun mounted on top. Two soldiers in the back of that one. I wonder why I am the only one alone?

Captain Yurchenko walks from the rear of the convoy to the front. "Calling all brave Russian soldiers, move 'em out!" he yells and makes a sweeping motion with his right arm. He opens the driver's side door of his truck and steps up on the running board. He points right at me. "Verstakov, listen up."

I stand at attention. "Yes sir."

"You've got Asef for this trip. Pick him up outside the gate. He's been hanging out there all morning," says Yurchenko.

I hear chuckling and snickering all around. What is this, the fourth grade? One soldier, I don't know who, pelts me in the back of the head with something. I turn back to see a lighter on the ground. Annoyed, I go to grab it so I can throw it back, but it slips from my sweaty grasp and lands behind me. Now they are all laughing at my expense. Someone yells out, "Hey Verstakov, is that how your wife yanks your dick? No wonder you hang out with that A-rab all the time!" Someone else yells out, "Maybe that Towel Head knows how to fuck you just right!" Now I grab the lighter and hurl it to no one in particular. "No, he don't, but your girlfriend sure does!" I yell.

Now I am laughing, I know Yurchenko is watching but I can't help it. We are all hollerin' and swearin', and throwin' stuff at each other. One of the soldiers in the gun-mounted truck stands up and thrusts his hips forward several times and pounds his chest like a primate. The other guy looks like he's going to fall off the edge of the truck. Mikhail Astafurov stands there stifling his laughter. All in all, this entire convoy has devolved into a rowdy group of hooligans. We are ridiculous and stupid. Man, this is fun.

But one stern glance from Captain Yurchenko and we all immediately straighten up. "Listen up, dickheads," he barks sharply from the running board. "We need Asef. That kid may just save all of our lives up there. Who else here can speak five languages? Anyone? Show of hands, can anyone here speak five different languages? Hell, sounds like basic Russian is a challenge for most of you idiots."

I feel like shit. Of course, I can't speak any other language; I can't do much of anything. That's why I'm in this hellhole, because I am nothing. Yurchenko then adds, "And no more referring to him as the A-rab or Towel Head. His name is Asef. We can be professional, got it?" We all stand silently still.

Yurchenko steps off the truck and walks over to me. The top of his beret comes to my shoulder. He looks up with that icy blue stare of his and says, "Verstakov, you want to know why I pair you with Asef all the time? Because Asef sees you as a brother. I saw that right away. He's more comfortable with you than with any of these other jokers, that is why I've been keeping him with you most every day."

He puts one hand on my shoulder and says, "Listen to me, Verstakov, you are an old soul; far smarter and stronger than you give yourself credit for. You don't have to resort to this juvenile mentality."

All I can say is, "Sir, yes sir," and give him a salute. Fuck, now I feel even worse than shit.

He walks back to his truck, all the while calling out, "Calling all brave Russian soldiers, I said let's move 'em out!" He climbs in the truck, slams the door behind him. I get in my truck and start the engine. The convoy starts to move. Bloody hell, I may be an old soul, strong and smart, and whatever the hell Yurchenko said, but I have to spend all day with that dork. All day with Asef Wazir.

***

The jail cell became blurry through hot tears. Vlad closed his eyes and let the noise fill his head, did not fight it. *Blast. Gunfire. Commands. Blast. Gunfire. Commands.*

15.

The door labeled 4-C in shiny, metallic characters, swung open to the inside. There stood Raisa Petrova, ever so petite, wearing a beet-splotched apron over a prim green housedress; sensible beige shoes on her feet, her burgundy hair neatly done up in a bun. She glanced up and gasped. "Zhanna!" She gently took Zhanna's arm, ushering her inside.

Zhanna's face was a red, swollen mess, her right eye puffy and purple. A row of stitches kept her upper lip together, another row of stitches ran along her forehead. A bruise circled her right forearm in the pattern of Vladimir's splayed fingers. Multiple cuts marked her neck and shoulders, remnants of the mirror shattering over her body.

Raisa did not make any judgment, only reached up to smooth her daughter's hair, as tears filled her own hazel eyes. She helped Zhanna take a seat at the little kitchen table. She then busied herself preparing a pot of tea. The smell of Mom's famous beet *borscht* already filled the apartment; freshly baked bread sat steaming on the counter. Mom always spent Saturdays cooking for the week ahead. Nothing had changed.

For the first time in months, Zhanna felt the tension melt from her shoulders. Her stomach untangled. She could breathe easier. "It's been bad for about a year," she said with a heavy breath. "I guess I thought it would get better."

Raisa set down a cup of tea. Zhanna took a sip, but cringed as the heat stung her lip. "Mom, I'm pregnant," she said into the tea. "But there was a lot of blood. The doctor doesn't think the baby is still alive."

Raisa fought back tears and held her daughter close. "You are safe now. That is the important thing."

Zhanna hugged her mother while looking at the black-and-white photographs adorning the walls. In one picture, a six-year-old Zhanna and her mother smiled next to a batch of freshly baked sugar cookies, her first entry in the annual Communist Youth baking contest where she won a second-place trophy. In another, an eleven-year-old Zhanna with two long braids stood smiling on a river dock next to her younger brother, Alexander, who held up a fish, caught during a state sponsored outing for "afflicted kids."

Next to that one, a twenty-six year-old Zhanna standing between her lanky father and short mother, holding up her diploma on the last day of hair-cutting and styling school.

Through her tears Zhanna couldn't help but stare at that photograph. Shortly after that photograph was taken, she and some friends went to the Red Torch Pub for a graduation celebration, and there she had met Vladimir and fallen hard in love with him.

Vlad's irresistible green eyes; his messy hair. The way he swaggered up to the dartboard. His mere presence left her feeling inspired, as if she could do anything she set her mind to. But of course, that was before the war. Before the angry outbursts, before the pills, before the drinking, before he jammed a gun to her head.

But still, just thinking about him made her feel more alive. However much she wanted to hate her husband, she could not.

16.

20 January

Fifty minutes after his release from jail, Vladimir stepped off the city bus and walked three blocks under the icy Soviet sky to his and Zhanna's apartment. Finally home after a horrid twenty-four hours.

The first thing he noticed was the lingering essence of Zhanna, her warm vanilla scent. But of course she would not be at home. She was too smart to be here waiting with open arms for her asshole of a husband to get out of jail. Without her, the apartment seemed nothing more than a sixty-square-meter void, eerily stagnant. Even the sound of the door shutting behind him echoed throughout the place. The muddy footprints of Rogusskii and his deputy, now dry and clumpy, trailed down the hallway where they made a left into the bedroom.

In the bedroom, remnants of the carnage were everywhere; bloodstains combined with shards of shattered glass on the carpet, the broken tea cup, top dresser drawer pulled open so far it leaned downward. A smear of dark blood ran down the edge of the dresser where Zhanna had slammed her head. This was home now, once full of yellow flowers on the towels, now a scene of such brutality.

Where a husband had left to fight a war, only to return home a monster.

He bolted to the bathroom, yanked open the left-side drawer and watched as the bottle of little white pills rolled to a stop. A welcome sight, especially since a bottle of vodka waited patiently beneath the sink. He brought the bottle up and opened it.

It had become automatic, going for vodka and little white pills at the first feeling of agitation. A handful could calm the nervousness; dampen the guilt and stop the noise, if only for a while. Once the pills were gone, there would be more; there were always more. The army doctors handed them out like candy. He wondered how many pills it would take to erase the non-physical kind of pain. Two hadn't done a thing; four couldn't stop the noise. Maybe six pills this time. Eight pills spilled from the bottle onto his right palm. Okay, eight. He took time to study them, arrange them neatly within his palm, all of them facing up. Eight perfect little white dots ready to work their magic.

***

There are just a few clouds in the sky. They look like little white dots. Otherwise, the sky is a brilliant blue and goes on forever. Slowly, our convoy creeps out of the gate into the parched outskirts of Kabul. Captain Yurchenko is ahead of me. He must have taken his beret off because I can see his platinum blond hair through the rear window.

Mikhail Astafurov is out front in the armored vehicle. We have to stay well behind Mikhail and his crew in case he hits a land mine. The armored vehicle can withstand a blast but our trucks cannot. Four more vehicles behind me. A black helicopter is well ahead of us, whirling above, checking for mujahideen activity as we go along.

***

Eight little white pills neatly in hand, Vlad looked them over again, thought this was probably what his father had done countless times. Vlad, too, ever since the army doctor handed them over, took to those pills like a starved peasant. Vladimir grabbed the bottle of vodka, took a hefty swig, ready to wash down the pills.

***

I take a swig of water from my canteen, then fold my lips in to get every last drop. Because it's so dry and dusty out here, our water is strictly rationed. Russian engineers are drilling wells throughout Afghanistan to get more water for the soldiers. This is crazy; there's not enough water to fight this war.

"Vlad-ee-meer, Vlad-ee-meer!" I hear a voice. It's male but rather high-pitched, like his voice is still in the process of changing. "Vlad-ee-meer! Vlad-ee-meer!" I know that voice. I know it well. Been hearing it all summer. It's our translator, Asef. He is standing outside the gate, wildly waving his arms. He calls out, "Vlad-ee-meer, hi!" He is smiling like crazy. Way too happy. "Hi, Vlad-ee-meer! Hi!"

I see the back of Yurchenko's head in the truck ahead of me as I stop. He gives me a little wave and speeds off. I bet he is laughing to himself at my expense right now. I'll get him back at poker tonight. Maybe I'll take that nice watch of his. Then we'll see who's laughing.

I stop just outside the gate, reach over to push open the passenger side door. "Get in, Asef," I say, more than a little annoyed that I have to spend the day with him, "And stay off the side of the road. Don't you know how many mines we've buried around here?"

Asef's goofy grin slowly fades from his face. "Oh, yes, I always forget," he says as he starts to climb in the truck. He looks at me, adjusts his glasses; the goofy grin returns.

Asef is just out of high school. Started hanging around the base earlier this summer sporting a nylon backpack and had a stack of Russian language books tucked underneath his arm. Said he could translate for us. Pashto to Russian. Russian to Pashto. The kid's a genius, fluent in Russian as well as his native Pashto and a bunch of other languages, to boot. Yurchenko hired him on the spot to accompany us on supply transports and other non-combat missions. He's translated for us many times, gotten us out of some squabbles in the villages. For all of his gawky goofiness, I have to give him credit; he's got a lot of talent.

Asef is taller than me, but not by much. He's close to two meters tall but I must outweigh him by at least twenty kilos of solid muscle. Maybe even twenty-five. His ribs show through from underneath the white T-shirt he's got on, and those old cast-off camouflage pants he's wearing don't stay up very well. This kid is painfully thin and much too tall for his own good, constantly tripping over his own huge, T-Rex feet.

He gets in the truck and I start to drive forward. It takes him forever to get situated. His glasses keep falling off his nose and that stupid backpack he always wears gets in the way. It's bulging at the seams with way more books than he'll ever need. Some fall out on the seat, some fall on the floor. He swings the backpack around to the front of his body so he can finally sit back. "I should just wear it like this all the time. It would be a more convenient way to get to my books," he says, so proud of himself.

I take one look at that pitiful little situation. "Nyet. Nyet. God, Asef, don't wear your backpack on the front, man, just don't do that okay?" I am rolling my eyes and reaching for a cigarette. "Why don't you get yourself a briefcase or something like that?" I say, flicking my lighter. "That would look more professional." I take a drag and exhale.

Asef nods eagerly, "Oh yes, a briefcase. That is a good idea, Vlad-ee-meer. I should try a briefcase." More of that goofy grin. His glasses are huge. I wish he would stop grinning.

***

Vladimir gagged on the stagnant vodka sliding down his throat. He leaned over and spit it out into the sink, turning the water faucet at the same time. After washing his mouth out, he stood up and looked at the pills. The pills never cured a thing. Even with a daily dose, the flashbacks kept coming, the noise remained. Downing more and more pills would not erase the guilt he felt over the deaths of so many good men. His anger over what happened in Afghanistan always found a way of lashing out. Two years of pills and vodka had not solved a thing. Vodka never helped his mother; pills certainly had done nothing to help his father.

Vladimir slowly tipped his hand. One by one, eight little white pills tumbled into the sink, swirling down the drain with a gush of water. Next, he picked up the pill bottle. The remaining pills met the same watery fate. He swiped the bottle of vodka off the counter, poured a sparkling stream into the sink.

Find an Iskra or you're dead. Those were Rogusskii's exact words. "Damn," Vlad said, as he shook the remaining drops from the bottle. "That burly old cop was right." He turned off the water. He leaned forward on his open palms, looked his reflection dead in the eyes and stated, "You have to become a better man."

Vodka would not be his Iskra. Fistfuls of pills would not be his Iskra.

17.

21 January

Vladimir let his work boots drag over the gravel as he gradually brought his black '82 Dnepr motorcycle to a halt at the edge of the construction site Monday morning, ready to get back to work. After the horrid weekend, he needed to move, swing a hammer, pound some nails, sweat.

Across the gravel lot, a sliver of sun nudging up through the horizon highlighted the apartment complex Vlad and his crew had been erecting for the past four months. The building, a drab, five-story, square hunk of concrete, identical to all the other apartment buildings in town, stood tall and hard against the rising Soviet sun.

Once on site, he dove into work, framing the interior walls within the second-story units. Hours spent lifting, pounding, running up and down the two flights of stairs for more supplies. The physical activity felt so good, he didn't even take a break to eat or have a smoke with the guys.

Just as the naked, icy sun began to wane, Vlad put into place one final stud. But the stud would not stay straight; it kept leaning to the right. Vlad reached up, tapped the side of it with the hammer but to no avail.

He gave it a good whack but the stud remained tilted. Another pound with the hammer and the frosty January air felt like a sweltering desert. He took off his coat, threw it on the floor. Another whack with the hammer and the ground sank down, like sand. He wiped his brow. One more whack and the wooden pillar before him morphed into a four-meter-high, reinforced steel guard tower designed to watch for mujahideen rebels.

***

We are approaching a Soviet guard tower. There's a uniformed soldier up there, binoculars to his eyes, looking out for mujahideen. The mujahideen are Afghan rebels, claiming to be fighting the Russians in the name of Islam. They say they are fighting to bring back the Islamic Republic of Afghanistan. But they are nothing more than roving gangs of uneducated teenagers, high on opium, driving around in pickups, shooting their rifles in the air.

The Soviet Union is gradually pulling out of this war, that is why my reserve unit is here, one last push in an effort to win this fucking thing. But what will be left of Afghanistan after we leave? Nothing but mujahideen thugs? Shit, this place will go to hell overnight.

We pass the guard tower. In my rearview mirror, I see the soldier still has the binoculars to his eyes. Man, that's gotta be boring.

I glance over to Asef, who's got his nose buried in a paperback Russian phrase book. Haven't paid much attention to him all summer. We've always referred to him as the A-rab or Towel Head, but Yurchenko said Asef is more comfortable with me than with the other soldiers. Wouldn't hurt to get to know the kid, I guess. "So, Asef, how do you know so many languages?" I ask.

Asef eagerly puts his book down on his lap. "My father is a diplomat for the D.R.A, the Communist Party of Afghanistan. He's held that post for five years now. Before that, he was the general secretary, so we've had all kinds of Russian dignitaries in our house over the years. I learned Russian as a kid right along with Dari and Pashto. Just last year, my dad had to go to Moscow on official Party business. He took me with him because I speak better Russian than he does. That's where I got this nylon backpack, from a street vendor in the Arbat district. I just loved the Arbat." He looks at me with that goofy grin, pats his backpack.

I've never been to Moscow. Shit, I've never been anywhere. But I nod anyway.

Asef keeps talking. "I went to boarding school in London. Started when I was seven. Learned English there. And of course, one can't help but pick up French over there, too. Once I became fluent in French, then Spanish and Italian came easy. I mean, let's face it, once you learn one Romance language, the others aren't so difficult." He pushes his glasses up the ridge of his nose. More ridiculous smiling.

I cannot relate at all. Finished two years at college and quit. Academics were never my strong suit. All I can say is, "Uh, yeah. Sure. Those Romance languages." I roll my eyes. The dirt road is horribly uneven. We are bouncing all over.

***

Vlad stopped himself from pounding the tilting stud for a moment, took a deep breath. This was just the type of situation Rogusskii had warned him about. When the flashbacks took over, anger went unchecked, causing everything to go to hell. This is where an Iskra would help diffuse the anger. Vlad stared at the crooked stud trying to focus on something other than Afghanistan. Something to give him hope. Something he liked to do. But nothing came to mind. The agitation remained. The memory continued. So did the noise. *Blast. Gunfire. Commands. Blast. Gunfire. Commands.* Without an Iskra to calm him down, Vlad gripped the hammer and continued to pound the hell out of the wooden stud as dust flew all around.

***

Can't see the guard tower anymore, lost in the desert dust. The whole convoy is moving slowly. If Asef is a rich politician's son, then what the hell is he doing out here with us? His black hair is perfectly cut. He's clean. Obviously well taken care of.

"This is risky work you're doing, Asef," I say, exhaling a fat plume of smoke. "Not a whole lot of rich kids running around out here. Do your parents know what you are doing?"

Asef laughs. Of course it's an eager laugh. "Well, kind of! I told my dad I had a job translating for the Red Army. You should have seen him. So proud. Tells all of his politician friends that I am a big help to the Party, furthering the cause, but he doesn't know I am actually out in the battlefield with actual Red Army soldiers! He never asked the specifics, just as long as he gets to say that I have a prestigious job is all he cares about." He laughs again, but looks down, adjusts his glasses.

He turns away, looks out the window and says, "And as for my mother, she doesn't hear me. I don't think she has ever heard a thing I've said. You know, Vlad-ee-meer, sending me off to boarding school was the best thing to happen to her."

I get it. Asef wants to piss off his parents. I may not have seen the Arbat and speak all the Romance languages, but this is not hard to understand. Bet this is the first time he has ever done something of his own accord. He wants his parents to notice him. Wants to be heard.

He's quiet for a moment, and then turns to look at me. His ears stick out so far from his head that I think he may take flight. He smiles that big, goofy grin of his and says, "Vlad-ee-meer, this is so great! Working with you has been the best summer of my life. I will always remember this summer!"

He keeps smiling, adjusts his huge glasses again. I take a drag. Damn, Yurchenko was right; Asef does see me as a big brother. I had no idea.

***

"Vlad-O! Hey, Vlad-O! Anyone there? Verstakov! Calling Vladimir Verstakov. Vladimir Stepanovich Verstakov! Okay. Whatever. Supreme Dart Thrower Verstakov! Reigning King of Dart Boards Everywhere! Hello! Can you hear me? Vlad-O! Vlad-O!"

Oleg Maksimev was standing to Vlad's side, calling his name, but Vlad couldn't stop pounding on the stud, the memory of Asef, his silly backpack and goofy grin still very much alive.

"Vlad! Vlad-O! Stop with the hammer already! The stud is straight! I repeat, the stud is straight! Oh, for fuck's sake!" Oleg grabbed the hammer mid-swing. Vladimir jerked back hard. Nails spilled from his tool belt onto the plywood subfloor. Out of sheer panic, Vlad pivoted around, gripped the hammer with both hands, and held it overhead ready to pummel the rebel fighter who stood at his side. "Get away from me, rag head!"

Not fazed in the slightest, Oleg reached overhead, catching the hammer's claw, stopping it in its tracks. He yanked the hammer out of Vlad's hands and gave him a solid shove to the chest with it. "Vlad-O, what in the bloody hell is wrong with you, man? And who the hell you callin' a rag head?"

Vlad fell on his ass. He shook his head and quickly looked around. No more heat. No more sand. No more Asef. Just his longtime friend, Oleg, who was obviously pissed off. "What? Oh. Oleg. You scared me. Hey, shouldn't sneak up on a guy with a hammer," he said, lumbering back up.

Oleg stood a good ten centimeters shorter, but stockier, with biceps like tree trunks, a meter-wide chest. He had an unkempt mop of shaggy black hair, two missing front teeth, and a severely crooked nose, a result of too many hockey brawls as a teen. Gray dust flew from Oleg's overalls and hardhat as he spoke. "Sneaking up on you? Sneaking up? What the fuck, man? I've been standing here calling your name for the last five minutes, but you may as well have been a million kilometers away. And then you try to bash in my skull with your fucking hammer? Call me a rag head? Vlad-O, in case you've forgotten, you are the calm, cool one. You are the one who thinks things through; sensitive and thoughtful, all that shit. Remember? I'm the one with no self-control always doing stupid shit. That's me. My dear mother, rest her soul, said that just one Oleg Maksimev in this world is quite enough, no reason to have any more. She said it every day, ya know, just as she was shoving me out the door."

Vlad wiped his brow. "I'm sorry. You just startled me is all."

Oleg brought out a pack of cigarettes, tapped them in his palm. "Well, whatever, but listen, you better have a smoke. Boss sent me up here. That little prick says he wants to see you in the trailer, now. And Vlad-O, my friend, I gotta warn ya, he don't look too happy. Better have a smoke first."

Vladimir nodded gratefully, took the cigarette from his friend, and leaned in for a light. Oleg lit a cigarette for himself, still clearly pissed off. "Vlad-O, you remember the day you got your deployment notice?"

Vlad exhaled and nodded. "Of course, I remember the exact moment. I met Zhanna after work. Got home, there was a soldier waiting at our door. He handed me the notice and walked off. Why?"

Oleg exhaled a plume of smoke and let his arms fly to his sides. "Yeah, well I remember too. When you told me you were going to war, I was jealous. Maybe it sounds crazy, but I wanted to fight. As a kid, I fought like hell on the ice every day. Every chance I got, I fought for my team. After high school, I was ready to keep fighting, for my college, my team, my university. But I couldn't. They wouldn't let me because some stupid test showed I had a heart defect. Moscow State wouldn't touch me. Neither would Leningrad. Hell, I couldn't even get time on the ice at Tomsk!"

Oleg took another drag. "After you were called up, I went down to the military recruitment agency and tried to join. Those smug little uptight clerks took one look at my medical record and closed the file." He pounded his chest with one fist. "Look at me, I'm twenty-six years-old, and I never got a chance to prove myself, never got to fight! That's what men do, we fight!"

He took another hurried drag. "And here you are, Vlad-O. you got to fight and now that you're home, you barely acknowledge me, never play darts. Man, if I had a chance to go to that goddamn desert and kick some Muslim ass, I would be bragging to everyone about it!"

Vladimir looked down to the floor. It's bad enough when your wife knows you returned from war a complete monster with no impulse control whatsoever and that you barely have a grip on reality. The only thing worse than your wife knowing is if your hard-partying, vodka-drinking, dart-throwing buddy knows it, as well. "War is not all it's made out to be, Oleg. You're lucky you didn't have to go," was all he could manage to say.

Oleg slapped him on the shoulder. "Whatever. Don't forget to go see the boss. He said it's important." He started to walk away. But before his disheveled silhouette disappeared around the framed-out doorway into the dusty hall, he turned around, held his arms out, and shouted, "Hey, Vlad-O. It's been a while! Wednesday night. Darts. Be there!" Then he was gone.

Vladimir stood for a moment, hammer in left hand, cigarette dangling from his mouth. Wednesday night darts when the guys from work meet at the Red Torch to throw darts, sling back vodka, basically act like a bunch of overgrown teenagers; it was fun. But Vlad couldn't do it anymore; the light-hearted spirit wasn't there anymore, only bloody images and unbearable noise.

Vlad jerked his left foot back, ready to give the stud a good swift kick. But he kicked with too much anger and not enough forethought, bashing his knee hard into the corner of the stud. "Goddamn it!" he yelled, hopping around on one foot, losing his cigarette in the process. Foolish to think an Iskra would appear just like that and everything would be all right. He turned, gripped the hammer overhead with both hands, and brought it down hard, smashing it directly into the stud. The wood split down and all around, splinters flew out from the sides but the hammer's claw held fast, deep in the stud.

Vladimir left the hammer embedded in the stud and stormed through the framed-out doorway. Didn't even bother grabbing his coat, already so steaming hot with anger and frustration. He jetted down two flights of unfinished stairs, tossing off his work gloves one by one, throwing them against the bare wall.

Outside, generators chugged away. A bulldozer dumped a load of rubble in the distance. Hammers slammed in an offbeat rhythm. An idling crane hummed nearby. Workers yelled orders over the noise. Vladimir tore across the construction site, *Blast. Gunfire. Commands. Blast. Gunfire. Commands* ripping through his head. Hustling up the four metal steps to the trailer door, he wondered just what the hell the boss wanted.

After knocking twice, he pushed open the flimsy metal door and said, "Hey boss, you wanted to see me?"

18.

Timur Ioksim, the forty-two-year-old, state-appointed lead contractor and foreman for the apartment project, sat at his wobbly metal desk along the far wall, left hand resting against his temple, right hand jotting something on a white tablet of paper. He didn't even look up, just quipped, "Vladimir Stepanovich, well, take your bloody time, why don't you? I sent that idiot Oleg up there to fetch you over twenty minutes ago."

Vlad stepped in, looked to the ground. "Sorry boss, I just…just…Sorry it took me so long. If it helps, the first two floors are finished and ready for the plaster crew. I see the paint has been delivered. It's all in the custodial closet. Do you want me to get it read—"

Timur finally looked up, hardly impressed. "Shut up and sit down."

Vlad nodded "Yes, sir," and scooted the metal chair backwards to make room for his legs and sat down.

Timur sighed impatiently as he picked up a cream-colored file from the desk, took the time to put on his reading glasses. "Let's see. Looks like you had quite a weekend. Says here you were in possession of an unregistered firearm, resisted arrest, spent the weekend in jail, and, ah yes, how could I miss this dynamite little tidbit of information? You also beat your wife nearly to death!"

Timur slammed down the file and removed his glasses. "What the hell is wrong with you, Verstakov? You've been one of my finest workers, but the state won't let me keep you on the job swinging hammers and operating heavy machinery. You know that."

Vlad leaned forward, shook his head in an attempt to ignore the sounds, but the more he tried, the more his foot tapped erratically and the more he bit his lower lip. He stood up, began pacing back and forth. "It won't happen again, boss. Really, I can handle it. Can't you let it go this once?"

Exasperated, Timur shot up and quipped, "Let it go this once? I can't let it go! What do you think this is, France? England? The United States? Where everyone, la-tee-da gets to do whatever they want? This is Russia, goddammit! Communist Russia! There are no second chances here. The state says you have to go. But listen, you will be reassigned in due time to a different field of work, I'm sure."

Reassigned. Different field of work. Not a good choice of words. "Reassigned?" Vlad yelled. "Different field of work? To do what? To rot away at some factory with a bunch of gossiping old *babushkas* for the rest of my life? Nyet! Nyet! I can't do that! Boss, you know I work hard. I need to be outside. I need the physical exertion!"

***

My arm is hanging out the truck window. It's damn hot, but still, I like to feel the outside air. So glad I was assigned to a combat unit. I need to move, I need to be outside. I need the physical exertion. Asef looks up from his book and presses his glasses up to his nose. "So, Vlad-ee-meer. Where are we going?"

"Over the Salang Pass," I say. "We have to drop off supplies." He nods and goes back to his tattered book.

"So, don't you have nicknames in this country?" I ask. He looks over to me. He doesn't understand.

I motion with my hands. "You know, you call each other by a shorter version of your given name. Or make up a name that is more fitting," I say.

Now he nods. "Oh nee…neeck…neeck…names…neeck names! Yes, yes, we use those. Sure. My mother calls me Sefi for short. Dad never uses a neeck name. To him I am just always Asef."

"Well, no one ever calls me Vladimir. Maybe my boss does, or my mother when she wanted me to come back inside. But I've always been Viva or Vlad-O. Something like that."

Asef smiles. "Okay, Vlad-ee-meer."

I roll my eyes and chuckle.

***

"I appreciate the fact you need to be outside, Verstakov. I'll be sure to put that in your discharge papers. Vladimir? Vladimir? Hey, Verstakov, are you even listening?" Timur took a step away from the desk. "You're fired, do you hear me? The state says you have to go!"

Vlad automatically clenched his fist, lurched forward. But then abruptly stopped in his tracks. Stepped back, and slowly unclenched his fist. This anger, it must end. It ends right now. Find an Iskra, he thought.

But the noise remained. *Blast. Gunfire. Commands. Blast. Gunfire. Commands.* Vlad closed his eyes and tried to rise above it by thinking of enjoyable things, maybe an Iskra would appear. Fleeting images of riding dirt bikes with his buddies in the Ural foothills came to mind, but disappeared. An image of shooting pistols with Dad down at the shooting range drifted in, but drifted out just as quickly. Throwing darts with Oleg on Wednesdays at the Red Torch came and went. Nothing would stick. The agitation remained, as did the noise. *Blast. Gunfire. Commands. Blast. Gunfire. Commands.* Riding dirt bikes would not be his Iskra. Shooting pistols would not be his Iskra. Throwing darts would not be his Iskra.

Timur stepped back, touched the telephone. "What in bloody hell is wrong with you, Verstakov?"

Vlad took another step back, put his hands up to his sides, and pleaded, "I served this country with all my heart and soul. You can't just throw me away. Boss, please give me another chance."

Timur shook his head. "Sorry Verstakov, state says I can't. Get yourself some help, and then maybe you can come back."

Defeated, Vlad looked to the floor. "I'm...I'm sorry. It's the war, I have flashbacks. But I'll get better. If I can just find an Iskra, I'll get better."

Timur froze. "Huh?" he grunted. "You need to find a...what?"

Vlad held up both hands in total surrender. "I need to find something to believe in. It'll help. Maybe. I guess. I don't know. Shit, I don't know anymore." He flopped both hands back down to his sides, feeling utterly foolish.

Timur remained quiet for a second, rolling up his sleeves. "Whatever. Iskra or no Iskra, you need to go." He grabbed the telephone off the cradle. "Are you going to get the hell out or do I need to call the police?"

With the noise rising, Vlad clumsily shuffled backwards toward the door. "No. No, boss. I'm leaving. Leaving right now."

Outside with the generator and the crane and the workers, he cleared the metal steps in one stride then took off in a sprint through the dusty construction site, fueled by constant *Blast. Gunfire. Commands. Blast. Gunfire. Commands.*

19.

The flimsy metal door rattled to a close. Timur heard Vladimir's heavy work boots hit the gravel. Immediately, he bolted to the door and turned the lock. Peeking through the blinds, he saw Vladimir Verstakov sprinting across the site, off the property.

Timur stepped back to his desk and picked up the phone. The number he dialed belonged to a man by the name of Pasha. At least that was the name he went by. Timur had never met this Pasha, only knew that the guy periodically delivered a stack of cash to Timur's door. And it must have been Pasha who pulled the strings necessary to get Timur's daughter and two sons transferred out of the decrepit Mass School system, and into a much more distinguished District School.

All Timur had to do was call in with the names of some of the more troubled employees. The ones who angered easily, drank a lot, didn't have much to lose. Timur didn't know what Pasha did with the guys, didn't want to know. Cash came in on a regular basis, the kids were thriving, the wife was happy.

"Yeah, it's me," Timur said into the receiver. "Got another one for you, a real loose cannon. Name is Vladimir Stepanovich Verstakov. Big guy. High-strung. Criminal record as of this past weekend. Yeah. Went crazy, beat his wife. Oh, and he served in Afghanistan. Seems to be torn up over it." He paused. "No. I don't know what happened."

Timur hung up, closed the file. He placed it back on the pile, satisfied that another stack of money would be arriving any day now. He got back to his paper work.

Minutes later, he looked up. With one phone call, he had the ability to completely alter a life. The decision was solely up to him; he had the control. The thought filled him with so much satisfaction that he smirked to himself for no other reason than he felt great, complete, content.

Timur Ioksim had found his Iskra.

20.

The whole convoy slows. Yurchenko is up ahead, already out of his vehicle. So are Mikhail Astafurov and his crew. Mikhail and his men have their rifles, but Yurchenko is not armed.

There is nothing out here. We are on a single-lane dirt road strewn with rocks, big sandy ruts all over. Nothing but hot sand for kilometers in either direction. The sun is not yet at its highest point, but it glares at us with its fiery eye from above the horizon. Sometimes I think that thing just wants to taunt me.

Yurchenko motions for me to stop. "Why are we stopping?" Asef asks, looking up from a book. I kill the ignition; grab my rifle as I open my door. "I don't know, but stay here." I slam the door shut and head to Yurchenko. There is something blocking the road. An old, battered, white pickup, turned east-west, so we can't pass. Two men in there.

A man steps out on the passenger side. Olive skin, trim beard, probably around sixty, dressed in a flowing, white pirhan tonban, his head is covered with a small white cap. He calmly walks over to Yurchenko. They nod to each other and shake hands.

Mikhail Astafurov is motioning for soldiers to help him cover the front. Several hustle up there. Soldiers in the gun-mounted trucks are in position.

The Afghan man turns and points up the road where we are headed. He turns back and says something I don't under-

stand. Yurchenko appears to understand what the man said, and calmly replies in a horribly choppy Pashto.

After a few more failed attempts at conversing, Yurchenko holds his hands up and smiles a self-deprecating smile. He looks at me and says, "Verstakov, we need Asef to translate."

I respond, "Yes sir," and hustle back to my truck.

Asef is, as always, nose-deep in a book. "Yurchenko needs you," I say, twice slapping my palm against the hood of the truck. He looks up, his eyes get wider, and he smiles. He throws down the book, has to adjust his glasses again. He leaves his backpack on the seat.

***

A knock on the door. Then another. Vladimir barely opened his eyes. "Leave me alone," he mumbled, closing his eyes again. The brown couch provided enough cushion and support for a night's sleep, but it was not nearly long enough for his body. His legs draped over one end and every time he stirred, one leg dropped down to the floor. But he couldn't sleep in the bedroom, could barely even look at it without making himself sick.

Another knock on the door. *Blast. Gunfire. Commands. Blast. Gunfire. Commands.* Vlad swept the floor with his hand, found a fork resting on a plate. He grabbed the fork, hurled it toward the front door. "I said leave me alone!"

***

"I can go alone, Vlad-ee-meer. You don't need to walk with me over there," says Asef as he starts to shut the door. But the

weight of the truck's door combined with the uneven road is too much for his string bean of a body. Just as he pushes the door, he stumbles backwards into some brush. He lands on his skinny ass. I hurry over. He is nothing but a tangle of legs, arms, and ears. His glasses fall off. "Oh gosh. Sorry, Vlad-ee-meer! Sorry, I am so clumsy." I shake my head and roll my eyes. Typical Asef.

"It's okay; just stay on the road, all right? Yurchenko is right over there," I point up ahead, but I don't think he can even handle that much. I reach down to pick up his glasses, hand them over.

"Thank you," Asef says. He takes his glasses, slides them on, and stands up. He smiles that huge, goofy grin of his. "Okay, Vlad-ee-meer. I think I can manage from here."

***

More knocking on the door. It turned to pounding. *Blast. Gunfire. Commands. Blast. Gunfire. Commands.* Vlad fully opened his eyes. "What the hell?" he grumbled, tearing off the blanket. More pounding. "All right, all right, I'm coming!" Clad only in white underwear and socks, he wrapped the blanket around his body and walked to the door.

"Vladimir Stepanovich Verstakov?" came a smooth voice as soon as Vlad pulled open the door. "Are you Vladimir Verstakov, fired from Revolustia Construction this afternoon?"

Vladimir flipped on the light, rubbed his eyes. "Yeah. That's me. Now just who the fuck are you?"

"Pasha. Just call me Pasha. Sorry about the late hour but this is important. It concerns your career." At the door stood a man, not yet thirty, of average height, holding a leather briefcase at his side. He wore a long black coat over a white dress shirt and black slacks. Black necktie. Polished black dress shoes poked out beneath his slacks. He had some late-night stubble around his chin but otherwise he was clean-shaven with acutely defined cheekbones. Sandy blond hair, fast receding. Small hazel eyes. A soft but still manageable waistline.

Pasha took a step into the apartment, looked up at Vlad. "Heard you are out of a job. I'm here to help."

Vlad shook his head and shut the door. "Okay. Um, if this is about getting reassigned, I'm planning to file the paperwork during the week. Didn't know the employment division was so thorough. It must be after midnight," he said, repeatedly hiking the blanket up to cover his shoulders.

"It's 1:42 a.m.," Pasha said sharply, looking at his skinny watch. "I'm nothing if not precise." He started toward the den but stopped, staring in at the mess. "So. Mr. Verstakov, I take it you are single."

Vladimir scanned the room for his clothes. Spotted his hooded sweatshirt flung over the coffee table, jeans in a heap on the floor next to last night's supper plate. "Uh. No. I'm married," he said, scratching his head. "Zhanna's not here and she normally handles all the housekeeping. She's got her own way of doing things. I don't like to interfere."

"Clearly," said Pasha, rolling his eyes. He hesitantly brushed aside a pair of socks and sat down on the couch. "Mr. Verstakov, I'm not with any shit-for-brains state employment division." He placed the briefcase on the coffee table and looked up. "I'm what you could call a *biz-ness man* pure and simple. And I've come here to discuss some business with you."

Vlad swiped his sweatshirt off the table, began to turn it right side out. "Business? What the hell kind of business? This is the Soviet Union. We don't have any business going on here."

Pasha stared up at Vlad with a slight smile on his face. He chuckled. "Ah, yes, the mighty Soviet Union. A country run by the people, for the people. Workers of the world unite! and all that other bullshit they taught us in school. But the Soviet Union is dying, isn't she? Bursting at the seams with way too much debt, a bloody, useless war that went on ten fucking years. Even a new president with all kinds of ideas for change couldn't bring our boys back home. It's only a matter of time before Communism dissolves completely, paving the way for men like me to conduct some actual business. Good riddance to the Commies, I say. Soon, there will be no more state, only business. Profitable, profitable business."

Pasha unlatched the briefcase with both thumbs. "And this is the type of business I'm talking about."

Like a peacock proudly releasing its array of feathers, Pasha opened the briefcase. His slight smile grew wider as he swiveled the briefcase toward Vladimir. "Just take a look, Mr. Verstakov. Beautiful, isn't it? And it's yours."

21.

Stacks of US dollars, perfectly green and crisp, each neatly secured by a rubber band, filled the briefcase. Pasha reached in and carefully pulled out one stack.

He hefted the cash in his right hand, tossed it over to his left. "American dollars, right here," he said, placing the money on the table and pushing it along with one finger. "Hard currency in Russia. Will never go out of style. It's yours. Plus there's more when the job is complete."

Vlad tightened his grip on the quilt just to keep it around his body. "Hey, what...what exactly is goin' on here? I...uh...think you must have the wrong guy."

Pasha shook his head. "Nyet, nyet. I've got the right guy. One job and the money is yours." He turned the briefcase back towards himself, took out another stack of cash, and flipped through it with one thumb. "Beautiful. If the Americans understand anything in this world, it's money."

Vladimir lost hold of the quilt; leaving him standing there in his underwear and calf-high socks. "I have no problem with money. It's jail that makes me nervous. Whatever this job is, it can't be legal."

Pasha looked up and smirked. "Jail? Relax. I've got all the appropriate authorities on my payroll; no one is going to jail." He leaned forward, stroking the stack of cash with the back of his fingertips. Leaning back, he brought the cash to his nose and took a deep breath. "Ah, the look, the smell of money. There's just something about it."

Vladimir began to pull his sweatshirt over his head. "So, what is the job?"

Pasha, still staring at the money, said, "That apartment building your crew has been working on? I want it destroyed. Tonight. Before the morning crew arrives."

Vlad pulled the sweatshirt down, revealing his face. "You want me to destroy that apartment building? But why? It's almost done. I just finished framing the walls today. Why would you want it destroyed?"

Pasha let out an exhausted sigh and stood up. "You're asking a lot of questions for a guy in his underwear. Listen, I want that land. Right now, it belongs to the government like everything else in this shit-hole country, but our government is flat broke. If that building is declared a total loss, that's where I come in. I offer to take it off the state's hands, and it's mine. Once this pathetic country finally collapses, I turn around and sell that land for a tidy sum. Maybe to a British oil company. Maybe to an American bank or to a German auto dealer. Hell, perhaps I lease it back to a Russian orphanage at triple the price. Either way, I make a bundle of cash. And you will, too. Just burn the building down."

Vlad grabbed his jeans. "But there's security patrolling at night. There are people living in that area of town. I'll get caught," he said, stepping one foot into the pants.

Pasha shook his head. "Your boss gave security the night off, I made sure of it."

Vladimir zipped his jeans, thought a moment. "This could go bad. I already have an arrest record in my official file."

Pasha snapped the briefcase shut, stepped around the table. "What do you care about your file? What, are you worried about pleasing the government? Why? What the hell have those Commie bastards done for you? Oh, yes, besides shipping you off to war?" He looked up at Vlad with disdain. "What is it you were you fighting for over there exactly? Do you know? Did they tell you what you were fighting for before they sent you over there to get your legs blown off?"

Pasha paused. He turned around, took a few paces, and turned back to Vlad. "I know why your wife's not here, I checked. You are so fucked up from the war, she's afraid of you now. This government has turned you into some kind of a monster, and you stand here worried about your official file? Come on!"

Vlad's sweatshirt burned like the sun, his chest turned to cement. "Nyet!" he snapped. "Nyet. It's not like that. I'm not a monster. You don't know!" But his voice trailed off because he realized that, yes, it really was like that, and yes, Pasha did know. He turned away from Pasha, hoping to avoid any further discussion of Afghanistan. But the noise grew louder. *Blast. Gunfire. Commands. Blast. Gunfire. Commands.* He dropped his chin down, hands to his ears. "It's the noise. It's stuck in my head. I'm not a monster; I just can't stand the noise."

Pasha smirked again, so smug in his tailored suit and designer shoes. "Well, too bad that noise in your head is all for nothing. Too bad your marriage is over, all for nothing. What did it feel like to beat her, anyway? Does soft skin bruise easier? I bet it does. Too bad her pain was all for nothing. Twenty-five thousand Russian soldiers are dead. Thousands more returned home without limbs. Their lives ruined. Why? No reason. It was all for nothing!"

The noise kept coming, racing through like a freight train. Vlad snapped, "Nyet! It wasn't for nothing. We fought for this country. We fought for socialist freedoms. It wasn't all for nothing! Goddammit, it wasn't all for nothing!"

***

"Well, Vlad-ee-meer, here goes nothing!" Asef dusts himself off, moves his glasses up, and slaps my shoulder. He leaves to join Yurchenko and the Afghan man with whom he's trying to converse.

Now, this is odd. I can't figure this out. As Asef walks away, I see there are two big obstacles in his path. One is a rock, wide and jagged, as high as his calf. He sidesteps that one without any problem whatsoever. The ground is horribly uneven, strewn with gravel and brush. But he doesn't trip once, not even a stumble. There's also an old, felled tree on the other side of the road. He's going to trip over that thing and lose his glasses again, I just know it. But no, he steps on top of it. Right foot, left foot, and hops off. This kid's normally a nightmare on two feet, yet here he is practically gliding over to translate for Yurchenko and the Afghan man.

He reaches Yurchenko and gives both him and the Afghan man a professional nod. There's Asef, a willowy dark tower hovering over the compact, platinum-haired Yurchenko. He dwarfs our mighty captain and he's a full head taller than the Afghan man, too. But standing there, he doesn't look awkward. He doesn't fidget. He doesn't flash that goofy grin. He doesn't adjust his glasses.

Asef somehow looks older, poised like a statue next to Yurchenko. He's leaning forward, hands laced behind his back, listening to the language. Taking it in. Calmly turning his head to translate. What is it? He seems so different now.

***

"Language. That was Asef's Iskra," Vlad mumbled as the memory slowly faded. *Blast. Gunfire. Commands. Blast. Gunfire. Commands* still resonated in the background.

"Huh? What are you talking about?" replied Pasha, impatiently checking his watch.

Vlad snapped back to reality. "An Iskra is something you can believe in, that's all."

Pasha glanced up, let out an exhausted sigh. "Well, okaaaaaaayyyyy then, by all means, of course, let's forget everything and find a happy little Iskra! Perhaps we can all stand in a circle, hold hands, and sing while the goddamn Iron Curtain falls all around us."

He looked to the ceiling and back at Vlad. "What the fuck, Verstakov? You want something to believe in? You want hope? This briefcase here, this is full of hope. Green hope. Like I said, I'm a businessman. There is money to be made. I don't have time for some stupid Iskra, and neither do you. Now, if you want to subscribe to some New Age bullshit, do it on your own time. I need that apartment building burned down tonight. So tell me, Verstakov, are you in?"

Vlad took several labored breaths, closed his eyes, and tried to think of something to bring about calm. Fanning out a freshly dealt hand of cards, eyeing a straight in the process, lifting weights, fishing off the dock while Zhanna sunned herself atop a towel. All were good thoughts, but none would stick. The agitation remained, so did the noise. *Blast. Gunfire. Commands. Blast. Gunfire. Commands.* Playing poker would not be his Iskra. Lifting weights would not be his Iskra. Fishing would not be his Iskra.

Pasha cleared his throat. "I've got plenty of associates willing to do the job tonight. I'll ask you again, Verstakov, are you in?"

Vladimir looked at the stack of money, then back to Pasha. Pasha was real, the money was a sure thing. An Iskra may not even exist.

An endless expanse of scorching Afghan sand flashed before his eyes, a relentless sun overhead. Soviet bodies slumped in the sand, strewn over a blood-soaked desert. Vlad shook his head trying to erase the image from his brain. Everyone in the convoy had died a brutal death. The same went for countless Afghans, but that wasn't the worst part. The worst part was that this guy, Pasha, could be absolutely right. It could have all been for nothing.

Vlad walked to the side table, lit a cigarette, took one drag. "Yeah," he flicked his head back. "Hell yeah, I'm in."

22.

Vladimir flipped the ignition to neutral just before reaching Café Club, located five blocks north of the apartment building he was about to destroy. Still straddling his motorcycle, pushing side to side off the balls of his feet, he quietly guided the bike through the ally, and leaned it against a set of concrete steps next to the garbage cans behind the café.

Café Club was a new enterprise. Owned as a co-operative business between actual Russian citizens, not by the government. Zhanna absolutely loved the place, especially since the walls were painted in cheerful colors and were not lined with framed portraits of decrepit old Soviet leaders. Turned out, Pasha was one of the owners. According to instructions, he would be waiting inside, along with a bonus stack of cash when the job was complete. Vlad stashed the bike, tightened his coat around his torso, and took off toward the apartment building. With a stream of his own icy breath leading the way, he hustled past several other apartments, all of them dull, gray, and boxlike, just like the one he was about to burn down.

Along the cobblestone sidewalk, street lamps varied in their individual brightness; the few that worked properly made a constant, even-toned buzzing sound. The others only buzzed sporadically, flickering with random blips of light. Dim, useless light would not be a problem. No one was out. Too cold, too late. He pulled his fur-lined hat down over his ears as puffy white snowflakes began to sprinkle from the sky. The cobblestone gradually merged with gravel as he approached the doomed building. Vlad took a look around.

***

I look over at Mikhail Astafurov, who is across the road talking to some other troops. He stops talking to them and points me in the direction of the battered Afghan pickup. I nod to Mikhail and head up the road to keep an eye on the truck.

It's white, with patches of rust all over. Looks at least twenty years old. The engine is running and the driver is holding a radio to his mouth. He looks mid-fifties. He's got olive skin, a narrow face with a trim beard, and deep-set black eyes. His head is covered in a round little hat, just like the older man's. His eyes are on me while he speaks into the radio. I can't make out what he is saying, so I tap the windshield with my rifle and demand in Russian, "Better put that down!" He does. I demand he kill the engine. He does that, too.

"Who you talkin' to on that thing?" I bark, coming around to the open driver-side window. He pretends he can't understand, but as I grip my rifle and take a step closer, he starts talking. In halting Russian, he tells me that his three nephews are tending the neighbor's goats. A few of the goats have wandered and now they are on a trail. He is telling the boys not to go on that trail. He makes an exploding motion with his hands. I understand;

he's afraid the kids will trip over a land mine while tending the goats.

I stand at the open window. Do I believe him? He's talking to his nephew. Or is he bringing in reinforcements to slaughter us? He seems genuine. He's got a sincere voice.

***

Vlad snuffed his cigarette out beneath his shoe while the memory faded. The five-story partially finished apartment building loomed against a full moon shrouded in clouds. One spotlight illuminated the main double-door entrance. Either the other spotlight had burned out by itself, or Pasha had seen to it. No security in sight, just as Pasha said.

Vlad worked his way through the construction debris to the far west entrance, where it was darker. No doors yet.

The custodial closet was at the base of the stairs across from the main entrance. Five wooden shelves housed brand new cans of paint thinner, paint, wallpaper adhesive, and wood varnish. Several clean rags were folded neatly in perfect little squares.

Quickly he gathered the rags, threw them on the floor making two mounds of cloth. He grabbed a can of paint thinner, soaked the rags with the stuff. He took one final look around and ran over the plan one more time: Light the rags, run out the east side, use the back streets to return to Café Club. Collect the money. Ride home. Easy enough.

He pulled the lighter out of his coat pocket, squatted down, flicked the lighter, and brought the flame to one rag, then another, and another.

Vlad stood up and watched as the individual flames engaged each other to become a cohesive row of fire beneath the shelves. Flames crawled up the wall to the first shelf where a used paintbrush ignited into a ball of fire. He took a step back, felt the heat on his face, and watched the flames gradually eat up the closet.

***

I go to light a cigarette. The orange-red flame flickers, but it sputters out. I flick the lighter again. Another flame. This one does the trick.

I inhale, lean against the battered Afghan truck. The driver's not doing much of anything; just sitting there with his elbow resting on the open window. I look over. "Hey, you want a smoke?" I ask, holding up my cigarette.

The driver perks up. "Lotfan," he says with a pleasant smile. Lotfan, pretty sure that means please.

I reach into my chest pocket and pull out the pack of cigarettes. I slide another one out of the pack, hand it to him. I hold my lighter at window level. He takes the cigarette from me, shows me he's got his own lighter.

***

Vladimir shook the memory away while taking another step backwards. Clouds of thick, black smoke billowed from the closet, engulfing the area. Errant flames crept out along the linoleum toward the staircase. Vlad pivoted around, sprinted to the side door.

But he only made three strides toward the door when the first bullet rang out.

23.

The bullet hit the floor just short of his right foot. Vladimir buckled mid-stride, skidding down to his knees. Another bullet flew overhead. He covered his head, hit the floor. "Fuck!" he yelled into his chest. A third bullet rang out. He couldn't tell where that one hit, but it was close.

From somewhere inside the smoke, a rough male voice yelled out, "Security! This is security! Put your hands up!" He spoke Russian, but with a heavy Chechen accent. Vlad slowly lifted his head. Up ahead moved a dark figure; short, muscular, grasping a gun with both hands. He stayed in constant motion, walking forward, darting side to side, pointing the gun in random directions.

Vladimir quickly glanced right, then left. Too far from either side exit to make a decent run for it. The security guard was moving erratically all around the front. No way to make it outside before the guard took another shot. Probably best to surrender. Pasha would fix this. Hopefully.

Getting up on his knees, Vlad brought his hands up to his head and shouted into the thickening smoke, "I'm comin' out. Don't shoot, okay? Don't shoot!"

But security did shoot again, this time with much more accuracy. The bullet whizzed by, grazing his left shoulder. The guard came straight for him. Vladimir hunkered down, covering his head just as another bullet shot past his ear. He threw himself flat on the floor, interlaced his fingers behind his head. "What the fuck!" he whispered into the linoleum. "What the fuck! Fuck! Fuck!"

The guard stopped to reload. Vlad released his hands, propped himself up onto his elbows.

Straight ahead in the doorway, just under the lone spotlight, stood another guard. Taller and skinnier than the spastic, gun-toting one. The taller one stood stationary at the threshold, gripping a crowbar at his side. A ski mask covered his face. "Security!" he shouted. Obviously Chechen as well. The shorter one finished reloading and started darting around again, pointing the pistol in every direction. The taller one stood still, tapping the crowbar on the side of his leg.

No uniforms. No badges. A crowbar. A ski mask. Chechen. These guys were no security guards.

Vladimir dropped back down to his belly, shimmied backwards on his forearms while looking behind his right shoulder. The closet was obliterated, eaten whole by a solid wall of orange flame. Over his left shoulder, the row of fire in front of the staircase had risen to knee level. He could jump it, but only if he made a move for it right now. No doubt the two thugs would spot him as soon as he got to his feet.

No time to think. Vladimir jumped to his feet, whipped around and sprinted across the scorching linoleum to the staircase. He leapt over the knee-high row of flame, cleared it, and landed hard on his shoulder and hip on the plywood stairs. A scramble up the steps, a hard right, four more steps, and he set foot on the second-floor hallway.

Not as much smoke on the second floor, but it was rising fast. Vlad stopped to catch his breath, glanced down the hallway. From down the stairs came a heavy thudding sound. Another thud followed that one, but a high-pitched scream accompanied it. Most likely, the taller guy had cleared the flames, but the short one had seared his balls.

Vladimir sprinted down the hallway to the unit he had been working on yesterday. The plywood subfloor was hot. Beyond hot. Scorching. It was going to give way. One set of heavy boots pounded down the hall in a constant cadence. Probably the taller thug. His boots hit hard, creating a steady, heavy-toned rhythm.

***

Asef doesn't miss a beat. He's rhythmic. No lapses. He stands tall, confident, managing two languages with ease. Translating is automatic for this kid.

Yurchenko and the Afghan man are conversing now, in full, coherent sentences, thanks to Asef. I am leaning against the truck, smoking, watching them. Whenever Yurchenko speaks, Asef looks to the Afghan man, copies Yurchenko's words in fluid, flawless Pashto. His Russian is perfect and precise without even the slightest trace of an accent.

Russian is not a beautiful language, and neither is Pashto, but Asef makes them beautiful.

***

Vlad skidded but barely slowed down, made a left into the apartment unit. A full moon beckoned from outside the window cutout. Maybe there would be enough time to jump out the window and haul ass back to Café Club. But the tall thug and his crowbar were coming quickly down the hall. And that short, muscle-bound guy was around somewhere, possibly outside. Simply jumping out the window wasn't going to work; he needed a weapon.

Vlad felt his way through the thickening smoke, found the stud that had been the source of so much anger and frustration yesterday. He reached up with one hand. Sure enough, the hammer was still stuck in there. His fingers grazed over the hammer's handle. He jumped up twice, shoving the bottom of the hammer upwards. The claw loosened. With one foot against the stud, he yanked the handle out to free the hammer.

Vladimir moved cautiously back toward the window, blindly swinging the hammer out in front of his face. Once his hips hit the bottom of the cutout, he quickly turned, slid one leg to the outside, and then the other. The crisp iciness of Sverdlovsk had never felt so welcoming. Two stories down. Seven meters at most. Maybe drop the hammer first, he thought.

But the hammer flew from his grasp as a blazing hot crowbar slammed across his neck, jerking him backwards to the floor. "Goddamn it!" Vlad yelled, his head hitting the scorching floor. He quickly rolled to his left side, felt frantically for the hammer. No such luck. A strong hand grabbed Vlad by the bicep, flipped him over on his back.

A smoky silhouette of the taller thug with the crow bar at his side, his face shrouded by a ski mask, stood over him. The man dropped down hard, thrust a knee into Vlad's chest, crushing the crowbar down over his windpipe. With his arms pinned to his sides, Vlad tried to dig his feet into the floor and arch his back, but the floorboards softened and sunk down, making it impossible to find purchase. His heels kept sliding out only to flop on the floor.

The weakening floorboards did allow Vladimir to turn his head slightly and dig his right shoulder down into the floor, leaving a tiny gap between the bar and his windpipe. He took a quick breath. In one swift, adrenaline-fueled motion, he got a right-handed grip underneath the bar, then turned slightly to the left, and performed the same maneuver.

The thug's eyes widened beneath the ski mask. He pressed the bar down harder as Vlad tightened his grip. Dense drops of sweat, salty and musky, dripped from the holes in the thug's ski mask into Vlad's eyes. Vlad managed to talk, but choked on his own words. "Who. The. Fuck. Are. You?"

The thug said nothing, just huffed and cursed in his brutish Chechen tongue.

The floorboards creaked and popped beneath the struggle. There wasn't much time for either of them. He maintained his grip on the bar and pressed up against the tall thug's strength. The crowbar couldn't weigh more than five kilos, Vlad figured. The man must weigh seventy-five, eighty kilos.

***

"Hey Verstakov, how much can you bench press, anyway?"

I'm still leaning against the battered old truck watching Asef translate for Yurchenko. Funny question, how much can I bench press? Who is asking? I look over. "What?"

It's a soldier from the back of the convoy. He's walking up the road. Can't remember his name, not sure if I ever knew it because everyone here calls him Red. Red's got flaming red hair, lots of freckles. Can't be a day older than nineteen. Must have been drafted just out of high school.

"Our truck got stuck in the sand when we stopped, but it's so loaded down, we can't push it out ourselves," Red says. Of course he can't, his arms are too soft and squishy.

"But you look strong enough, Verstakov. How much can you lift, anyway? Eighty? Ninety kilos?"

I laugh because that is funny. Really, I find that hilarious. "Uh, Red, try a hundred and ten."

***

The memory faded, but infused Vlad with the strength to mutter, "You want to see how much I can bench press, motherfucker?" He followed through, jerking the bar straight up, slamming the taller thug square in the nose.

The man tumbled backwards into the unfinished wall, cupping both hands over his face. Vladimir shot up to standing, the crowbar swinging. He took a step toward the guy.

But a sharp stab of metal cut into the back of his neck. He pivoted around. The shorter thug was there, holding the hammer out in front of his body, gripping it with both hands. Must have lost the gun on the stairs. He swung it again, upwards at Vlad's cheek, but missed.

The entire floor abruptly sank down. Felt like at least two centimeters. The smaller thug wobbled in his stance, but swung again. The taller guy was still slumped along the wall, bleeding, gagging. The smaller guy stepped closer, took another swing, but Vlad stopped the hammer cold with the crowbar, shoved the bar forward out from his chest, and gave the guy a hard, left-footed kick to the gut. He faded into the smoke just as the floor dropped lower still, another two centimeters, at least. Vlad dropped the crowbar.

No time to look for it. He turned, took two giant steps to the window, guided only by the light of the full moon outside. Grabbing the top of the window cutout, he swung both legs to the outside. Behind him, a high-pitched scream, followed by a deafening crash. Vlad turned back just as the entire middle section of the subfloor collapsed into an open sea of vengeful flames. That short guy must have dropped like a bullet.

Vladimir hastily turned toward the outside. With both heels secure against the side of the building, he dug them in, lurching forward out the window. He, too, dropped like a bullet.

24.

Vlad dropped straight down, ultimately landing flat on his belly on a mound of dirt and gravel. He clambered up to his knees, heaving, retching, fighting against constricted lungs to take a genuine breath. Wads of black, tar-like substance spewed from his mouth. A thin stream of blood ran from the wound at the back of his neck to the corner of his mouth. "Son of a bitch," he muttered, finally able to speak.

Sitting back on his knees, he covered the neck wound with his blackened, ashy left hand and looked up. A solid mass of terra cotta-colored flame jetted out from the second-story window from which he had jumped moments ago. The flames gradually rose up to the third-floor window to merge with thick ribbons of black smoke.

No fire trucks approaching, no police, not even a siren off in the distance. Pasha hadn't been kidding around when he said he bribed all the right people. And the two thugs, were they Pasha's doing as well? "Son of a bitch," Vlad muttered again.

Vlad fell forward, hyperventilating, on his hands and knees. He spit out another wad of black mucous, his chest laden with it. A hefty, fist-sized rock lay just in front of his face. He grabbed it in case that ski-masked thug appeared.

He coughed again, released the rock. Not enough strength or energy left to wield it, anyway. Most likely, it would be used against him if it came down to another fight. He flopped down to one side.

A siren rang out in the distance. Vladimir pushed himself up, looked around. The grassy field behind the burning complex was dark enough and away from the street. It was the safest route of escape. A long loop around the neighborhood while the firefighters busied themselves, and then, if everything went well, he'd walk the back way to Café Club to collect the money. Vlad stood, decided not to run, but to walk calmly through the dark field.

***

I'm walking away from my post to go help push the pickup out of the sand. Should I call Mikhail Astafurov over to tell him about it? That I am needed elsewhere? No, he's way up the road talking to some village teenagers. He's handing them cigarettes and chocolate bars. Must be getting directions or some other useful information out of them.

Besides, Captain Yurchenko and the older Afghan man are heavily engaged in conversation, thanks to Asef. I don't want to disturb their flow. I can see Red's embedded truck down the road from where I stand; this won't take but a minute. One good shove and I'll be right back here.

Red is walking next to me. He's talking, but I don't hear. I turn around and walk backwards. The Afghan driver's got his head back on his seat, looks like he's about to doze off.

Red takes out his keys. "I'll start the engine; tell me when to hit the gas, okay?"

"Yep," I say as I toss my cigarette to the ground. I head to the rear of the truck.

***

Vlad had made it midway into the grassy field when the vicious sounds crept in again. *Blast. Gunfire. Commands. Blast. Gunfire. Commands.* He dropped to his knees, clutched his stomach, spit up another wad of black goop, and moaned, "My post. I left my post."

25.

Pavel "Pasha" Grachov placed his steaming mug of tea down on one of Café Club's shiny black tables. In his other arm, he balanced the café's cash register drawer and zippered money pouch. He slid them from his arm onto the table and sat down. Café Club had long since closed and Vladimir was not back, time to count the night's haul.

He grabbed a handful of cash, separated the rubles from the dollars, counted out a tidy sum, and secured it with a rubber band. "So easy," he muttered, tossing the bundle to the table. He took a sip of tea and gathered another wad of cash. "So fucking easy."

The trendsetting young adults of Sverdlovsk were hungry. But no longer for cold beet soup or broiled meat covered in sour cream. They wanted pizza, hamburgers, and French fries. Pasha provided it all. No longer satisfied with the chewy, chocolate-flavored, digestive biscuits sold in the state stores, they wanted real chocolate. Pasha provided that, too. Thanks to this era of Openness and Restructuring, anything that had roots in the West was red hot, selling at a sky-high premium. Pasha was more than happy to supply all of it—at a hefty markup.

Pasha secured a fourth bundle, tossed it down, and scanned the remaining cash. What would his father-in-law, that old Jew lawyer, say to all this? He chuckled, and gathered another bundle of cash, confident that he would surpass the old man some day.

The trendsetting young adults of Sverdlovsk were not just hungry, they were thirsty, too. But plain Russian vodka wasn't making the grade in these waning days of Soviet rule. Pasha quickly discovered that if he added a lime wedge to the inferior Polish vodka he ordered for fifteen rubles per bottle, watered it down with soda water, and described it on the menu as a cool and refreshing "Paris Cocktail," he could easily sell the stuff for seven rubles per shot.

Pasha secured the eighth and final bundle of cash. Next, he opened the zippered money pouch.

The trendsetting young adults of Sverdlovsk craved music, as well. But the usual patriotic hymns or crappy synthesizer medleys could no longer fill the void. To meet the demand, Pasha hired a hip, young, university kid with spiky blond hair and a decent collection of black-market record albums to spin songs by popular Western rock bands at earsplitting volumes, much to the crowd's delight. Because they were getting the added benefit of decent music, Pasha charged customers a twenty-ruble cover charge just to get in the door. That money went straight into the money pouch.

All total, fourteen stacks of cash gleamed like jewels on the table. The rubles would need to be converted to hard currency at once, before their value fell any further. Pasha checked his watch. His newly hired thug, Vladimir Verstakov, should be arriving any time now, the building destroyed. Yet another investment.

Push them a little, these Afghan war veterans. Touch upon their weaknesses, primarily the futility of the war, their anger, their guilt, and they caved. Most of the veterans were so far gone—addicted to painkillers and alcohol—that they practically fed from Pasha's rich hands. They were easy pickings. Push them a little, get them angry enough, wave some money or pills around, and they'd do anything. That deranged construction worker, Vladimir Verstakov, had been no exception. Guilt and anger were wonderful stomping grounds.

Pasha took another sip of tea, leaned back. And what was it Vladimir had been ranting about? Something to believe in? Ah, yes, an Iskra, that was it. Pasha smirked at the thought.

He placed the money in his briefcase, shaking his head in euphoric disbelief. This little co-op café was proving to be a virtual gold mine, far better than he had originally envisioned, and far, far better than he was leading his two business partners to believe.

Fyodor Druchek and Grigory Fomenko luckily didn't come around the café much; too busy pushing paper for the crippled KGB. Neither of them were comfortable in business, and this idea of a New Russia, a democracy, where people could go into business for themselves, voice their own opinions, and even protest the government, sounded crazy to men such as Fyodor and Grigory, line-toeing men who had been employed by the state their entire adult lives.

But the demise of the Cold War meant smaller, sporadic paychecks, and a freeze on pension funding. The world's most powerful spy agency was hanging by a thread. Pasha knew it and saw an opportunity. After a few meetings, Fyodor and Grigory readily handed over their existing retirement funds to invest in the café, authorizing Pasha to run the day-to-day operations. Every few months, he threw them a thousand or so to keep them quiet. The rest of the profits went directly toward his own real estate ventures.

And another investment beckoned, just as soon as Vladimir destroyed that hideous, totalitarian apartment building. Twenty-five thousand square meters of prime downtown property he could either sell or develop just as soon as the Iron Curtain fell by the wayside.

"So fucking easy," Pasha muttered again as he latched his briefcase shut.

"Easy? Hardly." Came a deep, gravelly voice from near the kitchen.

Pasha startled, knocking the chair over with his briefcase. Vladimir Verstakov was slumped against the wall, bleeding from his mouth and cheek. Worse, droplets of blood splattered upon the fine Italian tile. He had tracked mud through the place, and his clothes were covered in sweat and ash. "Verstakov," Pasha said, keeping a firm grip on the briefcase. "What the fuck happened?"

26.

"You look like bloody hell," Pasha quipped as he pushed Vladimir into the kitchen and shoved a dishtowel in his face. "Here, use this. You're dripping blood all over the floor."

Vlad held his head back but gagged on blood and ash. "I did it," he said, breathlessly. "But two guys jumped me, had a crowbar and a gun. They were Chechen. One's dead. He fell through the floor. Don't know about the other one."

Pasha stopped fussing with the towel. He pivoted around with his hands on his hips, walking away while shaking his head. "That doesn't make any sense, why... who...would..." he turned, slammed one hand on the steel counter. "Well, fuck me, those idiots have finally figured it out."

Vlad abruptly brought his head back to neutral and grunted, "Huh?"

Pasha exhaled. "It must be my co-op business partners, Fyodor and Grigory. They are sending a message that they are on to me." He looked away and shrugged. "Typical KGB, leaving the dirty work to their Chechen hired thugs."

Blast. Gunfire. Commands. Blast. Gunfire. Commands. The noise hit like a freight train. *Blast. Gunfire. Commands.*

Blast. Gunfire. Commands. Vlad threw the towel aside. "KGB! You're tangled up with the KGB? And sent me in there? You set me up!"

***

"Okay this is how we set it up. Red, get in the cab, I'll go to the rear. We'll push this motherfucker out of here in no time." Red jumps in the cab. I trudge in the hot sand to the back. Red's truck mate, Danil, is already back here. He nods, a cigarette dangling between his lips. Danil is from Vladivostok, twenty-three, a deep-sea fisherman like his dad. His forearms are huge.

The truck rocks back and forth as Danil and I push, but it's not even beginning to move from the rut it's in. Both back tires are completely buried in sand. I slap the side of the truck and yell, "Hey, Red, kill the engine, will ya? We gotta dig this out. You got a shovel in here?"

I glance over to the battered Afghan truck. The driver's still got his head back against the seat.

Red jumps out, rummages through the cab. He pulls out a triangular army-issue spade. Danil says he has one, too. I fetch another one from a nearby truck and the three of us start digging. I keep glancing over at the Afghan driver. He's not doing anything.

Maybe five minutes go by; the tires are free. We are burning up. Red is breathing hard even though Danil and I did most of the digging. Danil takes off his blue-and-white-striped shirt, ties it around his head to catch the sweat.

"Okay, Red, get behind the wheel. Let's push the motherfucker out!" I yell. He hops in.

Danil lunges back, places both hands on the bumper. I toss the shovel aside and wipe my brow.

***

Pasha had his hands up. "Okay look, I may not be the most honest businessman in the world. Been skimming off the top for my own real estate ventures, but I didn't set you up, Verstakov, really. I didn't know the partners would do this." He stood still for a moment, watching. "Hey, you know what I'll do? I'll throw in an extra grand for your efforts. Consider it hazard pay." He then walked over to a cabinet, pulled it open. "Here, let me get you a drink. Got my own stash here. Only the best stuff will do after a night like this."

Vladimir took a deep breath, tried to quiet the noise. *Blast. Gunfire. Commands. Blast. Gunfire. Commands.* No more anger. No more anger.

Pasha poured two shots of Stoli and slid one over. He took his glass and started pacing. "They are coming after me next. There must be a way to keep Fyodor and Grigory away from the café, away from the books, and the hell away from me."

Vladimir stared at his glass, reached out and touched it, one drink, no one would know. But ultimately he pushed the glass away and pulled a pack of cigarettes out of his coat pocket. "I can't drink. Got a little problem with the stuff." He tapped one cigarette out, stuck it in his mouth. "You need security," he said, searching the other pocket for a lighter.

Pasha stopped, snapped his fingers. "Of course, that's what I need. Security. Rich men need security." He threw back his shot and set it back down on the counter. "Be my bodyguard. Three hundred per week. Cash. American dollars, of course," he said.

Vlad shook his head while lighting the cigarette. "Shit, Pasha, I don't know, I almost got killed tonight."

"Okay, five hundred per week," Pasha snapped. "That is damn good money, and last I checked, you were out of a job. You think your wife is going to come sauntering back? Back to the man who beat her? Oh, and look, now he's broke and out of a job. What the fuck, Verstakov! You've got nothing else!" He poured another shot and downed it.

Pasha set about pacing and planning. "Bodyguards need to stay in shape, so I'll pay for a membership at the Soviet Boxing Academy. They let regular people exercise there now, not just hand-picked elite athletes anymore."

Vlad took a drag. True, he had nothing. Nothing but violent memories and noise. And here was Pasha. This guy was throwing around money as if it were nothing; he wore a tailored suit and sported a five-hundred-ruble haircut; his mother surely never lied; his father had not blown his head off; he wasn't sent into an endless war. Most of all, Pasha did not have the *Blast. Gunfire. Commands. Blast. Gunfire. Commands* running through his head, making him so crazy that he couldn't tell his wife from a rebel fighter.

Perhaps enough cash would calm the noise, erase the memories, and bring Zhanna back.

Vladimir blew out a cloud of smoke. "Sure, I'll be your bodyguard," he said. "But show me how to make money, too."

Pasha stopped, crossed his arms and smiled. "You want to be rich?" He laughed. "Sure. I'll teach you everything I know. Work for me and get rich."

Pasha reached for the bottle, threw back another shot. Vlad looked at his glass longingly, but did not touch it. "Okay, Pasha, You've got yourself a bodyguard," he said, pointing one finger. He tapped his cigarette in an ashtray. "Now, give me one rule every good business man ought to know."

Pasha stood still, staring straight ahead. "Okay, here's one for ya, listen up," he said, rolling up his sleeves. "Paying too much interest will bury a man. Always minimize any interest you must pay. Don't pay it. Earn it."

Vlad took a drag. "Okay," he said, despite the irrelevancy of the advice given. The apartment had come courtesy of the government after he and Zhanna married; his motorcycle was a result of a series of wise trades. He had second-hand furniture and nothing but jeans and T-shirts to wear. But he filed the advice away. "Don't pay interest. Got it."

27.

23 January

"There, almost done. Just one more little piece right here." Zhanna leaned in, took one final snip off her new client's bangs, then stepped aside. "So, what do you think?"

Olga Slavakova had walked in off the street two hours ago, a tearful mess. No makeup, no jewelry, a scarf over her frizzy, salt-and-pepper strands. Said she just found out her husband had slept with a slew of women throughout their marriage, and was not planning to stop any time soon. Young office interns, short-skirted file clerks, bleached-blonde reporters, the occasional waitress; apparently, the man was not discerning in the least.

After undergoing Zhanna's handiwork, Mrs. Slavakova now stared silently at her reflection. Her locks smooth and shiny, cut to a neat and tidy shoulder length, blow-dried away from her face, light wispy bangs, all dyed a deep, rich chocolate color. She brought her hands up and lightly patted her new hairstyle, almost bursting into tears again. "Zhanna, I love it!"

Zhanna placed her scissors down and breathed a silent sigh of relief. New clients were always nerve-wracking, especially the rich, well-connected ones. "I'm glad you like it, Mrs. Slavakova. It's best to come in every six weeks to touch up the color and trim the ends. That way, you always look put together."

Zhanna pulled open a side drawer, pushed around several tubes of lipstick, and decided on a plum color. "And if you don't mind, your lips are screaming for color!" She leaned down to apply the lipstick, stood up. "Your skin is a little dry and flakey. Make up a mixture of one part oil to two parts salt. Scrub it on your face every other night for the remainder of the winter. That should do the trick."

Tension and sadness slowly melted from Mrs. Slavakova's face. "Zhanna," she said, staring at her reflection. "I am fifty-three years old. For twenty-two years, I was the dutiful daughter of an ambitious politician. For the past thirty-one years, I have been the loyal, adoring wife of an even more ambitious politician. My children are grown, and I have considered myself done. Just plain done. I never thought I could look this good again."

Zhanna tossed the lipstick back in the drawer. "Don't ever say you are done, Mrs. Slavakova. Twenty-three, fifty-three, or a hundred and three, women are never done. Women have too much to do in this world."

Zhanna stopped for a moment with the drawer still open and looked up at her mirror where a few photographs of her with Vladimir were taped to the glass.

In one photograph taken at their wedding, Vladimir stood so tall and handsome in his black suit. Closely cut auburn hair, those intense Slavic green eyes shining into the camera. He held her in his arms, cradling her with a warm, gregarious smile on his face. Zhanna's gown, which she designed and stitched herself, flowed down to her ankles, white satin, with little, yellow, satin flowers around the neckline. In her right hand, she held a single yellow rose. But she was not looking into the camera at all; she gazed only at Vladimir.

"That must be your husband," said Mrs. Slavakova.

Zhanna looked down, shut the drawer. "That's Vladimir. We're...apart right now."

"And is Vladimir where your split lip came from?" asked Mrs. Slavakova. "Your makeup isn't hiding a thing, my dear."

Zhanna swiped a bottle of hairspray off the counter, looked at her client in the mirror and stopped. "It's strange, Mrs. Slavakova, I know I can't go back. But I still love him." She pumped the bottle a few times into her client's new hairstyle. "Oy, I may be the most foolish woman in all of Russia."

Mrs. Slavakova shrugged. "Join the club, my dear, join the club."

She stopped with the hairspray and stood still. For the first time in days, Zhanna laughed.

28.

9 September

"And here's another tip, V.V., if you're interested," offered Pasha, with one hand on the steering wheel. They cruised along in Pasha's cherry red, two-door Lada on their way to another job. Vlad sported a new tailored suit, complete with silk tie, a sleek leather briefcase, and a cool pair of wraparound sunglasses. Going about life as a sharp-dressed man was one of Pasha's tips, an integral step, he said, in the acquisition of wealth.

Vlad turned to Pasha. "Yeah, I'm interested, boss. Let's hear it."

"Okay, it goes like this," said Pasha. "All the money you make must go back into the business. Every bit of it. Especially in the beginning. That's how your business grows."

Pasha made a right turn on Sobolunksa Street and headed east. "For example, my wife's parents gave us five thousand rubles as a wedding gift. I invested that money in black market items, televisions, record albums, stereos, chocolate bars, you name it. More than doubled my initial investment. I took that money, invested half of it in home appliances and the other half in the typical vices—cigarettes, alcohol, girlie magazines. Got a 300 percent return that time."

Vlad thought for a moment. "You didn't go on holiday? If Zhanna's parents gave us that kind of money, I would have taken her on a trip. Maybe to Georgia. She's always wanted to go there."

Pasha sighed. "That is precisely why I am a millionaire and you are not. Now pay attention." Pasha went on, gesturing with one hand. "Investing is what you need to be doing. You've got some cash now. Invest it!"

He made another right. "The Communist forces were finally put down last month. Boris Yeltsin will be the leader of a New Russia, and he is going to fucking blow this country apart. You need to gather your cash, buy up goods while you still can. I'm talking toilet paper, toothpaste, pussy plugs, diapers, towels. Go raid the charitable groups if you have to. Jack up the price and sell the stuff on the open market. I guarantee you'll more than double your investment. See how it works? Make your money work for you every hour of every day."

Pasha pulled alongside the curb and pointed straight ahead. "This is it, your next assignment. There's an extra grand in it for you."

Vladimir took a look. Just another ten-story apartment building, gray, utilitarian, made of concrete, just like all the others in town. "What am I supposed to do here?" he asked.

Pasha explained. "This is where my partner, Grigory Fomenko, lives. He and his family occupy the two apartments on the top floor. You need to break in and get some information for me."

Vlad shot his head around. "You want me to break into a KGB agent's apartment? Are you fucking insane?"

"Relax. It'll be fine," said Pasha, raising both hands off the steering wheel. "Grigory is on vacation. He took the whole family for a cruise down the Volga. They won't be back for five more days. Plus, I've got the keypad code to get in. It'll be easy."

Vlad leaned back. "But what do you want?"

Pasha killed the ignition and looked around. "My head cook says Grigory was waiting outside the other night, asking about the café. He wanted to know the daily operating expenses of the kitchen and so on. And just this morning, Yessica, you know the waitress with the legs that won't stop? Well, she said Grigory approached her in the park with questions about how many people come into the café on an average night."

Pasha slammed the steering wheel. "I can't have that obese Commie lurking around scaring my staff! I need to know what information he has. Maybe I can use it to throw him off."

Vlad's head hurt just thinking about it. "This man is an agent for the most powerful spy network in the world. You don't think he knows exactly what is in his office, and exactly what has gone missing?"

Pasha laughed. "Correction. The KGB *was* the most powerful spy network in the world. Now, it's running on fumes. The agency and its agents are limping right along with the rest of the country. Any agent worth his salt defected back in the eighties. Besides, Grigory was never a ruthless Cold War killer. He's made a career out of shuffling papers and making sure the real spies have enough tea to keep them awake during interrogations. Relax."

Vlad lit a cigarette. "A grand?" he asked.

Pasha nodded "Yep. Cash. I'll drive around the block, meet you back here."

Vlad stepped out of the car, briefcase in hand. A few leaves still clung to the trees. Blades of brown grass grew sparsely through cracks in the cobblestone. Two women passed by, one with a toddler in her arms. Once the women strolled out of view, Vlad stepped inside the building. To the left stood a flight of wooden stairs. To the right, an elevator. Exhaling, he pressed the button and waited for the elevator to open.

29.

Vlad waited, one hand in his pocket, sleek briefcase brushing his shin, for the door to slide open. The metal door showed a muted reflection of a sharply dressed man on his way to the acquisition of great wealth. The clunky door jerked along its track, making a muffled buzzing sound upon opening. Inside, two flickering fluorescent rods lighted the cramped space.

Inside the elevator stood a redheaded man, a black duffel bag tossed over his shoulder, a bottle of Coca-cola in his hand. His build was soft, his face full of freckles, and his hair glowed a bright fiery orange beneath the fluorescent light. He looked to be in his twenties. The man stepped off the elevator, and nodded to Vlad with a friendly smile. "Good afternoon," he said, sliding past.

***

Red hops out of the truck. His hair looks like a wild flame next to the black metal of the truck. He smiles and raises his hand to Danil and me. "Thanks guys, I appreciate it!" We were successful in pushing the truck out of the sand. Now it sits crooked on the road with Red standing next to it, smiling.

***

Vladimir startled, so much that he dropped his briefcase to the floor, where it landed amongst dust and muddy shoe tracks. He lurched toward the front door and grabbed the man's elbow so hard the man spun around. The cola splashed out of the bottle, splattering onto Vlad's fitted shirt and silk tie, but he didn't care. Instead, Vlad broke out in a huge grateful smile, so relieved to finally see a familiar face, someone who understood the demons of war.

"Red! Oh, my God, Red! It's you!" he shouted, towering over the guy. "But you were shot in the stomach. I carried you out...but you survived! You're alive. I can't believe it!"

The redheaded man tried unsuccessfully to pull his arm away. "Um, do we know each other?" he asked meekly, eyes darting all around. He lost his grip on the cola bottle, it gushed over one of Vlad's shiny shoes. The poor guy was close to panic. Obviously, the man was not Red. Vlad abruptly let go of the man's elbow, took a step sideways into the puddle of cola. He held up both hands and stepped back, his foot crunching on his sunglasses. "Oh, hey, man, I'm sorry. Thought you were someone else."

The redheaded man walked backwards until his duffle bag hit against the glass door. "No problem. Really, it's okay," he said, scurrying out the door.

Vlad stood for a moment staring out the door, and then bowed his head. Of course that hadn't been Red. Red died in the ambush. They all died. No one was left.

Vlad took a deep breath and looked down at his expensive new suit. Shirt and tie drenched in sticky cola, one shoe covered in the stuff. He picked up his briefcase, wiped off the dust and mud. One corner was scuffed from hitting the ground.

He focused on his filthy suit and tie. Could get them cleaned. Could buy another briefcase. But the noise persisted. *Blast. Gunfire. Commands. Blast. Gunfire. Commands.* His stomach churned, chest turned to cement. The swanky clothing didn't matter. When he saw Red, or the man he thought was Red, that's what mattered.

Going about life as a sharply dressed man would not be his Iskra.

30.

The elevator door rumbled to a close. Vlad gathered his things, still reeling from the memory of Red. But a hurried voice shouted from the entrance. "Hey, catch the elevator, will ya?" Vlad looked over. The voice belonged to a middle-aged man running toward the elevator. He wore a brown business suit, carried a briefcase in one hand and a rolled up newspaper in the other. With just a tiny sliver of fluorescent light showing through the elevator door, Vlad quickly reached out and stopped it.

"Thanks," said the man, a little out of breath. He looked up at Vlad with a pleasant smile and said, "This elevator is painfully slow and I only have a half hour for lunch." The man stepped inside. "Where ya going?" he asked, glancing down to the panel of buttons.

Vlad put his left foot inside the tiny compartment and glanced at the man. "Ten. Please. Tenth floor. Thank you," he said weakly.

With one foot in the elevator, the fluorescent light overhead emitted a scorching heat so bright he had to shield his eyes. So hot, his skin burned. He stood motionless while the floor turned to sand. Slowly his foot sank in, up to his knee, under a blazing Afghan sun.

***

Danil and I trudge through the sand, back up to the road. This stuff is almost up to our knees. Danil is ahead of me; he's got his blue-and-white-striped shirt wrapped around his head. It's soaked through with sweat. We step onto the road. Danil retrieves his canteen from the truck, takes a good hefty swig. Red pulls his canteen off his shoulder and hands it to me. "Here, take a drink," he says. I nod in gratitude, toss the spade aside, and take hold of the canteen.

Danil lowers his canteen to his chin. He nudges me in the ribs and points to the battered old Afghan truck. "Looks like your driver's got company there, Verstakov."

I look up the road to my charge. He's got his handheld radio to his mouth, talking into it. "Shit!" I yell, thrusting the canteen back into Red's hands. "Come on!" I sprint up the road, my rifle clanging at my back. Danil is right behind me; I can hear his heavy foot strikes.

I stop in front of the truck, swing my rifle around. "Thought I told you to put that radio down!" I've got the rifle aimed at the windshield. The driver's eyes are huge. He immediately drops the radio.

Danil comes around to the driver's side. He's gripping his rifle, too. He opens the door and yanks the driver to the ground. He stomps on the guy's back with his bulky leather boot. The driver is frantically trying to lift his head, yelling in Pashto. I step forward; aim my rifle at the back of his head. Danil kneels down, his knee pressed into the man's shoulder blades. "Just shut up!" he yells. I maintain my aim on the back of the man's head.

Red appears at my side, breathing hard.

Mikhail Astafurov comes running over. The gold wedding band around his neck bounces side to side. "What's the problem here?" he asks. I tell him I left the driver to push Red's vehicle out of the sand and then I saw the driver talking on the hand-held radio. "The radio is in the truck," I say.

Mikhail pulls his pack off, places it on the ground. From it, he takes out a length of coarse rope and tosses it to Danil. Danil lets up on the driver's shoulder blades and ties his wrists together behind his back.

The civil conversation between Captain Yurchenko and the Afghan man is rapidly deteriorating, thanks to our little scuffle. The Afghan man is visibly upset, pointing and yelling. We've got his friend tied up, a rifle to his head. Guess I can't blame him.

Yurchenko is trying to smooth over the situation, but he's glaring at us with that steely blue stare of his. He's pissed. Asef is having a hard time translating because the two men are talking at the same time. He keeps looking from one to the other, doing the best he can with the situation.

The driver keeps turning his head side to side, pleading and yelling. Danil pats the guy down. He pulls a knife out of the driver's waistband. "What's this? What are you doing with this?" he barks, and tosses it beyond the man's reach. The knife hits the sand. It's a medium-sized blade, black handle with a band of gold on the tip. Danil yanks the driver up to his knees. He's got sand in his beard and his head covering is askew.

Now the older Afghan man is walking over, fuming. Captain Yurchenko, who is not very happy either, follows him. Asef is shuffling behind them, trying his best to keep some kind of conversation going.

As soon as Asef approaches, the driver calms down, despite the fact that his wrists are bound, and he's got a rifle aimed at his head.

Danil looks up at Asef and points to the knife. "Ask him why he's carrying around that knife!" Asef translates accordingly, then looks back toward us. "He says it's for slaughtering sheep. All the men in the villages have a knife like that."

Mikhail pokes his head out of the truck, holding up the radio. "Captain, I spoke a few words into this, and a kid answered." Asef translates that much to the driver. The driver responds frantically.

Asef looks at Yurchenko. "He says he is keeping in contact with his two nephews who are on their way to purchase some goats for him from a person across the village. They must walk back with the goats and he's worried if one wanders off, the boys may go after it. He was giving the boys instructions to stay on the well-beaten path even if a goat wanders away. Many kids from his village have been killed by land mines and he wants to keep in constant contact with the boys."

I grip my rifle, take a step toward the driver. "Captain, that is not exactly what he told me! He told me it was his two sons and they were tending a neighbor's goats. The goats wandered to a trail and he was telling the boys not to go. The land mine part is correct."

Asef translates in Pashto. The driver hurriedly responds.

Asef turns to Yurchenko. "He says his Russian is rudimentary, at best. He may have gotten his words mixed up, but he is telling the truth. And Cap-teen, if I my comment, Pashtuns consider everyone to be a neighbor. It is not uncommon to use the terms 'person across the village' and 'neighbor' interchangeably."

Yurchenko takes his time to think. He looks down at the driver then at me. "Verstakov, stand down." I do so immediately.

He looks to Danil. "Untie him. Let the man stand up." Danil follows orders. Yurchenko picks up the knife, hands it back. "So you can feed your family," he says. Asef translates that much. The driver nods gratefully.

***

At once, Vlad's heart jumped to his throat. Enemy approaching, time for battle.

"Um. Are you okay? Sir? You said you're going to the tenth floor, right?" The man in the business suit stood staring at Vlad, who remained stuck, left foot in the elevator, right foot in the lobby.

Vladimir abruptly retracted his left foot from the tiny elevator compartment. The noise grew louder still. *Blast. Gunfire. Commands. Blast. Gunfire. Commands.* "I can't go in there!" he yelled. "I can't go in there!"

Keeping an eye on Vlad, the man reached down and repeatedly jabbed his chosen button; most likely readying himself to jump out of there if this crazy veteran were to actually get inside.

Vlad heard the man's sigh of relief as the door rumbled to a close. He pivoted around, looked to the staircase.

31.

Fifteen minutes later, Vlad watchfully stepped out of Grigory's apartment, his briefcase full of files, and looked around. "Hell, no, I'm not getting in that thing." he muttered, breezing past the elevator to the staircase. He ran down the first flight, and the next. He kept up the quick pace, slowing down to a casual stroll only whenever anyone climbed past.

***

I head down the road to my truck. Asef stumbles down the steep grand until he is at my side. "What was that about?" I ask.

Asef comes to a clumsy halt. "Those men are from the next village," he says. I don't think this kid can walk down hill and talk at the same time.

I get to the truck, open the door.

Asef slides in on his side. "The man Yurchenko spoke with is named Farood. He is an elder of the village; he has the most sheep and the most wives. The driver is his cousin, Osman. Farood told your captain that his village is normally very quiet. The people are good, decent, hard-working Muslims who have grown weary after years of war with the Soviets."

"Can't say I blame them," I say, starting the engine. "So why did they want to speak with Yurchenko?"

Asef turns to me. "Seems their village has become a rebel stronghold. Many Soviet convoys have fallen victim to hijackers, or worse. They were warning Yurchenko."

Bloody hell, we are driving straight into a mujahideen stronghold. "But why are they warning us? Aren't they part of the resistance, too?" I ask as I check the side mirror.

Asef shakes his head. "Farood and Osman are from a small tribe of Pashtuns. Very religious, extremely disciplined. Strict followers of the Koran. As religious people, they are offended by the rebel mujahideen who claim to be fighting in the name of Islam, but are little more than thieves and rapists." Asef leans back and chuckles. "Don't get me wrong, Vlad-ee-meer, they don't like you Soviets much, either, but even more so, they are offended by the hypocrisy and chaos the mujahideen have brought to the country."

Dust flies everywhere as Yurchenko pulls out onto the road. "So what do these Pashtuns want with us?" I ask, waiting for the dust to settle.

Asef explains. "Farood still carries a lot of sway within the area. The rebels leave him alone. He's assured Yurchenko a safe passage through the village."

Now I look to Asef. "Yeah? Safe passage in exchange for what?"

"Weapons. They want rifles to fight back at the mujahideen."

I start to pull out. "So Yurchenko has agreed to give a small tribe of Pashtuns some of our weapons so they have a fighting chance against the muj. In exchange, we get safe passage through the village?"

Asef nods. "Yep."

I think about that for a moment. "Well, I guess that makes sense."

32.

Damaged briefcase in hand, Vladimir hurried outside the apartment building. He took a quick look around before opening Pasha's door. "What took you so long?" Pasha snapped. "And what happened in there? Your clothes are a mess. Is that stale cola I smell? Awful."

Vladimir slid in. "I seem to have a problem with elevators. Tight spaces, in general. Can't stand them anymore."

Pasha rolled his eyes. "You seem to have a problem with tight spaces?" he quipped. "Tight spaces bother you? Tight spaces? Those waitresses I hire at Café Club, now there are some tight spaces! What the hell is wrong with you, anyway?"

Vlad set the briefcase on his lap. "At the elevator, a redheaded man stepped off and it triggered a memory of this guy in my convoy. Just like that, I was transported back to Afghanistan. I tried to get on the elevator, but my legs wouldn't move, felt like they were stuck in sand, the sun was beating down. Couldn't breathe, couldn't move."

Pasha turned toward his door. "Oh, bloody hell! Here, you take the wheel. Drive around the block. I'll go up there myself."

But Vladimir popped open the latches on his dusty briefcase. "There are stairs, you know. I can still handle those." He pulled out a cream-colored file folder. He handed the file to Pasha. "For a KGB agent, Grigory doesn't hide things very well. This was sitting in the middle of his desk."

Pasha took the file. "You walked up ten stories?"

Vlad nodded. "Two hundred and sixty-eight steps, to be exact." He lit a cigarette and looked out the window as they pulled away from the building.

33.

12 September

Vladimir leaned against the thick concrete foundation, which held a towering cast-iron statue of another, much more notable man named Vladimir. Lenin. The founding father of Communism held his steely arms outward, gazing longingly over the city, as if trying to maintain his hold on a country that no longer wanted him, or his system of governance. A fresh load of bird crap ran down his iron face. The plaque on the foundation beneath Lenin's feet read, "Workers of the World Unite!" Beneath the plaque, scrawled in faded white spray paint, were the words, "Fuck the Bolshevik."

Vlad stood waiting, a white envelope in hand, without much hope that Zhanna would meet him here in October Park. Since February, he had penned her several letters, addressed to the October Woman salon, asking her to meet at the Lenin statue. He always waited; she never showed.

Last week the white envelope containing divorce papers arrived. This morning, Vlad signed them and took the envelope to the post office, but at the last moment, dropped by the salon and told one of the stylists that he would be waiting under the Lenin statue if Zhanna wished to talk. After thirty-five minutes of waiting, he looked up at Lenin and said, "It's over, you know, for you, and for me." He snuffed out his cigarette and walked away. The post office would still be open.

"Hello, Viva," came a sparkling voice. Vlad pivoted. Zhanna was standing beneath Lenin's open arms, her hair draped over one shoulder of her flimsy coat. It looked blonder. She stood straight and unwavering; yet she failed to make actual eye contact.

"Zhan," he said, quickly striding to her, "I didn't think you would come."

She shivered in her thin black coat as the wind picked up. She steadied her blowing hair and bit her lower lip, still looking away. "I told myself I would never see you again, that I would forget about you, but there I was, rolling curlers into an eighty-year-old woman's hair, and I thought, what the hell. So...here I am. Did you sign the papers?"

Vladimir looked to his feet while he handed over the envelope. "Yeah. I signed everything. You can have the apartment. I'll move out."

Zhanna took it with a curt nod and slid the envelope into her purse. She tightened her coat around her torso to shield against the chill. "No. You keep it. I'm renting a basement apartment. I'm fine there."

Vladimir nodded as he took off his heavy coat and wrapped it around his wife's shivering body. He leaned in and kissed her right cheek, then her left cheek. Zhanna did not protest but gave nothing in return.

"You look nice, did you streak your hair or something?" he asked, taking a step back.

Zhanna relaxed a bit and smirked. She looked up. "They are called highlights, not streaks, but thank you. I did them myself. I've had a lot of time lately, you know."

Vladimir put his hands in his jeans pockets. "So, you want to get some tea, sit down somewhere?"

She shook her head. "I have to get back. The salon is booked solid all day. A wedding tomorrow, a high school social next week. It's crazy."

Vlad looked off toward the steely Lenin. "Funny, even in the worst of economic times, women still get their hair done, don't they?"

She nodded and looked to the ground. "Yeah. Probably even more so."

He turned back toward her and touched her blonde strands. "Hey, for what it's worth, I haven't had any pills since January. And I've sworn off drinking for good. I just quit altogether. Not one single drop. No more."

Zhanna kept her gaze down and nodded. "That's good." Then she looked up. "Where is the gun?"

Vlad looked her in the eye. "The police took it. I don't want that thing in my life anymore. It's gone." He took a breath. "Look, I know I don't deserve it, but please, wait to file the papers. Just a few months. Maybe we could just talk. I can't even say how sorry I—"

Zhanna abruptly looked up. "I was pregnant."

Her comment brought on the noise. *Blast. Gunfire. Commands. Blast. Gunfire. Commands.* Vladimir released her hand, stepped back. "What?"

Zhanna continued. "Back in January. I was close to four months along. I knew it, but I didn't tell you."

He shook the noise away. "Why didn't you tell me?"

She wiped her eyes and looked away. "I didn't say anything because I was planning on leaving you." She looked back at him, her mouth trembling. "If only I had. The doctor said the baby died of blunt-force trauma. I had an operation to remove the dead tissue. Dead tissue, they call it. That was a baby." She stifled tears. "I will never forgive myself for not leaving earlier."

Vlad reached out and touched her cheek. "You should have told me, I would have been there for you."

Zhanna locked her gaze upon his, her eyes all of a sudden on fire. "Don't you dare say that!" she snapped. A stinging slap across the face stopped the noise at once.

Another stinging slap. "For almost two years, I tried my hardest to take care of you. I gave you everything. You did nothing but fuck it up!" Another slap. "Don't say you would have been there for me! Don't say it!"

Vlad stayed silent and took the hits, unable to disagree.

Zhanna stepped back, biting her lower lip. "Being there is a lot more than just words." She closed her eyes as thin tears leaked out around the corners.

Vlad tried to touch her shoulder, but she flinched.

"I have a feeling it was a girl," she said, her voice trailing off. "And I've named her Karina. Sounds ridiculous I know, but somehow it helps me cope if she has a name."

Vlad took a breath and nodded. "That's a good name. It's a good name."

Zhanna sniffed. "It's crazy, Vladimir." She looked down at her feet. "Sometimes I think you could beat me to the ground and I would still love you. You could shoot me a thousand times, and I would come back." She looked up at him. "You have a pull on me that I can't resist. And I hate myself for it."

Vlad held Zhanna's waist and pulled her in closer. Of course, she did not resist.

He whispered into her ear. "Don't blame yourself. None of this is your fault."

Gradually, Zhanna's entire body relaxed in his arms.

Vlad gently pulled away and tilted Zhanna's chin upwards. "Listen, we can't just end things like this. Let's meet on a regular basis. Just for a few months. If it doesn't go well, then go ahead and file the papers."

Zhanna looked at him hesitantly. "You mean we would have dates?"

Vlad nodded, feeling more confident. "Yeah, we'll have dates. I'll write you a letter every week and tell you when and where to meet."

Zhanna thought for a moment, but looked down again. "No. I don't think that's a good idea. I can't," she said, wiping the stray tears running down her face. "It's too late."

Vlad took a deep breath. "Okay. I understand," he gave her a kiss on her right cheek. "Take care of yourself, Zha-Zha, okay?" He kissed her left cheek.

Zhanna gently pushed him away and said weakly, "Good-bye, Vladimir."

Never had she looked so small and vulnerable. He couldn't leave her like this. "Hey," he said, running a hand through his own hair. "I learned something from all of this. It may be silly, but perhaps it can help."

"What is it?" she asked, sniffing.

"It's called an Iskra."

"Huh? What is that supposed to mean?"

"An Iskra is something you can believe in," he explained. "Something to bring about hope when times are tough. Maybe you can find an Iskra and it will get you through these hard times."

Zhanna sighed. "Well, can't hurt to try, I suppose." She looked toward the October Woman salon across the street, then turned back to him. "I'd better go."

"Good-bye, Zha-Zha. Please, remember the good times. Don't hate me," he said, kissing her cheek for the last time. She looked up with eyes of liquid. "Viva, I don't hate you, but this is over, for both of our sakes, this needs to be over."

***

This is over. Yurchenko told us to stand down. The Afghan men are leading the way in their battered old truck.

"I'm learning so much this summer by translating for you," Asef says with his hand out the window. "This has been a great experience."

I light a cigarette, then check my rearview mirror. "Yeah, Asef, that's great," but I'm hardly listening. I shift into first. The truck drags a bit, but eventually the sand spits us out to the road.

***

Zhanna looked out across the street and sighed, pulling the envelope out of her purse. "Maybe these could wait until the end of the year," she said, obviously exasperated with herself.

Vlad smiled. "And, so, what about the dates?"

Zhanna thought for a moment, then nodded. "Okay. I'm willing to give it a try." She paused for a moment and looked him dead in the eyes. "But I will write the letters, I will tell you where and when to meet. You better show up, or I mean it, we are over."

Vlad nodded. "I will, Zhanna. Write the letters. I'll be there."

She walked away, gradually merging with the crowd crossing the street. Vlad turned around and walked back through the park. All the while, the iron Lenin stood over the city of Sverdlovsk; arms wide open, hoping for things to get better.

34.

13 September

Vladimir stood staring at the leather, teardrop-shaped punching bag hanging at eye level before him. He punched the front of the bag with his left fist. The bag wobbled back and forth three times. He punched the side of it with his right fist. Again, the bag wobbled three times.

As part of Vlad's employment, Pasha paid for a membership at the Soviet Boxing Academy. With so many emotions and not nearly enough control over them, maybe a regular routine of exercise would help quiet the mind, he thought. He punched the bag again. Another three wobbles.

After ten minutes of punching and wobbling, Vlad stopped.

He looked around the busy boxing gym. All men, except for a curly haired woman at the front desk. The gym obviously used to be an oversized garage of some sort with its high ceiling and large, metal overhead doors at the entrance. Mats, benches, and a rack of weights. Lockers leading to a steam room on the other side.

In the middle of it all stood the boxing ring. Square, defined by ropes. Two gloved men sparred in the ring, both extremely fit, one with a light complexion, the other one with short, black hair and a salt-and-pepper beard.

Several teardrop-shaped punching bags hung around the gym, each with a man behind it. The men were leaning back slightly, hitting the bag on the front, not on the sides. Each blow was really a series of three small, quick punches, hitting the bag on the rebound, and then switching fists. No wobbling bags. They punched with the side of the fist, not the knuckles. They shuffled their feet forward and back within the lunge.

Vlad stepped back into a slight lunge and hit the bag again. Left fist. 1,2,3. Right fist, 1,2,3. The bag was loud and clunky with each punch, but it didn't wobble. Left fist. 1,2,3. Right fist, 1,2,3. Left fist. 1,2,3. Right fist, 1,2,3. With each successive bout, punching the bag became less awkward, more of a smooth motion. Left fist. 1,2,3. Right fist, 1,2,3. Left fist. 1,2,3. Right fist, 1,2,3.

Left 1,2,3. Vlad narrowed his eyes, focused on the bag.

Right 1,2,3.

Left 1,2,3. He started to shuffle his feet.

Right 1,2,3.

Left 1,2,3. His fists moved faster, hit harder.

Right 1,2,3.

Left 1,2,3. He paused, loosened his neck, rolled his shoulders.

Right 1,2,3.

Left 1,2,3. A rush of adrenaline warmed his body.

Right 1,2,3.

Left 1,2,3. His heartbeat rose.

Right 1,2,3.

Left 1,2,3. The bag swung in a predictable three-beat rhythm.

Right 1,2,3.
Left 1,2,3. Fists flew. Harder and faster each time.
Right 1,2,3.
Left 1,2,3. He shook the sweat from his brow.
Right 1,2,3.
Left 1,2,3. Anger melted away.
Right 1,2,3.
Left 1,2,3. Guilt melted away.
Right 1,2,3.
Left 1,2,3. Disappointment melted away.
Right 1,2,3.
Left 1,2,3. Joy gradually morphed into calm focus.
Right 1,2,3.
Left 1,2,3. Remorse melted away.
Right 1,2,3
Left 1,2,3. No emotion.
Right 1,2,3.
Left 1,2,3. Life. All of it happening right here, right now.
Right 1,2,3.
Left 1,2,3. Nothing but the fist.
Right 1,2,3. Nothing but the bag.
Left 1,2,3. Nothing but the fist.
Right 1,2,3. Nothing but the bag.
Left 1,2,3. Nothing but the fist.
Right 1,2,3. Nothing but the bag.
Left 1,2,3.
Right 1,2,3.
Left 1,2,3.
Right 1,2,3.

***

Tap, tap, tap. Tap, tap, tap. Asef is looking down at a book but tapping his fist on the open window frame. He taps in threes. Tap, tap, tap; tap, tap, tap. But it's a horribly uneven rhythm. Tap, tap, tap; tap, tap, tap. I can't stand it. My nerves are already frayed after that stop; seeing the Afghan driver use his radio after I told him not to. Was he really talking to his two nephews who were on their way to corral a few goats? Tap, tap, tap; tap, tap, tap. Or setting up an ambush? Tap, tap, tap; tap, tap, tap. I've had enough.

"Asef, quit it, will ya? Shit, I can't stand it!"

We are in the truck, driving slowly. I'm trying to avoid all the deep ruts and rocks along the dirt road, but it's impossible.

"What is it, Vlad-ee-meer? What did I do?" Asef is looking at me. He looks so concerned for my welfare.

"The tapping, man, just stop the tapping. It's making me fuckin' crazy!" I yell.

He stops the tapping at once, places his hand on his lap, and looks down. "Oh, I didn't even realize I was doing that. I'm so sorry."

Oh shit, now I feel bad. Asef is a lost puppy with his big, sad eyes, constantly needing attention, always looking for validation. I just snapped at a lost puppy.

"Sorry, I didn't mean to snap at you," I say, cresting a small hill. "It's just, when I was a kid, I used to tap my utensils on the table, or against my milk glass. Dad didn't like it at all and made me stop. But Mom thought I should be able to freely express my creativity."

"Ah, Vlad-ee-meer, perhaps you are turning into your father," Asef says, smiling. "As much as we fight it, I am sure it happens to us all."

I nod, "Yeah, looking back on it, I think that's exactly what my dad was worried about, that I would turn into my father. It makes sense. At some level, he must have known all along."

"And what exactly do you mean by that?" Asef asks. He is looking at me as if I am a crazy person.

"It's nothing," I say, waving my hand in his direction. "Hell, I've talked enough already."

"Well, perhaps you are turning into your mother, then," Asef says, mischievously raising his bushy eyebrows.

"Oh please, no. Don't say that!" I say, shaking my head. I take a breath and raise one hand from the steering wheel. "My mother is a very complicated person, that's all. Let's just leave it at that."

The wheel sharply jars to the right. We are heading straight into a deep pothole and despite my efforts, I can't control it. The truck violently lurches forward as the passenger tire hits the edge of the crater. One corner of the tarp snaps off the bed of the truck. Supplies are flying out of the truck. Asef is bracing himself against the dashboard. I am frantically turning the steering wheel. "Shit!"

The truck jerks left. I gun the gas and we are out of the hole, then I stomp on the brakes. Asef crashes chest-first into the dashboard, and then slams back against the seat.

I take a deep breath and close my eyes. Asef says nothing, but I hear him breathing hard. Another thing I can hear: the right front tire whizzing, relieving itself of air. "Fuck!" I yell, slamming both palms against the steering wheel. Out of frustration, I pat around, looking for my pack of cigarettes.

Wide-eyed, Asef turns to me. His glasses are askew, hair a mess. He holds his hands up and starts to laugh. "Okay. Vladee-meer, I get it. Your mother is a complicated woman and you have issues with your father. I get it. Now, can you please keep us on the bloody road?" He keeps laughing. "I meant what I said, Vlad-ee-meer. This really is the best summer of my life! I will never forget this summer!"

Behind me, boxes of bandages and cans of beans are strewn along the dirt road. Red's truck is coming into view. Danil is leaning out his window, pointing his two middle fingers up in the air, a huge smile on his face. "What the hell happened, Verstakov?" he yells. "Getting a blow job from the towel head or something?" Red is all over the road, hunched over the steering wheel, laughing. I think he just ran over a can of beans.

Here I am, sitting in the middle of scorching Afghanistan, smoking a cigarette inside a truck that has a flat tire because talking about my mother makes me crazy. My redheaded comrade is trying to navigate his truck around my lost cargo. A boisterous, deep-sea fisherman is giving me the finger. Next to me sits a privileged Afghan teenager who is laughing his ass off because this is the coolest, most exciting thing he's done in his entire life.

This is all too surreal. Now I start laughing, too.

***

Left 1,2,3.
Right 1,2,3.
Left 1,2,3. The memory of Asef, laughing, happy, with his huge glasses askew, faded away.
Right 1,2,3.
Left 1,2,3. Anger rose up again.
Right 1,2,3.
Left 1,2,3. The guilt returned.

Right 1,2,3.
Left 1,2,3. Joy and focus completely disappeared.
Right 1,2,3.
Left 1,2,3. Agitation returned.
Right 1,2,3.
Left 1,2,3. Blast.
Right 1,2,3.
Left 1,2,3. Gunfire.
Right 1,2,3.
Left 1,2,3. Commands.

Vlad took a step back and punched the bag one time with all the raw strength he had. "Fuck Afghanistan!" he yelled. "Fuck the muj!" He hit it again. "Fuck the war!"

35.

The bearded man in the boxing ring suddenly stopped sparring with the blond man. He walked to the side of the ring, leaned into the ropes, and called out, "Hey, tough guy, quit your trash talk or get the hell out of my gym! And take it easy on the speed bag. It's hard enough to make a living these days, ya know!" He hopped up and down within his stance, rolling his shoulders. He looked about forty-five years old; a very fit, very quick forty-five years.

Vlad stopped mid-swing, looked over. He quickly steadied the bag. "Oh, uh. Sorry about that. I'm trying to quiet some demons inside my head."

The man shook his head, chuckled, and raised his gloves. "Aren't we all, tough guy. Aren't we all! He made a sweeping motion with one arm. "Well come on, glove up and get in here! Show me what you've got!"

Vlad found a pile of gloves in a bin next to the ring. "I've never boxed before," he said, climbing through the ropes. Inside the ring, the man was already shuffling around and throwing punches to the air. He didn't stop moving about the ring, but said, "Don't worry about it, tough guy, you look like a natural. Besides, anyone can do it." The man shuffled over in a hunched position, fists beneath his chin. "Name's Roman Belov. I manage this place," he said, taking a quick punch to the air.

Vlad stood up straight, not sure of what he needed to do. "Nice place. I'm Vladimir Verstakov."

Out of nowhere, Roman threw a sharp right-handed punch to Vlad's jaw, so hard that Vlad stumbled back into the ropes. "Damn!" he exclaimed, holding his cheek with the bulky glove. For a man twenty years older and ten centimeters shorter, Roman could land a solid hit.

"That's called a jab," Roman said, not the slightest bit out of breath. "It's a quick and powerful punch. Starts from the shoulder. Now let's see yours." Roman shuffled backwards, throwing more jabs into the air. Vladimir held up his left glove, stepped forward and aimed it at Roman's nose. Too slow. Roman ducked easily, responding with two quick jabs, one to Vlad's chest, the other to his cheek.

"Whenever you manage to get a body shot in, always follow through with a hit to the face. It keeps your opponent perpetually off balance," instructed Roman.

Vlad shuffled forward and quickly slammed Roman in the chest and chin with a left-, then a right-handed jab. Roman stumbled but caught himself. "A lefty, eh? You've got a distinct advantage there," he said. "The opponent doesn't see it coming. Focus on your counterpunch, that's where you'll win."

Vladimir wasted no time following through with a hit, directed to the tip of the chin and upward. Roman's head shot backwards.

"An uppercut!" Roman exclaimed. "Now that's more like it! Very nice, tough guy, very nice!"

Roman kept shuffling around, hunched over, fists tucked beneath his chin. "Tall fighters need to stay tall, so straighten up. Stay tall."

Vlad straightened up, but Roman moved in with a right, then a left uppercut to the stomach. Immediately, he pivoted and landed another slam to the temple.

"That's a triple combination right there," Roman exclaimed, taking a break. "Top that off with a sharp elbow jab to the neck, and you've just knocked your opponent out cold."

Vlad stepped back, but quickly lurched forward, throwing two strong left jabs. Roman, taken by surprise, lost his balance for a moment. Vlad used the time to land another uppercut to the stomach. Roman teetered. Another two right jabs, and he had Roman securely trapped in the corner of the ring. Vladimir raised his gloves in a V and let out a victorious, "Ha!"

Unfazed, Roman cupped Vlad's elbow, leaned forward, and shoved it to the side, turning his own body ninety degrees. Roman then followed with a vicious left hit to the ear. Vladimir stumbled sideways into the ropes and flopped to the floor.

Roman took off one glove, reached down to help Vlad stand up. "So tough guy, what brings ya to the gym?" he asked, sparring lightly.

Vladimir tried for a jab, but missed. "Like I said, I've got some demons. Thought some physical exertion would help. And it does. This feels great, just what I needed."

Roman shook the sweat from his eyes, still sparring. "That's exactly my vision for this gym, to open it up to the public. Remember back to primary school when we had sports training every day? The whole point was so the Communist Youth Sports League could find those kids with elite athletic potential. Those kids were sent to the Sports Academy for intense training."

Vlad nodded, then pivoted and went in for a right hook. "Yeah, by fifth grade the athletes were weeded out, and we didn't have exercise in school anymore."

Roman easily blocked Vlad's hook with an uppercut. "I was one of those kids weeded out, and because of the superior training at Sports Academy, I went on to become middleweight champion of Omsk four years in a row." He came out of his athletic stance, took a breath. "Physical activity has always served me well, and I'm not just talking about my livelihood. Training made me a better student, gave me internal discipline. I'm a better manager and father because of my athletic training."

He went to the ropes, grabbed a towel, and threw one to Vlad. "I believe everyone should be able to reap the benefits of exercise and sports, not just elite athletes. Now, thanks to the reforms, I'm able to run my own gym." He picked up a bottle of water, brought it to his mouth. "I have so many ideas for programs to get people to start exercising. Just thinking about it makes me feel optimistic; it breaks through the drudgery of everyday living."

Vladimir wiped his brow. "You have an Iskra. Encouraging people to exercise. That's your Iskra."

Roman withdrew the water bottle, water trickled to the floor. "Huh? Iskra? What are you talking about?" he asked, as if suspicious Vlad was a crazed killer.

Vlad tossed the towel to the floor. "Sounds silly, but an Iskra is something to believe in, that's all."

Roman wiped the sweat off his face, relieved. "Well now, I guess I do have an Iskra. Never thought about it that way. So, let's hit the weights, shall we?"

36.

16 September

As usual, Vlad spent the evening guarding the coveted entrance of Café Club, keeping an eye out for the business partners and deciding which of Sverdlovsk's trendsetting youth were worthy enough to pay the stiff cover charge and enter for a night of over-priced revelry.

Friday night, the club was in full swing by 7 p.m. The bartenders slinging the counterfeit vodka; cooks busy serving up American-style pizza marked up at least 200 percent; the spiky-haired DJ dancing around behind the turntable, spinning his collection of tunes from the West.

A blaring "Sweet Child O' Mine" hit the turntable as Pasha stepped outside, his arms wide. "Hey, V.V. How's it going out here?"

Vlad nodded at the line. "Lots of people tonight, boss." The line was long, more men than women, a lot of denim jackets and big hair. Vlad checked the identifications of a couple from Revda and pointed them inside.

Pasha looked back over his shoulder, then leaned forward, "Hey V.V. No more couples, okay? They don't drink enough. If you get any more couples, just tell 'em the club is full."

Vlad nodded, "Okay, boss." A group of young men stepped up, identifications in hand. Vlad motioned them inside.

Pasha crossed his arms, put up one finger, "Let all the men in, especially those in groups, and any man who looks middle-aged. They spend more."

Again, Vlad nodded. "You got it, boss."

Two girls appeared next, neither of them a day over sixteen. They cheerfully giggled, said they had forgotten their papers. Vlad looked away, shaking his head. "Nyet," he said, ready to send them back home to their parents where they belonged.

But Pasha nixed that idea right away. He stepped forward, so warm and welcoming, and ushered the girls inside, even motioned for the bartender to serve them a drink on the house.

"Okay, so V.V. all the men, all right?" said Pasha, looking back into the café. "And girls. That's what the men want, lots and lots of girls. But only if they are in a group of at least two, ready to party, and only the young ones. No wedding rings and no women over the age of thirty." The way he said "woman" and "thirty" in the same sentence made it sound like some kind of disease.

Vlad laughed and said, "So, what you want is an endless parade of cheap and easy pussy."

Pasha smiled and slapped Vlad's shoulder. "That's exactly what we need in this place, V.V! Hell yeah," he laughed. An endless parade of cheap and easy pussy! I love it. Keep it up!" He turned to go back into the club. But he whipped back around just as a blonde woman in her early twenties, legs up to her neck, dressed in skin-tight, leopard-print pants and a red top, stepped up and handed over her identification. Pasha reached past Vlad to take the woman's hand.

"Viktoria. Viktoria. Viktoria," Pasha said wistfully, looking her up and down.

Viktoria smiled and wrapped her arms around him. "Mmmm, Pasha, downstairs. Thirty minutes?" She turned back, plucked her card from Vlad's hand. "And you, too, security guard. My, oh my, where did Pasha find you? You are a doll!" She swiped a hand across Vlad's cheek and licked her own lips before slinking past Pasha to go inside. Pasha kept his eyes on Viktoria's leopard-print ass. "She was here last weekend," he said. "Just get her drunk and that woman will do anything. And I mean anything. You want a hand job? Blow job? See her with another woman? She'll do it. Just say what you want. Give me twenty minutes, okay? Then you can have your turn. I'll watch the door." Pasha slapped Vlad again on the shoulder and walked back into the club.

A group of four guys flashed their papers; Vlad let them in. A happy couple holding hands, Vlad turned them away. A raven-haired girl with purple eyeliner and two slutty-looking friends at her side, in they went.

Another girl, very tall with heavy makeup, stepped forward. She had on a tiny skirt, sky-high heels, and a tank top. Nothing more. She smiled coyly and opened her purse, which rested against her hip. "I know my identification is in here somewhere," she said, taking out a tube of lipstick and a lighter. "But it's all the way at the bottom."

The girl straightened up, her nipples poking out from her tank top. She placed her hand against Vlad's hip, where his T-shirt met his jeans. Ruby-red lips lingered just below his own lips. "So, do you think we could come to some sort of an arrangement, or are you going to make me take everything out of my purse?" she asked.

***

"We are going to have to take everything out, goddammit," I say, shaking my head, looking at the flat tire. My hands are on my hips, cigarette dangling from my mouth.

Asef and I are standing outside the truck. He will be of absolutely no help, I can only imagine. "Pick up the stuff along the road, will ya?" I say to Asef.

"Okay, Vlad-ee-meer," he says with way too much enthusiasm, and runs down the road to fetch the lost supplies.

Red and Danil have stopped. After giving me some more shit for blowing out a tire and bringing the convoy to a halt, they grab their rifles and head out in front of the truck to keep a look out. I toss Danil my pack of cigarettes as a consolation. He catches it in one hand, puts up the other hand in a gesture of gratitude. The other supply trucks in the convoy are coming into view, slowing down. The gunners in the back can guard the rear.

The soldiers in the supply trucks exit their vehicles. They are laughing, giving me shit about this. I give it right back to them. We are all young, muscular, and strong, hearty Russian stock. Invincible. This won't take long. I unlatch the gray tarpaulin from the bed of the truck and we all get to work unloading the crates.

***

"So, what do you say?" asked the girl. "Do I need to take everything out, or can we come to some kind of arrangement?"

Without thinking, he touched his fingertips to her bare thigh. She had goose bumps. Not only was this girl willing, there were dozens more inside the club. Indeed, he had an endless parade of cheap and easy pussy at his fingertips.

But the noise crept in; his head pounded with each beat. *Blast. Gunfire. Commands. Blast. Gunfire. Commands.* While his body wanted that woman, his soul was not in agreement. The permanent pit in his stomach expanded up into his throat; sweat filled his brow and armpits, leaving him to shiver. He looked up to the night sky, but saw only a pulsating sun. Its severity made him squint. The line of people waiting to get in slowly morphed into an angry mob of mujahideen rebel fighters clad in baggy clothes and armed with stolen Soviet weapons.

Immediately, he stepped back from the girl and snapped, "Just go in, okay? Go in and don't come back. I don't want to see you again tonight." The girl happily shut her purse, tapped Vlad on the nose, and stepped jauntily into the club. Vlad stood a sweaty mess, reeling from the memory. Obviously, an endless parade of cheap and easy pussy would not be his Iskra.

37.

17 September

Zhanna stood at the front desk, scrolling through her appointments for the week. Booked solid. Not only was *she* booked up, but all of the stylists in the shop were busy. The door swung open and in walked her next appointment. "Mrs. Slavakova!" said Zhanna, quickly walking out from behind the desk. "How nice to see you again." She held her arms out to catch Mrs. Slavakova's coat and scarf.

"Oh, Zhanna dear, I need help. This is dreadful. Just dreadful!" exclaimed Olga, thrusting her coat into Zhanna's arms, then tossing her scarf on top. "I have to speak this evening at the Woman of Russia annual banquet and I have nothing to wear, absolutely nothing! This rain is going to wreak havoc with my hair. And just look at my makeup! Why, I'll have to skip mascara altogether."

Zhanna hung Mrs. Slavakova's things on a hook and poured a cup of tea. She motioned for her to sit, handed her the tea, and gently rubbed her shoulders. In typical Zhanna fashion, she started rambling.

"Just relax, don't worry about a thing. I will have your hair and makeup looking fabulous. A little loose powder goes a long way in keeping makeup in place. I can wrap a clear bonnet loosely around your head and send you home with a dome umbrella. I keep a few in the back just for days like this. And go without mascara? Don't even say such a thing! I've got waterproof mascara. Bought three tubes from a street vendor. I think it's from France. And as far as an outfit, have you taken a look across the street lately? That dress shop used to sell nothing but ankle-length gray frocks and orthotic shoes, but I can't believe the selections now! I have a little time after your appointment. If you want, we can go over there together and pick out something. A flowing red dress, oh, I can just see it on you now! We need to find you something in red! And black accessories. Yes! Your hair should be up."

Zhanna finally took a breath. "Mrs. Slavakova, you will be the pinnacle of elegance tonight. I guarantee it," she held up her scissors, snipped them together twice, and immediately got to work.

Mrs. Slavakova sipped her tea and smiled. "I knew I was in good hands."

Ninety minutes later, Mrs. Slavakova stood up from the chair, indeed a picture of sheer elegance with her hair swept up and away from her face in a French twist that was loose enough so that a few strands of hair framed her face. The hairstyle accentuated her blue eyes, which Zhanna had made even bluer with two coats of black, waterproof mascara.

Zhanna shuttled over to the front desk where she found a clear plastic bonnet.

Mrs. Slavakova brought out her wallet. "I think I'll skip the dress shop today, Zhanna. I must have something at home to wear," she said, peeling off American dollars.

"With the Communist Party hanging by a thread, my husband's job is also. He'll find a post in the New Russia, I'm sure, but for the time being, I better cut some corners." She laid a stack of US dollars on the counter and smiled. "But no matter how bad it gets, I will never miss my hair appointment. It's the only time I have that is just for me."

Zhanna carefully situated the bonnet over Mrs. Slavakova's new hairstyle. "We women take the brunt of the world. Nothing wrong with a little reprieve now and then."

She stopped with the bonnet. Mrs. Slavakova's comment brought to mind something Vladimir had said when they met at October Park. *Funny, even in the worst of economic times, women still get their hair done, don't they?*

Zhanna finished tying and stepped back while looking around the salon.

"What are you thinking about, dear?" asked Mrs. Slavakova as she patted her bonnet.

"I just had an idea. I want to own this place," Zhanna said bluntly. "We can own a business now, right? Just regular people? Is that such a crazy idea for me to own the beauty shop?"

Mrs. Slavakova shook her head and reached out to touch Zhanna's arm. "No. I think it's a wonderful idea, dear; you could do wonders with this place. But please, whatever you do, give it another name. October Woman, that is just so...so...so...Communist! Nothing with red, or October, or revolution in it. I can't stand it anymore!"

"America," said Zhanna. "That's what Russia wants to emulate right now, isn't it? America. I will rename this place Salon Americana. We'll have a yellow sign outside, all lit up."

Mrs. Slavakova threw her head back. "I love it!" She quickly got to business. "Now you need to get yourself down to the Office of Restructuring. There are loans for this kind of thing. My husband says there is a name for it, an English term, oh yes. Free mar...ket eco...no...my. That's it. Free market economy. It's hard to pronounce because we have no Russian equivalent. The Soviet Union is bankrupt; they need us off the dole, so they are encouraging this concept of a free market economy."

Zhanna's inspiration flowed like water. "The fluorescent lighting would have to go away; we'll play popular music; no more Soviet hymns. Likewise, no more framed pictures of old politicians on the walls. A fountain, of course we must have a fountain. More of an open space around the front desk; formal coffee and tea service in a separate, waiting area. My husband Vladimir could design much better-looking and better-functioning cabinetry. He and his friend, Oleg, could do the construction. We'll have hairstyling, manicures, makeup, a steam room. And all just for women! A place for a woman to escape, if only for an hour. Mrs. Slavakova, I have never thought about it before, but I think I love this idea of a free market economy!"

Mrs. Slavakova nodded enthusiastically throughout Zhanna's rambling of ideas. "My dear, I think the question is not whether Zhanna Verstakova is ready for the New Russia, but rather, is the New Russia ready for Zhanna Verstakova!"

38.

18 September

Sunday. Café Club was closed, chairs on top of tables, cash register open, the entire place dark. Vladimir searched for Pasha downstairs in his makeshift office. No Pasha. Upstairs in his other makeshift office. No Pasha there, either. Vlad knocked on the bathroom door, poked his head in the empty kitchen, and scanned the dining room. There was no sign of his boss anywhere in the café. Pasha had called earlier in the evening, said he had another job that would net another three grand. Three grand sounded good. The only problem was finding Pasha.

The business partners had been sending letters through their lawyers, demanding to see their rightful share of the café's profits. Pasha had held them off for a while, claiming the café wasn't doing as well as expected. But Pasha could no longer make excuses. Being career agents of the KGB, the partners were privy to anything happening in town. Fyodor and Grigory knew damn well how much the place was making and they wanted their cut.

They resorted to sending KGB moles to spy on Café Club, but Vlad spotted them each evening, kept them away from Pasha, and sent them packing. It was working for now, but as the business partners were becoming more problematic, Pasha was becoming increasingly elusive, always taking refuge in a new place.

Vlad shook his head as he checked the tiny broom closet. "This is crazy," he muttered, pushing open the double doors of the café. Next door, in a newly rented studio apartment, he finally found Pasha, sitting at his desk, a cup of tea at his side, reading the *Daily Pravda* that was spread out before him. He didn't stir when Vlad walked into the apartment, just flipped the newspaper back to the front page and said, "About damn time you got here, V.V."

Vlad closed his eyes and shook his head. "You're not that easy to find anymore."

Pasha folded his paper neatly in half and held it up. "Just look at this, goddammit! Those sneaky agents are at it again, trying to cut into my holdings." He slammed the *Pravda* back down on the desk.

Vlad stepped up to see what in the newspaper had made Pasha so upset. Pictured on the front page was a large garden plot, fenced off on all sides, half of it neatly tilled, the other half still dug up. In the foreground stood two women, somewhere in their fifties, both dressed in overalls, their hair pulled back and covered with scarves. One held a shovel; the other wore leather gardening gloves. The caption beneath the photograph read:

Mrs. Svetlana Drucheka (L) and Mrs. Galina Fomenka ready the soil in anticipation of Sverdlovsk's unique Garden for the Children project. The ladies have tilled the garden plot and gathered volunteers from the Ural Technical Institute of Agriculture to grow several different types of vegetables, starting in the spring. The vegetables will be donated to Russia's area orphanages where nutritional standards are sorely lacking. When asked what inspired them to create such a garden, Mrs. Drucheka replied, "We wanted to give something back."

Reading the caption and looking at the picture, Vladimir wasn't feeling Pasha's rage. "It's a garden. Two nice ladies are growing vegetables to give to orphans. Why are you so upset about this?"

Pasha swiped the paper from Vlad's hands, held it up, and hit it with the back of his hand. "These nice ladies are the wives of Fyodor Druchek and Grigory Fomenko! The two business partners I've been ripping off! And that garden is on my land! Remember the apartment building I hired you to burn down back in January? This is that same land! Druchek and Fomenko, with the help of their lawyers, no doubt, fenced off part of it in an attempt to get back at me. I've received letters threatening they would do such a thing. I just didn't think it would happen so quickly. And now they have allowed their wives to start this...this...this fucking...garden for the...fucking orphans or whatever kind of bullshit you want to call it! That's my land!" He threw the paper back on the desk and took a gulp of tea.

"They say they want to give something back. Give something back, my ass! They're feeling guilty, finally seeing Russian blood on their own hands from all these years of being married to the scum of the earth, KGB agents. Now they think they can redeem themselves and their husbands? It won't work. That land is mine! I've already been in talks with a German hotel chain to put up a luxury hotel on that land within three years. With Boris Yeltsin in office, the hotel deal is going to happen, but you have to get rid of that garden first. Rich jet-setters don't need to know of our orphanages. It makes them feel guilty and they don't spend as much."

Vlad took hold of the newspaper again, got a better look at the picture. Sure enough, it was the very same land he had trespassed upon nine months ago in the middle of the night. No evidence of the apartment building he burned to the ground, or of the two hired thugs who tried to kill him.

"They've only taken a part of the land for the garden, Pasha, and you do owe both Fyodor and Grigory a good deal of money. Why don't you just sign the plot over to them? It's a lot better than always looking over your shoulder for KGB assassins, and hiding in three different places. They are going to catch you, Pasha. This is the KGB we are talking about! Just pay them. That's all they want."

Pasha ran his fingers over his receding hairline, shook his head, and sat down. "I do have the money; you're right. I've got more than enough to pay them off. But I can't. I just can't do it."

"Why the hell not?" Vlad yelled, throwing the newspaper down.

Pasha calmly took another sip of tea. He placed the cup down, leaned on his elbows and said, "V.V., remember the night I first came over to your apartment to hire you for that arson job? You became upset when I hinted that the Afghan war might have been for nothing. I remember how you closed your eyes and tried to think of something to calm you down. Something to believe in. That's how you put it. You told me you needed to find an Iskra."

Vladimir nodded impatiently. "Yeah, of course I remember. And what in the hell does that have to do with this garden and the KGB wives?"

Pasha hit his desk. "Everything! I thought finding an Iskra was total bullshit at first, V.V. With you I thought I had a real nut job on my hands. But after that night, I got to thinking."

He leaned forward, straight-faced, his eyes searing into Vlad's. "The acquisition of wealth. That's it. It's so pure and simple," He stood up. "I'm a magnet for money. It finds me. I find it. It gives me hope, a reason to live. Now that I understand this concept of an Iskra, I am more focused than ever. Now I can see that this co-op café business is only a stepping-stone. There are much bigger things in store for me out there in the New Russia. I'm talking about corporations. I'm talking about a board of directors in black suits. I'm talking about huge profits. I'm talking about cars, houses, my own plane, women catering to my every need, the biggest yacht you've ever seen. I will have it all before I turn thirty-five and my Iskra will guide the way."

Pasha stepped over to his file cabinet. He turned around, and pointed a finger. "Our whole system of government is changing, the Iron Curtain is falling fast, and I am perfectly poised to make a killing. Just watch, V.V. One day, I will be Russia's richest man. I know it; I can feel it." He tapped his fingers atop the file cabinet. "I've known it for as long as I can remember. As a kid, sharpening tools for the neighbors for extra money; I knew it as a teenager hawking British cigarettes out in the park for twice the price. And I knew it when I met my wife. She's a nightmare to live with, but you know what? She comes from the right family, has all the right connections. That's all that matters."

He shook his head and smiled. "It's all so easy." He tapped the file cabinet again, walking away. "So fucking easy."

He sat down and folded his hands. "Now I have a name for it. Iskra. The acquisition of wealth is my Iskra."

Vladimir dropped his head into his hands. "It's your life, Pasha." Swindling two KGB agents out of their retirement funds was not a good idea, Iskra or no Iskra. He straightened back up and sighed. "You say you are going to make a killing in the New Russia? I say you are going to be killed while you are still in the old one. This is the KGB!"

But employment options were few, especially for a crazy Afghan war veteran with a criminal record, so Vlad agreed. "Okay," he said with a sigh. "I'll ruin that little garden. I can make sure nothing ever grows on it. Do you have any more information about the fence?"

Of course he did. The fence, according to Pasha's best estimate, was two and a half meters high and spiked on top. It had only one gate, which was secured with a very sophisticated lock. "You know how to pick a lock, V.V?" Pasha asked, looking directly at Vlad as if his Iskra depended on it, because it very much did.

Vlad shook his head. "No. But I can figure it out."

***

"I can't figure this out, Vlad-ee-meer. Something is not right. I can't figure this out."

Asef is walking toward me, balancing the lost cans of beans and boxes of bandages in his arms. I have the truck jacked up; just loosened a lug nut. I glance over to him through the buckets of sweat falling from my brow. What the hell can't he figure out? Walking and holding stuff? That much is true. He's stumbling all over the place.

"What is it, Asef?" I ask while loosening another lug nut.

He drops the cans and boxes to the ground and holds up a book.

"This," he says.

I wipe my brow and straighten up. Asef is holding the Muslim holy book. The Koran.

***

Vlad snapped back to reality. The memory of Asef holding up the Koran gradually faded. Pasha was holding up the newspaper again.

"You can see in the background there is a set of underground irrigation pipes ready to be buried. A fairly modern system, from what I can tell," Pasha said. "The partners, or the Agricultural Institute, must have put some good money into that. You gotta ruin those pipes. They'll never be able to grow vegetables on my land without the proper irrigation. If they can't grow vegetables, the Institute will pull out. The wives won't be able to do it all themselves, so they will give up on this little do-good project and go back to shopping all day. I need that land free and clear."

Vladimir nodded, knowing full well that he was digging himself even deeper into a life of crime. "You got it. I'll get it done tonight."

39.

I grab the Koran out of Asef's hand. "Where did you find this?"

"I found it on the road back there while I was gathering the lost cans," Asef replies. "There are more, too. And I also found smashed cans of American soda and empty packs of cigarettes, also American."

I look at the book. The Soviets have destroyed these holy books by the thousands. In the early days of the war, Soviet soldiers offered food and medical supplies to the peasants in exchange for their Korans. Captain Yurchenko himself said he commissioned piles of these books to be burned. No more religion to keep these people stuck in the Stone Age, so say our politicians and generals. But a Koran is here; I'm holding it in my hand. If the book is here, that means other people have been through here. Just what we need: uneducated Afghan rebels fueled by the Koran.

I hold the book up to Danil, who is keeping a look out. "Come look at this!" I shout to him. Danil walks over. His striped shirt is soaked with sweat.

All of a sudden, everything dawns on Asef. "I know where these Korans have come from, Vlad-ee-meer. From the United States. My father went to a conference at the United Nations regarding aid to Afghanistan and he told me all about it. The CIA has secretly been planting these holy books in schools and around the countryside in order to instill a resurgence of Islamic pride in the Afghan people. The American government has also been shipping weapons and other supplies to the rebel mujahideen so they can effectively fight off the Soviets."

Asef pushes his glasses up the bridge of his nose and laughs. "This is Rambo Three *come to life!"*

Danil and I look at each other. Our faces go blank. We both look to Asef. "What the fuck is Rambo Three*?" Danil asks.*

Asef laughs again. "Oh, yes, I suppose the Soviet government would be wise to ban that one from its cinemas! I saw it in London before school let out for the summer. Rambo is a CIA operative who goes to Afghanistan to stir up the mujahideen. Gives them weapons and holy books. By the end, the people embrace their religion and fight off the evil Russians. Good movie, lots of action. I didn't think the plot was very realistic, but here we are. We are living a movie."

And the weapons? Where are the American-supplied weapons? Danil looks up the road. I look into the mountainside.

Danil shakes his head. "Aw, shit. We are supposed to be a military superpower but I guess we are nothing more than a second-rate movie out of America." He turns and walks away. "We can fight the Afghans, sure, but we can't fight the Americans. There is no way we can fight Americans."

Asef is not laughing anymore. Everything his dad has told him and the movies he's seen are making sense now. All summer, he thought traveling around with a bunch of hearty Russian soldiers was great fun, but now he sees that this war is real.

"It's going to be okay, Asef," I say. "We are better trained than any muj street gangster with a gun from America."

Asef relaxes, but he is thinking. The kid is always thinking. "My father told me the Americans do not see the whole picture; they stand so passionately against Communism that they fail to see how fanning the flames of Islam will create a much bigger problem for their own country in the future. He thinks the Americans will regret their involvement."

I glance at the book. "Yeah, well, Asef, your father is probably right." But I think about that scenario for a second. It makes me laugh. "Someday, Asef, maybe another brilliant Afghan teenager will be right here at this very same spot, translating for an American soldier."

Now he laughs. "American soldiers here? I don't think that will ever happen, Vlad-ee-meer."

***

Vladimir sat next to Zhanna on a padded bench inside the Sverdlovsk Museum of Fine Arts, Zhanna's first idea for one of their daytime dates. Her voice was off in the distance, below the memory and below the noise, but becoming clearer by the second.

"So, I want to call it Salon Americana. I am meeting with the Restructuring Loan Board to finalize the papers this evening after work. Since I don't have enough cash for what they call a down payment, I have to pay 9 percent interest instead of the usual 6 percent. But the loan is for ten years, so I don't know if the interest rate makes a difference. I'll tell you what, Viva, if I didn't love shoes so much, I would have that down payment. What do you think? Do you think a Salon Americana is a good idea?"

A prolonged pause. "Viva?"

Another pause, followed by a nudge to the ribs. "Viva? Are you listening to me?"

Zhanna scoffed and shoved Vlad in the shoulder.

Vladimir jolted back into the present time; the image of Asef laughing faded, and there sat Zhanna, staring, hardly amused by the inattention.

He took Zhanna's hand. "Yeah. Zha-Zha, I was listening. You qualified for a government restructuring loan to buy the October Woman beauty shop and you have plans to turn it into a place for women to escape if only for an hour. You will keep the same staff. You will offer hairstyling, manicures, makeup application, maybe a line of skin-care products. You asked me to design and construct some cabinets for the place. You want to call it Salon Americana and your loan is at 9 percent interest instead of 6 percent because of a lack of a down payment due to your shoe habit."

He took a breath. "To answer your questions, yes, I will make the cabinets for you. I'll get Oleg to help, and yes, I think the name, Salon Americana, is a good one." He released her hand, swung his arm around her and kissed her forehead.

Zhanna pulled back, tapped him on the nose. "You really were listening, weren't you?"

She had recently permed her hair, so her strands were big and soft and flowed down her back like gold. He kissed her temple. "I hear every word you say, Zha-Zha. In fact, I hear everything," he said, pulling away. "That's part of my problem. Every sound comes through. Something reminds me of the war and I go right back to Afghanistan. I don't know what's worse, the images or the sounds."

Zhanna swept the hair from her face. "I've been thinking," she said, looking down. "The war may have triggered this, yes, but what about your father? He never went to war and—"

"I know," Vlad interrupted. "He was sick, too," He looked at Zhanna, his resolve strengthened. "But he catered to his demons. I refuse to do that anymore. I quit drinking, quit taking pills, I will beat this. I am much stronger than my father ever was."

"Maybe you should go talk to someone, then," Zhanna said, placing her hand on his shoulder. "Not every professional has fled the country yet. Go talk to someone. It can't hurt, and I know you are strong, but people can't do this by themselves. The images and noise may never go away, and Vlad, we can't live like that again. I won't do it."

Vlad stood up, shoved his hands in his pockets. "I'll think about it, let's just go look at some art, shall we?"

Zhanna sighed heavily, looking away. "But Viva, really I –"

He reached down, taking her hand. "I know, I hate myself for all of this. Let's just look at some art and talk about this later."

Slowly she relented. A slight, annoyed smile flashed upon her face as she nodded.

Standing before Gerasimov's "A Kolkhoz Celebration" with its colorful garden scene, Zhanna turned. "Oh, you know, this painting reminds me of something I read in the paper. Did you hear about the Garden for Children? Someone destroyed it the other night. The irrigation pipes were punctured with huge holes and the motor for the automatic sprinklers is completely dead. The college can't afford to buy new equipment, so the project is over."

Vlad immediately released his wife's hand. "Yeah, that's awful. Just awful," he said weakly.

"It was such a lovely idea, too," Zhanna said. "Those women really had a vision to do something positive for Russia. The strange part is that the garden was located on the same land as an apartment building that was burned to the ground back in January. Oy, that land must be cursed." Zhanna moved on to look at a collection of Kasli castings.

Vlad stayed back at the Gerasimov painting, looking at the floor, cursing himself for working for Pasha in the first place. He had to do something. "Hey Zha-Zha," he called out, walking over to the castings. "Paying too much interest will bury a person," he said, taking her hand. "Never pay interest."

Zhanna's expression went blank. "What?" She, too, born and bred in working-class Soviet society, had never dealt with issues concerning business or loans or rates of interest.

"I've been working for a co-op millionaire. He knows these things," Vlad explained. "I have cash. There's enough for a down payment, I'm sure. Let me give you the money for the down payment, then you won't pay so much in interest."

Zhanna immediately shook her head. "No, Viva, I need to do this by myself. I'll pay the 9 percent interest. I don't think it makes much of a difference, really."

"No! Zha-Zha, it makes a huge difference. You should earn interest, not pay it. Listen, Pasha has been giving me financial advice. He may be a crooked scoundrel without morals of any kind, but when it comes to money, he knows damn well what he is talking about."

Zhanna curled her lips inward and thought for a moment. "Well, I suppose it makes sense to make as much of a down payment as you can."

Vlad nodded. "Yeah. And here's another thing I learned. Whatever profits you make should go right back into the business."

Zhanna looked up, her eyes wide. "Everything?"

Vlad nodded. "More so in the beginning. That's how your business grows."

"I can't buy shoes?"

"No shoes. Not for a while. Take the money, make the down payment and plunge all the profits into the salon. After a while, when the money is flowing, you can buy all the shoes you want."

Zhanna slowly nodded. "I suppose that makes sense."

He took both of her hands. "After everything I have put you through, please let me do this. Take the money, make the down payment with it."

40.

1 October

Pasha managed to bribe all the right officials, thus was granted permission to leave the country for three days. Off to Germany, he said, to engage in talks with owners of a luxury hotel chain. He hoped to break ground in Sverdlovsk on his own land within a year.

With Pasha gone, the café was closed and Vladimir had three days off. Three days in which to design and build Zhanna's cabinetry for Salon Americana, which was due to open next week.

Vlad swung one leg off his motorcycle, shoved the keys into his coat pocket. Armed with a tape measure clipped to his jeans and a rough schematic of the cabinets in his hand, he stepped into the lumberyard on Sverdlovsk's industrial west side. It must have been the fourth one built in the city, as evidenced by the plain black letters printed across the awning: State Lumber Yard #4.

Two cabinets, she said. One on each side of the salon, eighty-nine centimeters wide, double doors, no more than 185 centimeters tall, with shelves thirty to thirty-five centimeters deep, maybe in a light finish. Vlad walked into the lumberyard confident in his woodworking ability. His first word as a green-eyed tot had been "hammer." At ten, he made a three-tier bookshelf. At twelve, he constructed a fully operative clock. At fifteen, he helped his dad at the furniture factory every day after school. Putting together a few cabinets to hold shampoo bottles and curlers would be easy.

The plan was to select the materials here at the lumberyard, and then meet up with Oleg, who would drive over in his pickup. Together, they would build the cabinets in Oleg's powered-up storage shed.

Oleg had sounded so happy on the phone. "Sure, I can help build cabinets. Sounds great, Vlad-O!" Even better, he had a new album from the US, Metallica, and some kind of Canadian beer he bought from a downtown kiosk. It would be a good time. Oleg's exuberance made Vlad feel even worse for still not making it back to their regular Wednesday night dart tournaments.

Vladimir headed to the fiberboard, figuring eight panels of medium-density fiberboard should be enough for two cabinets and leave some for trim at the top. Two coats of a honey stain would look nice. But the shelves that once carried sheets of fiberboard were empty, save for two pathetic looking scraps of thin plywood. Obviously, the floor manager at Lumber Yard #4 was trying his best with what was available. Onto the next best thing, twelve-centimeter thick plywood. Gone. Typical Russia, collapsing in on itself, nothing left. He dreaded resorting to thinner plywood, but started to look for some anyway.

Outside, beyond the awning, some panels of solid birch stood upright, filed in a row. Three sheets of the stuff. Hideously expensive, but the birch would give the cabinets a smooth, silky look. Zhanna would really like it. And just one coat of a clear finish would be fine since the wood was of superior quality. He unclipped his tape measure and measured each panel. Not enough here to make two complete cabinets, but he could build with the plywood and use the birch for the fronts. There should be enough left over for solid birch trim. "Yeah, that may work," he mumbled to himself.

Just then, Vladimir felt a tap on his back. "Excuse me, mister, could you hand me that box of nails way up there?"

He turned around to see who was talking and had to look down. It was a kid. A boy. Maybe ten years old. Blond as he could possibly be. Long and skinny. Bright blue eyes. Vlad turned back around, reached up, and grabbed a box of nails from a shelf next to the birch panels. He brought it down and handed it to the boy. "Here you go, kid."

The kid took the box. "*Spasiba*, mister." He turned to go.

Curious as to why a ten-year-old needed nails, Vlad called out, "Hey, what are you doing with those, anyway?"

The kid turned and looked up, squinting from the sun. He had freckles on his nose, crooked adult teeth crowding out a few remaining baby teeth. His jeans came up past his ankles. "My family is moving into a different apartment," he said enthusiastically. "Now we will be on the first floor. Dad is making a ramp for my brother so he can get in and out of the apartment easier. We used to live on the sixth floor, but the elevator was too small for my brother's wheelchair. Dad always had to carry him.

My mom put our name on the transfer list years ago, and yesterday our name finally came up! We get to move in this week."

Vladimir thought for a moment. "Hmmm, well, if you want nails for a wheelchair ramp, I'd go with the galvanized ones. They are much more resistant to decay. Hold on." He shoved a few other boxes of nails out of the way, ultimately finding a box of galvanized nails. "Here, take these to your dad," he said, holding out the box. The kid grabbed the box, gave the other one back, and said, "Okay, thanks."

The kid turned toward the covered area and pointed. "Oh, hey, that's my brother right there."

Under the awning, standing around a stack of plywood, were a mother and a father. Three other blond, blue-eyed boys of varying heights surrounded them, all between the ages of twelve and twenty. The father, long and lanky, was inspecting a wooden post, holding it up and letting it fall into his hand. The mother had sandy blonde hair covered partially with a scarf. She kept looking down.

Judging by the father's age and the ages of the boys, the mother had to be somewhere between forty-five and fifty, but could have easily passed for sixty. She did not just look prematurely aged; hers was a tired face trying to appear okay with the world, her sad eyes on the verge of breaking down but keeping it together for the sake of another.

This mother's spirit had taken a big hit. That much was certain.

The young boy ran up, met with his family and held up the box of galvanized nails to show. The father took the box, looked it over, and nodded in approval. The family moved on slowly. As they did, the four blond boys gradually dispersed to reveal a fifth brother. The oldest one. Also very blond with blue eyes. His mother was pushing him in a wheelchair.

The oldest brother had no legs, and only one arm.

He looked to be Vlad's age. Maybe a year or two younger. He wore an army-issue camouflage jacket with the left arm pinned up. Dog tags dangled around his neck. Two stumps where his legs should have been were covered in army-issue camouflage trousers, folded over. His hair was still clipped in telltale military fashion. Vlad looked at the long fingers on his only hand, at his extended torso. He should be standing taller than his father, but this guy would never stand.

As the family made its way to pay for the materials, the father stopped. He held up the box of nails and smiled. "Thanks for getting these nails. They're just what I needed and I didn't even know it."

Vladimir nodded. "Sure," he took a few steps forward and thrust his hand out to the wheelchair-bound man, introducing himself. "Vladimir Verstakov. 1988. 51st infantry. Bagram. Sent over as part of the final push."

The blond guy looked up, something he surely never had to do before losing his legs. He whole-heartedly reached out his single arm and shook Vlad's hand. "Matvei Ivaniev. 1986. Called up just after high school. Served with the 126th in Kandahar. That is, until that damn muj land mine tore me apart," he smiled a weak, self-deprecating smile while shaking his head side to side. "Served with some of the finest men in this country.

If I didn't have them to talk to, I would be completely insane." Matvei's eyes brightened as he spoke of his time at war and the men with whom he served, even made light of the land mine that took his legs and arm.

His mother, however, seemed to age another five years right then and there.

The family moved on. Vlad went back to his birch panels feeling weak and foolish. So many men returned from the war horribly broken, yet he was the one who couldn't keep his shit together. The noise came out of nowhere, louder than ever. *Blast. Gunfire. Commands. Blast. Gunfire. Commands.* He shook his head, wiped the sweat from his brow and tried to focus on the wood.

***

"I don't know what kind of wood you'll be able to get, Asef, but oak would be nice, or maple. Wait, what am I saying? You'll be in the United States; you'll be able to get any type of wood over there."

As we drive along, I am instructing Asef on how to make a simple desk. At the end of August, just a few weeks away, he's leaving for New York to take part in the United Nations Interpreter Training program. He's also enrolled full-time at New York University and has declared a double major, linguistics and European history. Said he wants to work as a professional interpreter and live in Europe for a while, and then go back to Kabul, earn a doctorate, and teach history at the university level.

Asef ain't going to be making any desk. He'll buy one in America or his parents will special-order a whole office set and have it shipped from wherever beautiful furniture is made. Maybe Italy.

But he seems genuinely interested in this kind of stuff. He's writing all my instructions down in his notebook. "Thanks, Vlad-ee-meer. I've never made anything with my hands before. I'll send you a picture of it when I'm done. I can send a letter to you, can't I?"

"Sure," I say. "It may arrive two months later and already opened by government agents, but I'll get it."

On second thought, I think he will *make that desk. He will make it and he will send me a picture of it. I chuckle at the thought.*

***

Vladimir clutched his stomach, had to squat down next to the wood panels. Breakfast was churning in his belly, threatening to come back up. Frantically, he ran to the far edge of the lumberyard, where he vomited twice on the grass. He leaned his forehead into the fence while fighting off the noise. *Blast. Gunfire. Commands. Blast. Gunfire. Commands.*

"Vlad-O! What the hell are you doing? Don't ya know we've got work to do?" Vladimir looked over to see Oleg, arms wide open, truck keys in hand, a huge smile on his face. His dark hair looked more like a mop than ever. Same old crooked nose, two missing teeth. Relieved to see an old friend, Vlad tried his best to move, but all he could do was hold one hand up and say, "Hey, Oleg. Yeah, I'll be right there." The thought of making cabinets could not penetrate the noise or guilt.

Woodworking would not be his Iskra.

41.

8 October

Zhanna folded the last of the brand new, fluffy, yellow towels, and placed it on an open shelf above the sink. She turned and smiled, looking out over the newly renovated salon. Stylists dressed in identical yellow aprons scurried around readying their stations; the receptionist was already on the phone setting up an appointment. Salon Americana was just about to open its doors for the first time and the place looked absolutely fantastic.

New floor tiles in a rich mocha, recessed lighting, vanilla-colored walls with clean, white trim. A bouquet of yellow flowers sat in a vase on the front desk. A tranquil fountain separated the front desk from the waiting area, where a comfortable couch lined with pillows beckoned women to sit and relax. Magazines were fanned out on a spacious, dark, cherry wood table. Freshly baked *bliny* in a basket, a samovar for tea, a pitcher of fruit juice, and a stack of paper cups awaited the morning's clients.

The light birch wood cabinets Vladimir and Oleg made had turned out better than she originally imagined. The guys even finished them off with classy crown and bottom molding made out of the birch. With the leftover materials, they made three individual shelves, one to go above each sink. A perfect addition.

Zhanna made one more visual sweep of the salon, and then clicked across the tile floor in her sleek black heels to check her appointments. "Ah, a free market economy," she whispered along the way.

But thick cigar smoke wafted out of the waiting area and into the main salon. Zhanna stopped in her tracks. A rough, mucous-filled cough drowned out the tranquil sound of the fountain. "Hello?" Zhanna called out, cringing. This could not possibly be one of Salon Americana's clients. Another rough cough. "Hello?" Zhanna called out again toward the waiting area.

Zhanna clicked past the fountain. She did not find a client in the waiting area, but the exact opposite: a portly, middle-aged man dressed in a cheap brown suit. He sat on the luxurious new couch, sucking on a stinky cigar. Another man, hugely overweight with a pink face and chubby lips, stood holding a paper cup of tea and stuffing a bliny in his mouth as if half-starved. Outside, a Chechen man in a leather jacket paced the entrance of the salon.

Zhanna took a hurried step backwards. "Um, can I help the two of you?"

The man on the couch pulled the cigar out of his fat lips and exhaled a plume of thick smoke into the air. Zhanna's knees weakened when he tapped the ash atop the nice, new, cherry wood table. The fat man quickly flashed a metal badge from his wallet and said, "We are from the Bureau of Building Inspection. Now, dear, we have a few questions and we will get out of your...your... what do you call this place?"

"It's a beauty salon. Just for women," said Zhanna, with an emphasis on *women*, hoping these two slobs would get the message and get out before any real clients walked in.

"Ah, yes, I see here you bought this place from the government. Formerly named October Woman. Is that right?" The cigar smoker reached forward and dragged his clipboard along the table, messing up the array of magazines in the process.

"That's right," said Zhanna, cringing.

"And exactly how did you pay for this, this, this salon as you call it, my dear?" piped up the obese man, grabbing another bliny. Crumbs and powdered sugar fell out of his mouth as he spoke.

"With a restructuring loan," Zhanna answered, trying to stay calm. "My husband gave me the down payment so I could secure the lowest interest rate possible."

"Oh, yes, and your husband would be...Let me see, here." The brown-suited man looked down at his clipboard. "Mr. Vladimir Verstakov, employed by one Pavel Grachov of Café Club. Commonly goes by the name of Pasha. Have I got that right?"

Zhanna nodded slowly, staring at the mess. "That's right." The cigar smell was making her sick to her stomach. So was watching the fat man cram another strawberry bliny into his mouth. It had taken two hours of waiting in line this morning just to buy those breakfast pastries. The cigar man spoke again. "So your husband,

Vladimir Verstakov, is using money earned from his job at Café Club to help you pay for this salon?"

Now completely fed up, Zhanna brought her hands up to her hips and glared at the men. "Yes, and may I ask, what does my husband or our finances have to do with the two of you inspecting the building? I want to see that badge again, if you don't mind." She held out one hand to the fat man, but neither man moved.

The men looked at each other and nodded in some sort of tacit agreement then looked at Zhanna. The smoking man snuffed out his smelly cigar in the puddle of tea left in the paper cup and stood up, leaving the cup on the table. "Our work here is done, my dear. Have a good day," he said, with a tip if his hat. The fat guy brushed the powdered sugar off his suit jacket and poured himself another cup of tea to take with him. He waddled toward the door. With that, the two men left Zhanna and the Salon Americana.

42.

20 October

All day a chopper has been flying overhead, ahead of us, looking out for rebel activity. It circles back occasionally. Right now, it's flying over my truck as it is returning to the head of the convoy. Yurchenko must have radioed the pilot, inquiring as to our whereabouts when we stopped to change the tire.

The spare tire seems to be handling the road just fine. I crest a small hill and I don't see Yurchenko's truck, but I'm sure he's up there waiting for us.

***

Vladimir cruised along on his motorcycle down Prospekt Lenina, weaving long and easy in and out of the sparse city traffic. Done with work, too restless to go home.

One of Sverdlovsk's many city buses rumbled down the street in the opposite lane. Up ahead, the cinema was letting out for the night. Across the street, the state-run ice cream parlor was dark; likewise, the record store. The co-op cafes spread along the city blocks were bustling, as usual.

Vlad's nose and feet froze in the late-night October air, but it was good to actually feel. It meant that he was still alive, which was more than he could say for thirty-two of the comrades with whom he had fought back in the desert.

Traffic thinned near Gorodskoy Pond. Vlad changed gears to pick up some speed. Nothing but speed. Maybe speed would keep the flashbacks away. He sped up. Living life on the edge of disaster may be a good way to ditch the demons. He sped up some more, hunkered down as he approached the pond.

A fierce wind picked up as he flew by the water. In an attempt to avoid getting kicked over by the wind, he hunkered down further, hit the accelerator. Up ahead, Prospekt Lenina veered to the left. Vlad leaned to his left side while pushing the left handle bar forward in anticipation of the turn.

***

I make a left-hand turn, snake up a few switchbacks. I can feel the truck strain with the rough road and the intense heat. Up ahead I see Yurchenko's truck. He's standing outside along with Mikhail Astafurov and the two Pashtun men. They are not talking, just standing around waiting for the rest of us.

I come to a stop. Yurchenko walks to the passenger side, kneels down. He stands up and gives me a nod. "Nice job on the tire." The helicopter pilot must have informed him of our flat.

He comes over to my open window. I apologize for the delay, but he doesn't seem too bothered by it. He asks me how many AK-47s I loaded into the truck this morning. I tell him twelve. He tells me that once we get to the village I should unload five of them and leave them with Farood. Leave plenty of rounds for each rifle, too.

I respond, "Yes sir."

Yurchenko heads down the convoy, presumably to ask Danil and Red to leave some of their rifles in the village, as well.

On the way back, he motions for Asef to exit the vehicle and come with him. Asef does, leaving his backpack and books strewn about the truck.

Asef and Yurchenko walk up the road to where Farood and Osman are standing. They engage in conversation, thanks to Asef who flows easily between the two languages. Farood is pointing up the road. After a while, all of the men nod. They shake hands.

Asef walks down the road, tripping over two rocks with his huge feet. He climbs back in the truck.

"What did you talk about?" I ask after he shuts the door.

"The Pashtuns have invited us to their village to share in some food and tea," he tells me quietly.

I think that is an odd invitation, Afghans inviting their hostile occupiers to share in a meal. But Asef tells me it's customary for the Pashtuns to be so welcoming. It's mandatory, actually. "They live by the Pashtunwali code," Asef tells me. "One tenet of the code is Melmastia, and it requires all Pashtuns to show hospitality and profound respect to all visitors, regardless of race or religion. Pashtuns are known to be the most hospitable people in the world."

"Well that's good, because I'm starving," I say. Up ahead, Yurchenko is moving, so I shift into gear and press my foot on the gas.

***

Hair flying in the icy wind because he lost his fur-lined hat on the last turn, which he took too fast, Vlad smiled to himself. Living life on the edge of disaster may just do the trick; the flashbacks were still happening, but so far, no noise. Peace. Just the sound of wind.

Maybe he could buy a fancier, tricked-out motorcycle, enter some of those wild, dirt track races on the south side of town. Go for the steepest, most remote ski hills; take up drag racing; jump out of an airplane. Anything to thwart the demons. Surely, with enough speed, the flashbacks would fade away. He leaned more to the left, pressed the accelerator harder, his head and torso sneaking over the centerline.

A set of headlights abruptly appeared around the corner. Vlad geared down and tried to right himself. But with all that speed and not enough distance between himself and the approaching car, returning his body to the upright position was impossible. The car screeched, sliding sideways into Vlad's lane, horn blaring. In panic, Vlad braked hard, but slid along the pavement, pulled by the weight of the bike. His left side kissed the asphalt, his leather jacket ripping open at the shoulder and his blue jeans burning up and down his leg. Vlad's entire left side was engulfed in heat and asphalt, his flesh on fire as the bike dragged him along the pavement. With his left hand pinned, he released the clutch, but stupidly hit the accelerator, causing the bike to whip out from underneath his legs. Headlights grew closer, brighter.

The bike careened down the road. Vlad cradled his head tightly with his right arm and rolled hard over the pavement. The car swerved. Vlad came to rest in the middle of the street, flat on his back.

The car screeched to a halt. A little old woman stepped out, shaking her fist. "What are you, some kind of moron?" she yelled in her granny voice.

The noise didn't just creep back in as usual, it roared back with a vengeance. *Blast. Gunfire. Commands. Blast. Gunfire. Commands.* "Goddammit! Motherfucker! Shit! Fuck! Fuck! Fuck!" Vlad yelled as he covered his head and curled up into the fetal position, not because of the intense physical pain he felt, but because of all the noise.

He managed to uncurl himself and sit up just as another car came speeding down the street, and he scooted away in time to avoid another collision. "Shit!" he yelled again, pounding the pavement. Clambering up to a standing position, he took a painful step forward, barely putting weight on his left leg. The bike had crashed into a grove of trees, and from what Vlad could see of it, the bike did not look at all salvageable. Tasting a mixture of blood and gravel in his mouth, he kept going, painfully hobbling down the street toward town.

Living life on the edge of disaster would definitely not be his Iskra.

43.

After the crash, the little old woman who had referred to Vladimir as "some kind of moron," demanded that he get in her car so she could take him to get help. He looked like her grandson, she spat, "Big and strong with a sweet face, and no doubt just as stupid."

Along the way, she told him it was a good thing his motorcycle was wrecked. Those things are a death trap; he should feel lucky to be alive after that. She had a cousin, Tomas, back in Leningrad, who crashed on a motorcycle and broke both legs, or was that Uncle Timur in Smolensk? She couldn't remember exactly, but regardless, "Those things are dangerous and should be outlawed." And there was an aunt who lived outside of town. She had a motorbike and the darn thing kept getting away from her, so she sold it and bought a proper bicycle.

The lady had numerous cousins and nieces and uncles spread throughout the country, and obviously felt Vlad needed to hear about each and every one. Vlad remained quiet for the entire trip into town, nodding while she ranted.

He planned to go home and clean up, but at the last second, he directed the talkative lady to drop him off at his wife's basement apartment. As she pulled up to the curb, the woman hit the brakes and looked at him quizzically. "Your wife has her own apartment? Now, why does your wife have her own apartment?"

She had her own apartment because they were going through a rough patch, he told her, nursing his scraped shoulder.

She held up her bony finger again. "Ah, a rough patch. Yes." And proceeded to inform him how her nephew, Leo, or maybe it was Viktor, and his wife had separated for three years before they got back together. "So, if you love her, don't give up," she instructed. "They are happy now. They understand each other. That's important, you hear me? To understand each other."

Vlad thanked the lady for the advice and hobbled, bruised and bloodied, out of the car to Zhanna's door and knocked. "Zha-Zha." It was the middle of the night, and he was a dirty, frightening mess. "Zha-Zha. It's me." He knocked again. "It's me, Zha-Zha. Please open up."

A sleepy Zhanna, dressed in a robe and slippers, opened the door. "Viva! What on earth!" she exclaimed upon seeing his beaten body.

"I crashed the bike," he replied weakly, trying to stand up straight despite the pain.

Zhanna leaned her temple against the door and sighed. "You crashed the bike. Here we go again, Viva. Here you are, a complete mess, and I am going to drop everything and try to fix you, aren't I?"

Vladimir gave a weak laugh, hunching over with pain. "Well, I suppose we understand each other, don't we?"

Zhanna closed her eyes and shook her head, all the while motioning for Vlad to come inside. "Oy. I may be the single most foolish woman in all of Sverdlovsk, perhaps in the entire Soviet Union."

In the bathroom, Vlad sat on the edge of the tub and gingerly pulled off his sweatshirt while Zhanna brought out a bottle of rubbing alcohol, some cotton balls, and bandages. Straddling the edge of the tub, she dabbed Vlad's shoulder with a cotton ball moistened with alcohol. One touch and he winced in pain.

"Oh, stop being such a baby, it's not that bad," she admonished, dabbing again.

"Say," she said, touching a moist cotton ball to his swollen lip. "Does your boss Pasha have any business dealings with a pair of building inspectors?"

Vlad shook his head. "No. I don't think so, why?"

"Two of them stopped by the salon the day of the grand opening. They asked about you and how we are paying for the place. Where the money is coming from, stuff like that. I thought it was a little strange, since they didn't even inspect the building. They were disgusting, too. One sucked on a god-awful cigar the whole time. The other guy was hugely fat and stuffed three blinys into his mouth right in front of me. Oy, I had to bribe the cashier a small fortune to get those pastries!"

Vlad immediately pulled back, brushed the cotton ball away. "Zhanna, I don't think those men were building inspectors. They sound like Pasha's business partners, and they just so happen to be KGB agents."

Zhanna's eyes widened. She dropped the cotton ball and stood up. "KGB! Viva, what in the hell are you doing wrapped up with the KGB?"

Vladimir stood up from the bathtub. "I'm not, but Pasha is. To open the café, he convinced those guys to invest their pensions. He's been taking their share of the profits all along."

"Well, obviously these agents know about you, too!" exclaimed Zhanna.

Vladimir pulled his sweatshirt over his head, ignoring the shooting pain in his shoulder. "That doesn't matter now. What worries me is that they know about you."

***

"So, what else do you know?" I ask out of the blue. Now that Asef has told me a bit about the Pashtuns, I'm curious.

Asef is leaning his temple against the doorframe. His black hair lifts and flutters with the hot breeze, his dark eyes look straight ahead. Now he looks at me. "Sorry, what did you say?"

"What else do you know? About these Pashtuns? If we are going to be sharing a meal with them, I need to know what to expect, so what else can you tell me?"

He perks up. "Well, here's something. This particular tribe of Pashtuns is different from the rest. There are only a few groups of them around Kabul. You know those trim beards both Osman and Farood have? Well, all the men of this particular tribe must have a trim beard, and they must keep their heads covered. It's part of their strict interpretation of the Islamic law. And this tribe is simple; they don't use any technology or celebrate holidays; their children are schooled at home, mostly with lessons from the Koran. They think of themselves as religious scholars."

"Religious scholars, huh?" I light another cigarette. A bunch of disheveled Soviet soldiers who have never stepped foot in a place

of worship are going to share in a meal with a small tribe of Pashtun religious scholars. "Now this should be interesting." I turn the steering wheel and go up a small rise. We begin to enter the village.

***

Engrossed in the memory, Vlad must have brushed past Zhanna, because he found himself in her tiny kitchen, reaching over the sink, making sure the window was properly locked.

"Vladimir? Vladimir? Listen to me! Don't you think this is a little silly? Of course I keep everything locked!" demanded Zhanna.

Vlad stopped, shook the memory of Afghanistan from his head. "This is the KGB we are talking about, Zha-Zha. They will do anything. You are not safe." Satisfied with the kitchen window, he sprinted over to the front door and began checking the lock. "I'm going to install a better lock in the morning. And you need more light by the door. No, better yet, move in with your parents. I need to know you are safe. You can't be here alone."

Zhanna whipped around, headed straight to the door. She grabbed Vlad by his bandaged shoulder and yanked him around, holding him against the door with one hand. "Vladimir, stop it! The door is locked. The windows are locked. A family lives above me. This is a well-lit, busy neighborhood. No one is going to break in. If the café partners are looking for their money, they will track down Pasha and take the appropriate measures. They have no reason to come after me. I will not move, and I sure as hell will not live in fear. Now stop acting so crazy!"

Blast. Gunfire. Commands. Blast. Gunfire. Commands. Vladimir closed his eyes while the noise took over. His body went so weak that Zhanna had to lurch forward and bring her other hand to his chest to keep him from slumping to the floor. "Viva, what is it?"

"You're right," he mumbled. "I am crazy." *Blast. Gunfire. Commands. Blast. Gunfire. Commands.* "I'm crazy. Just my father's son, I guess. Maybe it's not the war. Could be an Iskra isn't going to fix a thing. I'm just plain crazy."

Zhanna's face softened, her voice lost all trace of annoyance or anger. "Baby," she said, touching his face. "Come on, I didn't mean it that way. You know I don't think that."

Vlad steadied himself. "No. It's true. The vivid memories. The noise. None of it will go away. It's why I've wanted to put a bullet through my head. Wish I had, then I would never have hurt you, and I wouldn't have gotten wrapped up with Pasha and put you in this situation."

He took a deep breath. "I thought money would be the answer to this, but it isn't. No amount of money in the world can stop the memories and the noise, and what I did to you. I still have a stack of cash in the closet at home and I don't even care. Pasha fills a briefcase with cash every night and I'm not even envious. I just want my sanity." He pulled her in close. "You don't deserve any of this. The only thing I can't figure out is why you haven't completely given up on me."

Zhanna sighed and put her hands on her hips. "For your information, I haven't given up on you because for some strange reason, I still love you."

Vlad straightened up. "Let me stay here tonight. I can't leave you alone. Don't worry; I'll sleep on the couch."

"No! Absolutely not. You are not going to stay here!" Zhanna said, pushing him away. "I know what will happen if you stay, and…we can't…we just can't."

He took her hand. "I am not leaving you alone, not with those KGB agents out there. If you don't let me stay, I'll stand by your front door all night."

Zhanna rolled her eyes. "Oh, all right. But you are staying on the couch."

44.

Vladimir did not sleep on the couch. Not even a modest attempt was made, just as Zhanna predicted. Maybe it was Vlad's all-consuming concern for her safety; most likely it was that, combined with his torment that caused Zhanna to slowly mold her body to his, and kiss him as she wiped away the tear. Whatever the cause, Zhanna, as usual, could not resist the pull her husband had on her. He responded in kind, pulling her in closer, lifting her up by the waist so her thighs gripped his hips, and carried her away from the door. They made love in the drafty back bedroom, under a sea of blankets. Silently, more intense than ever before.

Afterwards, by the dim light of the moon, Zhanna sat naked on the edge of the double bed. She looked down at Vladimir, who lay sprawled out, fast asleep. She swept her hand across his face, always drawn to his face. "It's true, I still love you," she whispered. Exasperated with herself, she stood, tied her robe around her body, stepped into her slippers, and padded out to the kitchen.

Over a cup of tea, she found her journal sitting on the table and rifled through it. Inside, glued to the first pages, were magazine pictures of various hairstyles she wanted to copy. On another page, a sketch of an original design for a purse she planned to make some day. Near the middle of the journal, a snapshot of Vladimir slid out. Black and white, taken the day he left for Afghanistan. He stood so tall and strong next to the airplane.

After the photograph, there was just one more entry, the name Karina with a heart beneath it, drawn in black pen. She had written that name while recuperating from the miscarriage. The rest of the journal was blank.

She picked up the photograph of Vlad and tucked it in before the page with the purse design and closed the book. She took a sip of tea and touched her empty belly. They would be parents now. If Vlad hadn't lost all control that day in January, a warm little bundle would now be sleeping in a crib at the foot of the bed.

Zhanna set down her tea and opened the book. Again, Vlad's picture fell out. She picked it up and took another look at the purse sketch. She had drawn it years ago, her very own design; a small, rectangular purse, fun and colorful, with an outside pocket for a tube of lipstick, a feature that, much to Zhanna's dismay, never so much as crossed the minds of the dreary Soviet textile designers. The purse was functional enough, but most importantly, it was stylish.

Zhanna turned to the page with Karina's name written on it and slid her finger across the letters. "Karina, sweetheart, maybe your spirit is still out there."

She started filling up the pages, drawing the letter K in various scripts accompanied by different designs. Five pages later, one K, wavy and soft with a little heart at the bottom, stood out. She drew that same K again on a blank page. If Karina were alive, the two of them would go out to parks and museums and do fun things together.

There would be a lot to carry and Zhanna's design for a fashionable little purse would not do, but never in a million years would she wear a backpack. That purse can still be stylish, but bigger, she thought.

Zhanna stayed awake to greet the sun, feverishly revamping the original design. Two separate, zippered compartments on the inside. One for a change of baby clothes, another big enough for two folded diapers. One side pocket for snacks, another for a bottle, and a small compartment in the front in which to store safety pins. Still, the purse had enough room for a mother to keep her money and keys handy, and of course, the outside pouch for lipstick remained, because no woman, no matter how busy or tired she gets, should ever go without lipstick. "The Karina Baby Tote," Zhanna announced as she held up the completed sketch against the rising sun.

45.

Vladimir awakened with a newfound sense of calm and purpose, one that could only come from having the best sex of his life with the one woman he loved and wanted more than anything. He kept his eyes closed and slowly rolled over to touch her hair, to feel her smooth body, maybe have another go-around before work. "Good morning, Zha-Zha," he said groggily, reaching out his arm. But to no avail. Zhanna was scurrying around the apartment, pulling on a dress, looking for earrings, applying makeup, frantically organizing some sketches of a purse she'd drawn. She told him she was in the midst of great inspiration and had to go, had to look at fabrics and locate a crew of seamstresses, all before work. Tea and oatmeal were in the kitchen, and please lock up. Not taken aback in the slightest, Vlad was content to lie there and watch her scurry.

At work, a note awaited him in the kitchen. Pasha was at the Ipatiev house with an assignment. Vlad picked up the note and crumpled it. "The Ipatiev house? What the hell?" He shook his head, put on his coat, and headed out the door.

He crossed the street and walked six blocks along the cobblestones, and then took a left. He stopped to unzip his coat and crossed the street again. Not a day for such a heavy coat, but still, the sharp chill in the air was a dire warning of the pending Russian winter. Up ahead, the cobblestones gradually gave way to dirt and gravel. The dingy, white trim and cloudy windows of the infamous Ipatiev house poked up above the wooden fence surrounding it.

In front of the fence stood Pasha, hands in his pockets, dressed in a sharp-looking tailored suit. He was looking down at a pile of flowers at his feet.

Vlad stopped to light a cigarette. "Pasha!" he called out. "Your business partners are harassing my wife. You gotta call them off."

Pasha looked up. He held his arms out wide while the wind ruffled his suit jacket. "This is the place, V.V.," he said. "This is where it all went down, seventy-three years ago. Where we are standing right now, imperial blood once spilled. It pooled like crimson tea upon this very ground. The crime of the century, some say. The harshest of punishments, brutal beyond belief, and committed by our very own government." Pasha looked up to the sky, closed his eyes.

The late October sun shone brightly upon Pasha's face, making him appear almost angelic. "July 17, 1918, a Bolshevik leader by the name of Yakov Sverdlov gave the order to have an entire family murdered on this very spot. A mother, a father, four lovely daughters, and a son, Alexi, who was heir to the throne. Little Alexi was sick suffered from hemophilia. He was a mere thirteen years of age."

Pasha looked off in the distance. "And for what? Because they possessed wealth. The Bolsheviks couldn't stand it, so they gathered up the family and assassinated them in the basement. To add insult to injury, after the murder they changed the name of the city from Yekaterinburg to Sverdlovsk to commemorate Yakov Sverdlov for giving the order. Our city celebrates a blood-thirsty Commie!"

Vlad pulled the cigarette from his mouth. "Oh come on, up until Gorbachev took over, the entire country celebrated blood-thirsty Commies, and most of it still does!"

He stepped up to Pasha. "You're talking about the Romanov execution? Every school kid knows the story. The Romanovs weren't just wealthy; the family controlled all of Russia's resources for themselves, leaving Russians to starve to death. Plus, Nikolai the Second was the most inept czar we've ever had. A bumbling fool who couldn't make a decision, couldn't feed his citizens. With conditions like that, no wonder the Bolsheviks took over. I imagine it wasn't very difficult."

He put the cigarette back in his mouth, but abruptly withdrew it. "And, did you hear me? You gotta call off Grigory and Fyodor." Vladimir was in no mood to stand around and chat about the brutal misdeeds of the town's namesake when his wife could be in danger.

But Pasha wasn't through with the Romanov execution. He strolled along the mounds of flowers, still talking. "Legend has it that young Anastasia hid precious imperial jewels inside her corset. That's why she didn't die with her family; that's why she wasn't found with them. The jewels blocked the bullets, giving her a chance to escape. Not that she got far. The Red Army soldiers chased her down and made sure they finished her off with the butts of their rifles. The girl was seventeen."

He stopped and picked up a wilted daisy, put it to his nose, then tossed it to the ground, chuckling to himself. "Hiding imperial jewels in her corset, now there is a girl after my own heart. If Anastasia were alive today, she would be ninety years old. I picture her as a majestic queen, lounging amongst her riches, ordering her servants around with the snap of her fingers. I feel her spirit within the walls of Café Club, guiding me in my real estate ventures. After all, she and I share the same Iskra, don't we? That doomed girl and I, we appreciate our wealth. Her father may have been a complete fuck-up as a czar, but young Anastasia? No. No. She had that Iskra burning mightily inside her."

Vladimir took a deep breath, not at all amused by Pasha's theatrics. The man was taking the concept of an Iskra way too seriously. He crossed his arms. "Pasha, why in the hell are we here, anyway?"

Pasha stopped. He pointed off to the west. "See that?"

Vladimir looked over. Nothing other than a few people gathered around an ice cream trolley. "I see ice cream. So what?"

"Yeah, the ice cream trolley. For some reason, Russians love their ice cream, don't they? They'll line up at those trolleys even on the snowiest of days. Never understood that..." Pasha's voice trailed off as he spoke.

Vlad rolled his eyes. "What about the ice cream, Pasha?"

Pasha slapped one hand on top of Vlad's shoulder, causing a wave of pain to travel through his healing wound. Vladimir winced, but Pasha didn't seem to notice. "You know who loves his ice cream, V.V? Grigory

Fomenko, my obese business partner. I tell ya, it's like clockwork. He goes every day after lunch to that stupid little ice cream trolley over there to stuff his face. The guy really has a problem with food."

Pasha placed his hand inside his jacket. "Grigory is the more dominant of the two partners. If something were to happen to him, I think Fyodor would be too timid to move forward with trying to get his money back from the café. He'd give up and the business would be mine to sell. Then I could move on to bigger things, just as the spirit of Anastasia wants."

"So what do you want me to do?" asked Vladimir, completely exasperated.

Pasha pulled an object out of his jacket. It was wrapped in a towel. "Now, this won't exactly be the crime of the century, mind you, but it'll still shake things up a bit." He carefully handed the object to Vlad and said, "I want you to kill Grigory. With this."

46.

Vladimir didn't need to see the gun to know that's what it was. Military grade, muffled by a silencer. He took it in his hand, but kept the towel wrapped around it. "Where did you get this?"

Pasha said nothing; he just looked away and shrugged.

"It would be a beautiful murder," announced Pasha. "A Communist—the worst kind of all, a KGB agent—falling from a single gunshot emanating from a place where the Red Army murdered a wealthy family out of jealousy. But a rich and devout capitalist gives the order during the waning days of Communist rule. I can almost hear young Anastasia applaud my efforts. This is what you call poetic justice, V.V."

Vladimir held the gun close to his body and looked around. Killing Grigory would keep Zhanna safe, and it most certainly could work. If he could get into one of the dilapidated structures nearby, up on the third floor, most likely, he'd have a clear shot of Grigory standing at the ice cream trolley. Plenty of people milling around, Grigory would be a large target. Plus there was a silencer. One shot and blend in with the crowd. It would be an easy kill.

***

I haven't killed anyone yet. I wonder if I will? Still have three months left here in Afghanistan. When the draft notice arrived, that was the first thing I thought about: What would it be like to actually kill someone? If they were coming at me with guns blazing, would it be easy? Or would I stop and think? Would I panic? I just don't know because I've never killed anyone before.

These are my thoughts as we slowly pull into the Pashtun village. White stone structures scattered about; sheep wander around aimlessly. Shirtless boys are running around with an old tire. They stop and watch us drive by. They flex their muscles and laugh. Some run along with us, laughing. I wave. Yurchenko is waving. Mikhail Astafurov sticks his head out of the turret of the armored vehicle and gives the boys a salute. Some of the boys stop and salute in return. Ragged little girls are whispering to each other at the water pump.

I stop my truck and get out. The kids are all over me. I hand out a few trinkets, rubles, and gum because that's all I have in the truck. Yurchenko and Mikhail Astafurov do the same. Yurchenko is better prepared; he's got little toys and chocolate bars. I bet he misses his own kid. The rowdy boys scatter off to play.

Yurchenko motions for Asef to accompany him. I go to the back of the truck to unlatch the tarp. Both Red and Danil are out of their truck, as well, unlatching their own tarp. The other vehicles in the convoy are coming to a stop.

From what I can hear, Asef is already heavily engaged in multiple conversations between Yurchenko and men from the village. So many men are coming out to see what is happening. They are smiling, arms wide open. I smile back, and wave. Asef was right, they all have short, trim, little beards and their heads are covered. Every single one of them.

Another funny thing. I see plenty of children, but I don't see any women in this village.

***

Vladimir stood staring at the dilapidated structure from which he might shoot Grigory. "I've killed a lot of people, Pasha. I don't know if I have it in me anymore."

Pasha began to stroll away casually. "Think about it, V.V. There's good money in it for you. An extra five grand."

Vlad looked to the ice cream trolley and back to the structure, visualizing in his head how the whole thing would go down.

He took a drag from his cigarette and said, "Did you hear me? Your business partners have found my wife."

Pasha shrugged. "So, get rid of Grigory, and your wife will be fine."

No she wouldn't. There was still Fyodor, and the Chechen thug. This act would only dig him in deeper.

Vladimir handed the towel-wrapped gun back to Pasha. "I want my life back. I want my sanity back. I want my wife back. I can't do this anymore. Find yourself another bodyguard." Vladimir walked away. Living a life of crime would not be his Iskra. Money would not be his Iskra. The acquisition of wealth would not be his Iskra.

47.

4 November

Zhanna stirred her highlighting brush around the bowl to blend the two hair colors together. For Mrs. Slavakova, she preferred to use two shades of brown, one classic and the other more of a deep mocha. She combed Mrs. Slavakova's hair straight, parted it on the left. "So I see we have you down for a manicure today, too. Anything special going on?"

Mrs. Slavakova, nursing a cup of tea in her hands, sighed. "Well, my husband has been appointed to President Yeltsin's administration. Chairman of Domestic Policy, whatever that means. We leave tomorrow morning for Moscow to take part in a weekend of parties and state suppers at the Kremlin. I know it's a good move for him politically, but Zhanna, he'll have to live in Moscow at least while the *Duma* is in session. Those Moscow women are drop-dead gorgeous, and Karl, in all his years of holding political office, has never been able to resist a file clerk in a skirt." Her eyes fell while she sipped her tea.

Zhanna did her best to keep her client's spirits up. "Mrs. Slavakova, you are beautiful, too. Now let's give you some color and a sassy little cut, shall we?" She picked up the bowl of hair color, touched her brush to it.

But after taking another look at her forlorn client in the mirror, she set the bowl down. This woman cannot stay a brunette, she thought. Not for a weekend of elegance in Moscow. For her stay at the Kremlin, Mrs. Slavakova needs to be sleek and sophisticated, yet sultry, and just a little bit daring. No brown highlights, no sassy cut. She needs to keep her long locks and become a sexy redhead.

Zhanna held her brush in the air. "If you'll trust me with this, Mrs. Slavakova, I would like to turn you into a redhead. Give me a few minutes, and I promise you, those stuffy old politicians at the Kremlin won't know what hit them!"

Mrs. Slavakova raised her eyebrows and thought for a moment. "You know what, Zhanna dear? I'm tired of being the perfect wife, tired of playing it safe. Go ahead and work your magic on me!"

Zhanna happily clicked across the salon to the supply cabinet near the windows to mix up just the right shade of red. As she walked by, each of the five hairstylists in her employ was busy. The manicure station was full, as was the waiting area. No high-end shampoos or hair sprays stood on the open shelves yet, as supply chains were often broken, with the government in such disarray.

On the open shelves where the hair products were destined to go, Zhanna displayed several of her own Karina Baby Totes. Each one, made of soft, quilted fabric in a variety of colors, had the signature wavy K and a heart embellished in yellow on the bottom right corner. Priced at six hundred rubles for those still spending rubles, or twenty American dollars, she could barely keep the bags in stock. Clients marveled at the softness and functionality of the tote. They liked the cute logo and the upbeat color scheme. When picking up the totes, customers said things like, "How refreshing," "I have never seen anything like this," and "This does not look like it came from the government."

Stirring the hair color, she held the bowl up to the window. A deep, rich burgundy, perfect for Mrs. Slavakova's visit to Moscow; maybe one small touch of golden auburn to brighten it up just a bit.

Before she could look for the additional color, Zhanna abruptly brought the bowl down. Something outside had caught her eye.

Two men, standing on the sidewalk. They were looking around, occasionally pointing at the salon, engaged in discussion. It was the same two men who had dropped by a month ago, saying they were from the Building Inspection Bureau.

Zhanna looked again. Sure enough, it was the same men. One was hugely fat and eating something, a sausage maybe, wrapped in a paper napkin; the other wore an ill-fitting brown suit and puffed on a cigar.

She promptly put down the bowl of hair color and clicked, utterly annoyed, across the salon, out the door. "I'll be right back, Mrs. Slavakova. Sit tight."

Outside where the air was cold and crisp, Zhanna straightened her apron, did her best to compose herself. "Gentlemen, as you can see, I am running a fully legal establishment here. Private enterprise is permitted now, and I know that the two of you are not building inspectors, but KGB agents who were ripped off by my husband's boss."

The men did not stir. The obese one gulped a mouthful of sausage while the man in the bad suit tipped his hat. "Mrs. Verstakova, we realize you are an innocent party to all of this, but the fact remains some of our investment is tied up in your establishment. And much to our dismay, Mr. Pavel Grachov remains one step ahead of us, thanks to your husband. Now, we are only trying to come to the best possible solution to this problem."

Zhanna shivered in the cold but remained calm. "I sympathize with your situation, I really do. But my husband quit working for Pasha, and the salon has yet to turn much of a profit. Can't you leave us out of this?"

The fat man shook his head. "Afraid we can't do that, my dear. You are already involved."

Zhanna crossed her arms. "Look, my husband served this country well and is paying a steep price. The memories are debilitating, as is the noise running through his head. The only reason he took that job is because he thought money would make everything all right. But it didn't. He still has cash in his closet, and sees Pasha fill a briefcase with American dollars every night but he doesn't even wan—"

The two men perked up.

Zhanna immediately looked down, silently cursing herself. She had just let two KGB agents know that her husband had access to all kinds of money. She threw up her hands. "I'm finished talking about this. Send a lawyer if you have to, but I don't think I should talk to the two of you anymore."

The man in the bad suit tipped his hat again. "Well, then, have a good day, my dear," he said, and the men walked away.

Zhanna pivoted to go back to the salon. Poor Mrs. Slavakova was still waiting. But she quickly whipped around again. "Wait!" she called out. The men stopped, turned around.

"Wait!" She ran down the cobblestone in her high heels and met up with the men. "What if I can give you the down-payment money? That's the amount Vladimir gave to me. If I can come up with that much, would you call it even and leave us alone?"

The two men looked at each other, the fat one nodded. "Seems fair."

"Okay," Zhanna exhaled, out of breath from the exertion. "Give me some time. I have to meet with the bank, but I'll get your money. And my husband does not need to know about this. He worries enough about this already."

The men agreed to come back at a later date for the funds and walked away. In a frenzy, Zhanna slid off her heels and sprinted back to the salon to finish Mrs. Slavakova's hair.

48.

5 November

Left fist. 1,2,3. Right fist 1,2,3. Left fist. 1,2,3. Right fist1,2,3.

Vladimir had no trouble stepping up to the speed bag and getting right into his boxing routine this time.

Left fist. 1,2,3. No job.

Right fist. 1, 2, 3.

Left fist. No Zhanna.

Right fist. 1, 2, 3.

Left fist 1,2,3. No Iskra.

Right fist. 1,2,3.

Left fist. 1, 2, 3. But no more Pasha.

Right fist. 1,2,3.

Left fist 1, 2, 3. No business partners to worry about.

He punched the small speed bag, left and right, falling quickly into an energetic, cathartic rhythm.

Left1, 2, 3. Feet shuffling side to side.

Right1, 2, 3.

Left1, 2, 3. Heavy breathing.

Right1,2, 3.

Left 1, 2, 3. Sweat dripping.

Right 1, 2, 3.

Left 1, 2, 3. Nothing but the fist.

Right. 1,2,3. Nothing but the bag.
Left. 1,2,3. Nothing but the fist.
Right. 1,2,3. Nothing but the bag.
Left12,3. Nothing but the fist.
Right. 1,2,3. Nothing but the bag.
Left1,2,3.
Right. 1,2,3.
Left1,2,3.
Right. 1,2,3.

***

I grab three rifles from the bed of my truck. There are plenty more, but that's all I can grab right now. I lay down the gate, hop up, and search around for the crate with the bullets. Yurchenko is now standing by my truck. I hand down the rifles. He nods. He moves down to Red's truck. Red hands him two rifles. Yurchenko walks over to Farood and Osman, holding the rifles in both arms like a baby. He lays them down.

Together all three men are inspecting the rifles. Yurchenko kneels down on one knee. With the help of Asef, he is able to converse with the men about the rifles.

I step down from the truck with three more rifles in my arms. Red walks by me carrying another three. We lay them down with the others, then we both go back to gather the bullets. I find four crates with boxes of bullets inside. I take one of the crates and heft it over to the men. Red does the same.

Everyone present is in agreement. Farood and Osman are nodding. Yurchenko is giving a brief talk on proper rifle handling, with Asef following up in Pashto, looking extremely pro-

fessional and calm once again. Still can't get over how much Asef changes when he is translating. He truly is a different person.

The men all shake hands. They motion for us to go inside a nearby structure; it's white, made of cement. Farood says something to Asef, who in turn informs us the village humbly welcomes us as guests. They would like to share their food with us. Good, because I'm starving.

***

"Hey, tough guy, get in here!" Roman called from the ring, already crouched in fighting position, knees bent, fists guarding his face. He threw one straight punch, then another.

Vladimir stopped the speed bag from wobbling with his hand, headed to the ring. He threw a solid jab as soon as he stepped through the ropes. "This is probably the last time I'll be able to box. Quit my job, so there goes my membership. It's only a matter of time before my boss notices he's still paying for it."

Roman threw a right jab-hook combination. "Aw, sorry to hear that. I've so enjoyed kicking your ass!" Another combination, two left-handed jabs in quick succession, and Vladimir was backed into the ropes.

"Kicking my ass? What the hell are you talking about, old timer?" Vlad flew from the ropes with a right and a left uppercut to Roman's stomach. Immediately, he pivoted and landed another punch to the temple. Roman stumbled sideways, falling flat on his back.

He hopped right back up, put his arms up and said, "Ah-ha, tough guy, nice one! You got me with a triple combination right there. Top that off with a sharp elbow jab to the neck and you would have knocked me out cold."

They continued to spar and jab to the sound of weighted breath. "You're getting real good at this. I'd hate to lose you," Roman said, shuffling forward.

Vlad shook the sweat from his head. "Yeah, boxing makes me feel good, more focused. I really need that in my life right now."

Roman came in with a quick jab to the chin. "I could use some help around here. Maintaining the exercise equipment, showing new members how to use it, keeping the towels stocked, stuff like that. I can't pay nearly as much as a co-op millionaire, but I assure you, it's all very much legal. Plus, I'll throw in a membership."

Vlad blocked his face and moved ahead with a left jab, knocking Roman in the chest. "Yeah, that would be great. I'd love to work here. Thanks."

***

"Sta na shukira." It means thank you. Not sure I said that right, but I say it as I take a clay bowl of olives from the Pashtun man sitting next to me. He smiles and drops his chin down as he hands the bowl over.

We are all sitting on an earthen floor. Farood, Yurchenko, and Asef are sitting together, talking, eating, and laughing. From what I can understand, they are talking about futbol and how someone better beat Brazil next year. Asef is bullshitting his way through the futbol talk; he knows nothing about the sport, I can tell. I catch him a few times, roll my eyes, and shake my head. He knows that I know he's bullshitting. He shrugs and laughs in return.

Danil is sitting next to me. Takes a handful of olives, pops them in his mouth and leans in closer. He quietly says to me, "These guys are nice. So are they just softening us up for the slaughter or what?"

I tell him what Asef told me, that these men are not part of the mujahideen, but are a small tribe of Pashtuns who believe in living strictly by the Koran, and they adhere to a code of ethics that includes something called Melmastia, requiring all Pashtuns to show hospitality and profound respect to all visitors.

"Melmastia. Melmastia. Sweet, sweet Melmastia," Danil says looking upwards. He pops another three olives in his mouth. "Huh, I think I could get used to Melmastia." After all the food and tea has been passed around and everyone is full, it's time to get back on the road. We have supplies to deliver by evening.

Yurchenko stands up. So does Farood. Farood places a hand on Yurchenko's shoulder; he looks out at all of us and says with a warm smile, "Assalam u alaikum."

We all look to Asef, who immediately translates, "May peace be upon you."

***

Roman came in hard with a right jab to the chin, followed by a sharp left to the gut. "Pay attention, tough guy! Remember, you work for me now."

The memory of tea with the Pashtuns faded away. Vlad jolted back to reality to see Roman coming at him hard. With a guttural "Damn," Vlad hunched over after getting hit, but he struck back quickly, throwing a mighty upper cut to Roman's chin. Roman fell backwards, bounced off the ropes, and flopped onto the floor.

"Hell, yeah!" Vladimir bellowed, raising his arms up in a V. Boxing would be a good Iskra.

49.

8 November

"The circus. Good idea, Zha-Zha," Vlad said, approaching his wife, who stood waiting for him at the top of the white steps. The pristine, white lattice, steel dome of the circus arena hovered above, only a bit shorter than the unfinished television tower looming behind it. Hustling up the steps, his calves were sore from boxing, as were his arms, but otherwise Vlad felt invigorated after such strenuous exercise.

He leaned in to kiss Zhanna on the left cheek, then the right, and once again on the left. Out of habit, he unbuttoned his own warm coat, took it off, and wrapped it around Zhanna's shoulders because, as usual, she wasn't properly dressed for the weather in her heels, knee-length skirt, and fitted red blouse. Her coat hit at the hips with only one button in the middle.

Vlad situated his coat around Zhanna's shivering body and said, "I'm beginning to think you were right on the night we met when you said you are not a very good Russian."

She smiled, running a hand down his cheek. "Viva, whatever do you mean by that?"

Vlad crossed his arms around his own body to shield himself against the chill. "More than thirty Russian winters you have lived through, thirty! Yet you do not own even one decent coat. All of your clothing is fashionable, not functional."

Zhanna laughed. "Oh, I'm a decent enough Russian, but a terrible, terrible Communist! Functionality is severely overrated."

They purchased their tickets at the window for the special Saturday afternoon performance. As they waited in line to enter, they casually watched several children play on the steps with colorful balloons. One little girl, so focused on catching a wafting balloon, tripped while running up the steps. Blood flowed from the rip in her white tights. She wailed, holding her arms out for her mother.

The girl's frantic mother sprinted over, pulling her custom-made Karina Baby Tote off her shoulder as she ran. "It's okay, we can fix it, honey," the mom said in a cooing voice as she pulled out a small towel from the tote, pressing it to the girl's bloody knee. A stuffed animal from the special toy compartment and a cracker from the snack pocket kept the child occupied while the mother placed a bandage on the knee.

Vlad pulled Zhanna in close, kissing her temple. "She lives on in her own way, doesn't she? Our Karina." Zhanna smiled and stood a little straighter, looking more like her authentic self.

Inside the arena, they sat down with bags of popcorn. "I hope they do the trapeze. That's my favorite," Zhanna said. Vladimir mentioned he hoped to see fire juggling.

The lights dimmed, the audience hushed. A man with a whip hanging out of his waistband and carrying a large, golden hoop ran on stage to a cheering audience. He held the hoop up in front of his body, then overhead. The hoop caught the bright lights of the stage, causing it to shimmer. The man held the hoop stationary as tigers emerged from stage left, ready to jump through the shimmering hoop. Kids cheered, adults clapped, but all Vlad could focus on was the shimmering golden hoop.

***

Mikhail Astafurov is sitting across from me, eating from the bowl of olives. Around his neck, his wedding band catches the sunlight from the outside. The golden ring sparkles as it captures the bright light, and then fades as he moves.

Yurchenko instructs us it is time to move on; we've still got a lot of kilometers to cover. We all stand and say good-bye to our Pashtun hosts.

Now that I am standing, I can see out the square cutout. The women of this village are all outside. At the water pump, tending the animals, washing clothes, preparing food, feeding children.

Odd, they are covered from head to toe in black burqas; even their faces are covered. Wearing of the burqa has been outlawed by the Soviets. Even hair scarves are only moderately tolerated. Here, every woman is covered.

The sun is almost at its highest point. I have never been so hot in my life. These women must be miserable. We file out of the house. To my right a burqa-clad woman is walking toward the house from the water pump. The woman is carrying two pails full of water. A small boy is crying, pulling on the woman's burqa. When she sees us, she stops, looks down. Without thinking, I head over to help.

Suddenly, I feel a long, spindly hand on my shoulder accompanied by a hurried command, "Vlad-ee-meer, no!" The hand harshly yanks me backwards, so strong I almost fall over. It's Asef.

"Vlad-ee-meer, do not help that woman! Do not even look at her!" I can't believe it; I had no idea he could be that strong.

"What?" I start to argue. But Yurchenko is in his truck. Everyone is ready to go.

I climb into the pickup, start the engine, wait for Asef to get in. He's outside, hesitating. Mikhail Astafurov and his crew are already gone. In a cloud of dust, Yurchenko takes off in his truck.

"Are you coming or what, Asef?" I call out. Asef doesn't hesitate much longer. He runs across the dirt yard, climbs in, and we pull out.

"What in the hell happened out there? What is wrong with me helping that woman carry her water pails?" I ask, exasperated.

Asef adjusts his glasses. "That particular tribe of Pashtuns are strict followers of the Koran, Vlad-ee-meer. Every man must keep his head covered and maintain a trim beard."

He looks at me through those huge glasses. "The women have rules, too. A lot of rules. They must keep their bodies covered at all times. That is part of Sharia law, the core of their beliefs. They view woman as pure, perfect vessels of Islam. She becomes tainted if a man looks at her in any way. Thus, she diminishes the honor of the entire family."

I think that sounds rather stupid. In my country, no way would we let a woman carry something heavy. We open doors, we carry stuff, we fix things, we give women flowers after we do something dumb. It's called being a real man. Hear that, Pashtuns?

Now I laugh because the whole thing is ridiculous. "Okay, so, Asef, what would the Pashtuns have done to me if I had helped her with the water pails? Take away my goats for a week? Only let me have three wives instead of five? Really, I'm not scared of the Pashtuns." I find a cigarette and light it.

Asef shakes his head. "No. No, Vlad-ee-meer, you would be fine. Nothing would have happen to you. But they would probably have cut off that woman's nose as punishment. Most likely an ear, too."

Now, I slam on the brakes. Dust flies everywhere. My cigarette leaps out the window as the truck skids sideways. Asef smashes into the dashboard. He steadies himself and laughs, "Oh my, here we go again!"

But I am not laughing. Not anymore. "You better be kidding. Tell me you are fuckin' kidding me, Asef!"

He's not kidding. "It's their way, Vlad-ee-meer. Has been for centuries. Along with Melmastia, they also practice Namus, meaning honor of women, and Badal, swift punishment. Badal brings honor back to the family."

"But that's not the point!" I take a breath and calm down. "Not all Pashtuns are like that, right? You said this is just one small group." I straighten out the truck and find another cigarette in my chest pocket.

Asef nods. "Yeah, those Pashtuns belong to a very small group of fundamental religious scholars. They are Talibs. Together they call themselves the Taliban."

***

Vladimir let his bag of popcorn fall to the floor. By now, many tigers were jumping through several hoops. Some hoops were on fire. Trapeze artists flew overhead. Children were cheering. Circus music blared. A scary looking clown threw candy into the audience. Vlad felt sweat trickle down his temples. His throat closed up. The noise hit hard. *Blast. Gunfire. Commands. Blast. Gunfire. Commands.* "I have to get out of here," he muttered.

Zhanna turned to Vlad, dropping her own popcorn once she got a look at him. "Oh, my god, Viva, you are burning up!" she said, placing her hand over his forehead. "Breathe, just breathe."

He tried to take a breath but the noise wouldn't go away. "We had tea with this group called the Taliban. It was nice. After we left, mujahideen swarmed. They came out of nowhere. Killed everyone," He stood up. "I have to get out of here."

Zhanna turned to grab her purse. "Vladimir, wait!"

He walked out of the arena before the violent images and noise could take over.

Outside, the dim Russian sun barely cut through the icy air. Sitting on the top step, he breathed easier, but the nervousness remained. Behind him came the fast click-clack-click of Zhanna's high heels. She dropped down next to him saying nothing.

"I'm sorry, Zha-Zha. I didn't mean to run out," he said, dropping his head into his hands. "The memory, it was so real, I could even smell the tea."

She placed her hand over his and sighed. "Viva, I understand you are suffering and I want to see you through this, I really do. But I am thirty-one years old;

having these little dates and you coming over whenever you need me to fix you is not healthy. At some point soon I need to move on with my life, and so do you. Either together or apart, we both need to move on."

Vlad decisively brought his head up and declared, "Together. I want us to be together."

Zhanna brushed her hair back. "Then you need to help yourself. Go talk to a professional about the war. I can't see you again until you've done at least that much."

Vladimir nodded. "Okay, I will go talk to someone."

50.

14 November

Dr. Boris Zaslavsky, Psychiatrist. Licensed by the State. Specializing in Weakness of the Mind. So read the sign on the door, hanging so askew that Vlad could not stand it. He righted the sign and shook his head, exasperated by the weakling he'd become. He wrapped his hand around the doorknob, but immediately let go and took a step back. "I don't need help," he muttered to himself.

Another try, this time he held his grip around the doorknob a bit longer, but again, let go, took a step back. "I can do this by myself."

Finally, one more shot. Zhanna, after all was completely fed up, she was not going to let this slide. He stepped forward, grabbed hold of the doorknob, turned it halfway, determined this time to go inside if only to tell Zhanna he tried. But alas, he released. Took a giant step back. "I'm not crazy. Not crazy."

In a few days, Oleg and the guys would be throwing darts at the Red Torch Pub for their regular round of Wednesday night darts; couldn't that be enough? Go play darts, maybe mention the war with them over a few shots of vodka and call it good? Maybe Zhanna would approve of that. Vladimir turned away and walked on. He made it half-way down the hall before stopping, realizing that Zhanna would never approve of such a plan.

The door swung open. Squeaky, it needed lubricant on the hinges. "You must be Vladimir Stepanovich Verstakov. I've been waiting for you," came a voice.

Vlad pivoted to see the man who must be Dr. Zaslavsky. Tall and lanky, he wore black loafers, wrinkled gray slacks, a white shirt tucked in on one side only, and a black tie. No jacket. A head full of gray hair in disarray, with a moustache and beard to match. Small round bifocals. A cream-colored file in hand.

Vladimir stood still, put up both hands. "Okay, like I said on the phone, I have memories of the war. Sometimes the sounds in my head get so loud I can't control my emotions. My wife will divorce me if I don't at least talk to you. But I'm not crazy. Right?"

Dr. Zaslavsky looked him up and down. "No one ever said you were crazy, Mr. Verstakov. Now come sit down. We'll talk things through."

Vlad stepped into the office and stopped cold. Three of the office walls were covered with Dr. Zaslavsky's numerous diplomas, awards and certificates, most of them hanging horribly askew. The fourth wall housed a massive bookshelf loaded with dense textbooks. Books were stacked on top each other, forming piles that almost touched the ceiling. The whole thing looked like it was going to topple over at any second.

A small window looked out over downtown Sverdlovsk. A big desk stood near one wall but books and piles of loose papers made it unusable. One spindly leg was obviously loose. Two comfortable, oversized, leather chairs in one corner miraculously remained uncluttered. A stained-glass lamp hovering over the chairs and a samovar of tea on a table nearby made for a comfortable spot. Dr. Zaslavsky sat down with the file in his lap and motioned for Vlad to sit across from him.

But Vlad didn't sit, could not get his mind past the teetering bookshelf. Horribly sloppy, and dangerous, too. "Uh, doctor, I highly recommend you bolt that bookshelf to the wall, and take those heavy books off the top, or you are going to have a landslide in here some day."

Dr. Zaslavsky looked up from his chair and chuckled. "Oh. I never think about that. I just keep stacking and stacking." Vlad stared in disbelief. Obviously, this guy had no construction skills. "I can come back and do it for you. Won't take long. Your desk, too, that leg could use some—"

Dr. Zaslavsky cleared his throat, tapped the file on his lap, and again motioned for Vlad to take a seat. "I appreciate you taking the time to spruce up my office, Mr. Verstakov. My wife has been threatening to do it for years. But don't you think you are stalling, just a bit?"

A handyman defeated, Vlad grudgingly sat down.

Dr. Zaslavsky opened the file and immediately started writing. "What is your date of birth?" he asked, without looking up.

Vladimir, still looking around at the mess, said, "Uh, my birthday is nineteen April '63. I'm twenty-eight now."

"And you are a construction worker by training?" the doctor asked, keeping his eyes on the file.

Vlad nodded. "Yeah, but I've spent most of this year as a bodyguard for a co-op café owner, and as of the last couple weeks, I've been employed by the Soviet Boxing Academy, maintaining equipment, folding towels. Stuff like that."

"Education level?"

"Forty credits at college," Vlad said. "Took math and science classes. But I didn't finish. I like working with my hands, so I stayed with construction."

"Married? Any children?"

Vlad paused. "Still married. We are living apart, but my wife arranges dates periodically. We are trying to make another go at it. No kids."

Dr. Zaslavsky looked up briefly. "How about your parents? Are they both living?"

Vlad looked up to the ceiling, already bored. "My mother is alive. My father, well my father is dead, but Dad is alive. It's hard to explain. Well, not really, but… but…I don't know. It's complicated. That's all."

The doctor looked up with raised eyebrows, and jotted a note in the file. He applied a red tab to that page and turned to another. "That's all for the preliminaries. So let's talk about these memories you've been having. As I've said, I believe in talking things through."

Vlad described how and when the memories usually hit. "It could be a common situation, but something will trigger a memory and throw me back into the war."

Dr. Zaslavsky nodded. "Yes. Those memories you are having are called flashbacks and they are very common in war veterans or anyone who has experienced profound trauma."

Vlad went on to describe the noise that accompanied the flashbacks. How first came a high-pitched whine, followed by a deafening blast, another whine layered on top of the first, then a second deafening blast: two land mines detonating in quick succession. Soon after came the syncopated *rat tat tat* of AK-47 gunfire from all around, and through it all, the succinct commands of Captain Yurchenko, *"Return fire! Repeat, return fire!"* and *"Go! Go! Go!"*

"It keeps me up most every night and interrupts my days. Whenever it hits, I try to focus on an Iskra, but so far I have not found one strong enough to drown out the noise."

Dr. Zaslavsky abruptly looked up from the file. "Huh? Iskra? What's that?"

Vlad explained the advice given by Officer Rogusskii. How he needed to find something to believe in. "Find an Iskra or you're dead, that's what he said."

Zaslavsky looked back at the file, held his pen. "We should go to your time in Afghanistan. Start at day one."

Vlad exhaled, and stood up. "All right, um, I got off the plane and met Captain Yurchenko right away. He tossed me an AK-47. Mikhail Astafurov was there, too." He walked over to the samovar. Above it, a framed certificate hung horribly askew. He straightened it, stood back to get a better look. "Remind me to bring my level when I come back. All of your frames are crooked. I can fix these easy enough."

The doctor cleared his throat again. "Excuse me, Mr. Verstakov, you are stalling again. You were about to describe your experience in the war, remember?"

Vlad poured a cup of tea. "Sorry doctor. It's just that all aspects of construction and woodworking are important to me; it was a huge part of my childhood. Dad taught me all I know about it. I'm talking about my dad, not my father."

Dr. Zaslavsky uncrossed his legs and quit writing in the file. With a sigh, he turned back to the page he had marked with a red tab. "I knew it. All right, Mr. Verstakov. Today we are not going to talk about the war at all. You are going to sit down and tell me about your parents."

Vlad put down his mug in protest. "But they have nothing to do with my flashbacks or the noise."

"Perhaps not, but war and other traumatic events will add to and amplify any guilt or anger lying dormant. If you want to slay these demons as you so describe them, you must start at the source. It's good to talk thes—"

Vladimir threw his head back. "Wait, wait, don't tell me. Talk these things through. Right?"

Doctor Zaslavsky demurred with a slight grin. "Okay. Okay. Perhaps I overly use that phrase. I believe in it, that's all. Guess you could say it's my Iskra. Now, come, sit down, Mr. Verstakov and tell me about your mother and father."

51.

"All right," Vladimir smirked, putting his hands up in surrender. "I'll tell you about my parents." He topped off his tea from the samovar and sat down in the leather chair. "So, I'll start with Mom. My mother was originally from Leningrad. Both of her parents were teachers. When Mom was about fourteen, the government assigned her parents to Sverdlovsk, where her mother became principal of an elementary school and her father took an administrative position at the university. My mother completed one year of university before dropping out to marry my dad, Stepan Verstakov. Eight years later, they had me. I'm an only child. My childhood was pretty damn good. No complaints." He stood up and flopped his arms to his sides. "So, am I done?"

Zaslavsky smirked. "Sit down, Mr. Verstakov. You can do better than that."

Vlad sat down, held his hands out. "I'm only doing this for Zhanna, okay? I don't want my dart-throwing friends knowing I was here. They already think I've gone soft."

Zaslavsky crossed his legs and leaned back. "Don't worry about that. Just talk. Let's stay with your mother."

Vladimir leaned back too, and crossed his arms. "Okay. Okay. Let me see. Uh. Maybe it's because of her early years growing up in a big city, or having some college experience, I don't know, but my mother has always been, in a way, above it all; prettier, smarter, and a little more sophisticated than anyone else." He shook his head and went on. "It's not something she flaunts, and really, I don't think she's even fully aware of it. That's just her nature. She never wore a housedress, never discussed cleaning tips or traded recipes with the other ladies in the building. While I was growing up, she worked mornings in the university library, and that's where she discovered a love of poetry."

He leaned forward, ran his hand through his hair, and chuckled. "You know, Doc, I still remember this one particular spring day, there's this image I have of my mother I'll never forget. I must have been seven. She and I were out in our courtyard; she was standing near the swing set, apart from the other moms, who all sat gossiping at the picnic table. She looked like a true goddess compared to them; tall and willowy, dressed in ivory with her deep red hair flowing all around. I was sitting at the top of the slide."

Vladimir sat up and chuckled again at the memory. "Man, that slide was fun. It was steep and fast, would spit you way out, send you flying over the gravel landing right onto the pavement. Now that I think about it, that was one dangerous slide, but I loved it, all the boys in the building did."

"Stay focused," prodded Zaslavsky.

Vlad shifted his weight within the chair. "Okay, anyway, I liked to pile a bunch of gravel on the pavement, so that when I landed, I'd hit it, demolishing my pile, send bits of gravel flying. Did it over and over again, it was so fun. But this particular time I built the pile a little too high and too close. Instead of crashing into it, I tripped over the whole thing, fell flat on my face onto the pavement. As I stood up, blood gushed out of my nose, all over my shirt. Tore my jeans. Man, I was a mess."

Zaslavsky chuckled. "Oh, to have boys!"

Vladimir laughed. "Well, my mother came running over." He waved his arms overhead. "She was shrieking my name; "*Volya! Volya*!" That's what she called me. Still does. She ran over and kneeled down, using her nice white sweater to wipe the blood off my face."

Dr. Zaslavsky nodded. "Sounds like a caring mother."

Vlad smiled, and shook his head. "Yeah, well, I tell ya, Doc, I thought that crash landing was one of the coolest things I'd ever done in my whole seven years of life, so I started laughing, couldn't stop. Made the blood gush out even more. Mom fussed and fussed trying to clean me up with that white sweater of hers. But it wasn't doing any bit of good. Finally, she threw her sweater down and laughed, too. She hugged me so tight right then. Even now, I can still feel it." He leaned back in his chair. "Yeah, I still feel it. I know that sounds silly, but it's true. Oy, I have gone soft."

Dr. Zaslavsky shook his head. "No. That is not silly. Your mother loved you very much."

Vladimir nodded. "Yeah, she did. Ya know, she wanted me more than anything." He took a breath. "So, back in the apartment, my mother hefted me up on the kitchen counter to wash my face and take care of my bloody knee. While waiting for the water to warm up, she stood there looking into my eyes, had a slight smile on her face. She brushed my hair back, and said, "*Volya, your eyes are two fields of grass, kissed by the morning dew, sparkling like emeralds under the brilliant Slavic sun.*"

Vladimir looked away. "Huh," he muttered, "You know, she was always saying things like that. And commenting about my eyes. She was always jotting down her own poems as they came to her. To this day, the color green is the subject of much of her poetry." He leaned back. "Funny. While growing up, I never gauged the impact of my eye color. See, neither of my parents have green eyes."

He picked up the mug, then set it down. "And here's another thing I failed to gauge the impact of: my mother's drinking. Now that I have sworn off alcohol, I can see it clearly."

Zaslavsky turned a page in the file and glanced up. "Your mother drank a lot?"

Vladimir crossed his legs and nodded. "Still does. Come to think of it, I don't think I ever saw my mother actually pour herself a real drink; she's much too classy for that. But she was never without a dainty flask of vodka by her side, always taking quick little sips here and there. A quick nip, then she'd get back to reading my bedtime story; frequent little sips while we ran errands; another series of tastes while she checked my homework."

Zaslavsky nodded. "Vodka. Russia's great poison. It kills thousands every year, yet no one acknowledges it."

"She'd stash the bottles underneath the bed or behind the toilet," said Vlad. "Dad always found them. He never said anything to her, just found the bottles and threw them away. Invariably, Mom would buy more and the whole game started all over again."

Zaslavsky was sitting back, had his hands folded beneath his chin. "I see," he said, while leaning forward. "That's interesting. Now let's switch gears for a moment. Tell me about your dad."

Vlad looked to the ceiling. "Uh, okay. Dad. Like I said, his name is Stepan Verstakov. When he was twelve, his mother was crossing the street, got hit by a car and died. After that, his father, a plumber by trade, drank himself into oblivion every night. Dad had a younger brother, too, my Uncle Konstantin. But Uncle Konstantin was always involved with his music and didn't pay much attention to family matters, so it all fell upon Dad. He spent his teenage years cleaning up after, and making excuses for a pathetic drunken father."

Vladimir rubbed his scruffy face and looked to the doctor. "You know, Doc, now that I think about it, after a childhood like that, life with my mother must have seemed perfectly normal." He laughed and stood up. "It's all a little crazy."

Dr. Zaslavsky said nothing.

Vlad went on as he topped off his tea mug. "So, my dad is a very decent guy, hard-working, takes pride in a job well done. As far back as I can remember he's worked at a state-run factory making furniture. When we moved out of the communal apartment and into our own place in '80, he surprised Mom with a beautiful china cabinet made out of solid wood. She really loved it." He sat down and took a sip. "And that's exactly what Dad wanted, to make her happy. He's still that way."

The doctor nodded. "Hmm. One gives, one takes. Their type of relationship is certainly not uncommon. Don't begrudge them too much for that."

Vlad nodded. "Yeah, I know how all that works. I did nothing but take while my wife Zhanna gave all she had."

"We'll get to you and your wife in due time. Stay focused on your parents for now," instructed Zaslavsky twirling the pen between his fingers.

Vlad took another quick sip of tea and kept hold of the mug. "So, eventually, Mom's equal devotion to both poetry and vodka came at the expense of housework, and then cooking. But Dad picked up the slack. He made supper most nights. I washed the dishes while he helped her to bed." He looked down into his mug. "Man, my mother is damn lucky to have Dad in her life, isn't she?" He looked up, shaking his head.

Dr. Zaslavsky crossed his legs. "And now, in your own life, do you see any patterns?"

Vladimir shook his head and chuckled. "Shit, I'm a lot like my mother, aren't I? Never thought about it. And Zhanna. She gives and gives. I do nothing but take."

He dropped his head back and exhaled. "Aw hell, that's no good. I don't want to live like my parents," he placed the mug back on the table and ran his hand through his hair. "I gotta change."

Dr. Zaslavsky turned a page in the file. "Mr. Verstakov. Now, you mentioned your green eyes as being something of an issue. What did you mean by that?"

Vladimir hung his head and exhaled. "Uh, how much time we got left? Because this may take a while."

"Enough. We have enough time," assured the doctor.

Vlad sat down again and looked the doctor in the eye. "So, earlier I mentioned Dad's brother, Uncle Konstantin. If you want to know about my parents, you have to know about Uncle Konstantin. He's integral to the family, and now that we have talked things through, I'm pretty sure he's the reason for this sickness I have in my head."

52.

Dr. Zaslavsky once again picked up the file. "Go ahead, Mr. Verstakov, tell me about your Uncle Konstantin."

Vladimir nodded and began. "Well, there's a creative streak running through my dad's family. Dad himself a gifted woodworker, makes furniture so stunning, it could pass for art. But the creative streak really hit Uncle Konstantin the hardest. It certainly caused him the most torment."

Zaslavsky was writing in the file. "I see. Go on."

Vladimir stood up and walked to the samovar to pour another mug of tea. "Uncle Konstantin was by far the coolest uncle a kid could have. He kept his hair long, smoked cigarettes, rode a motorcycle. He had a huge collection of illegal rock and roll records. The Who, Rolling Stones, The Doors—he really liked that sound." He took a sip of tea and turned around, leaning against the table.

"At family suppers I always sat next to Konstantin because he was left-handed, too; it was the only time I wouldn't have to worry about jabbing someone with my elbow. Plus, he'd lean over and whisper dirty jokes in my ear. Got me laughing so hard." Vlad chuckled at the scenario while crossing the office to a crooked frame.

He put his mug down and began to right the frame. "So, as I became a teenager, Uncle Konstantin would frequently drop by unannounced, obviously a little high, and ask me if I wanted to take a ride on his amped-up motorcycle. Of course, I wanted to. Dad hated it, but he let me go anyway."

Dr. Zaslavsky cleared his throat. "Go on, Mr. Verstakov."

Vlad picked up his mug and turned to Zaslavsky. "One day, Uncle Konstantin dropped me off at home after a motorcycle ride around town. He was still on the bike, getting ready to take off, but he turned and asked me something peculiar. He asked if I ever heard music in my head."

"Music?" asked the doctor.

Vlad nodded, and started clearing a pile of heavy books off Zaslavsky's wobbly desk. "Yeah. Konstantin said he heard music all the time. Not just little tunes here and there, but huge, sweeping, complicated patterns that kept him up all night. He tried to write the music down, but most of the time, it came too fast. He said the music was toying with him, making him crazy." He stopped. *Blast. Gunfire. Commands. Blast. Gunfire. Commands.* He dropped a book to the floor and looked at the doctor. "I guess now I know how he felt." He shook his head and kept clearing the books.

Dr. Zaslavsky looked up from the file. "Your Uncle Konstantin was a musician, I take it?"

Vlad nodded as he stepped away from the desk. "The guy could play any instrument you threw at him. Piano, violin, guitar, you name it. But his true talent was that voice of his. Man, could that guy sing."

Zaslavsky quit writing, brought his hand to his chin. "Are you talking about Konstantin Verstakov? Say, I do remember him. Played with the symphony, right?"

Vlad wiped his mouth. "Yep. He played violin with the USSR State Symphony Orchestra for twenty years. At the end of each performance, he stepped up and sang the Soviet national anthem a capella in that deep baritone voice of his."

Dr. Zaslavsky's eyes brightened as he smiled. "Yes, my wife and I saw him perform several times back in the seventies. The man truly was a great, great, talent. What a wonderful voice."

Vlad took his mug back to the samovar, started to fill it up again. "Well, I tell ya, Doc, for all the talent he had, the guy was a sorry-ass mess at home," He sipped from the steaming mug and turned. "He could keep himself together for a few months at a time, just to get through a tour, but invariably he'd fall into deep bouts of loneliness and despair for weeks on end. His only solace, an acoustic guitar, whatever drugs he could find, and vodka, of course. Lots and lots of vodka. We wouldn't hear from him for months, then he'd emerge, strung out, a scruffy mess, looking for money. Dad always helped him out."

Zaslavsky nodded. "Hmmm. Sounds as if your uncle suffered from some kind of depressive disorder."

Vlad took another sip. "Yeah. Whatever you want to call it, Doc, he certainly had problems," He brought his mug down. "I remember, one night, Dad received a frantic call from Konstantin's girlfriend. She was really high and screaming about all the blood. Dad rushed over to find Konstantin in the bathtub; nearly dead after slitting his wrists. Did a pretty good job of it, too. His forearms stayed bandaged for weeks."

Dr. Zaslavsky nodded. "Go on."

Vlad walked over and sat down. "So, after that, doctors put him on medication, but he never took it. Said it made him flat and he couldn't write any decent music when on the stuff."

The doctor agreed. "Yes, unfortunately, the side effects of the medication are often times worse than the disorder itself."

Vladimir leaned forward, his elbows on his thighs. "So, these depressive disorders, do they get passed down in families?"

Zaslavsky nodded. "Sure they do. Mental problems are prevalent along family lines."

Vlad looked down to his mug. "Huh. Yeah, well, anyway." He stood up and quickly found another frame to straighten near the desk. "My dad did everything he could to help Konstantin, but it wasn't enough. Dad used to say when it came to Uncle Konstantin, nothing was ever enough. Even too much was not enough."

He stepped back to check the frame. "I think it still breaks Dad's heart that he could never fix his brother. That's what Dad does, he fixes things."

Dr. Zaslavsky was jotting in the file. "Let's stay on your Uncle Konstantin for now."

Vlad adjusted the frame one more centimeter to the left, stepped back. "Well, at some point during the seventies, Konstantin grew tired of the violin, and even more tired of singing that damn national anthem night after night. He made plans to take a hiatus from the symphony and put together a rock and roll group where he would play the guitar. More specifically, the electric guitar."

Dr. Zaslavsky raised his eyebrows. "Really, huh."

Vlad looked at Zaslavsky and nodded. "Yeah. He wanted to perform songs that had nothing to do with the greatness of Russia or the virtues of Communism. He wanted to sing about women, life on the road, and torturous love. The kinds of things musicians from the West sing about."

"I imagine the state did not approve of that," said the doctor with a slight laugh.

Vlad took a sip of tea and shook his head. "Hell, no. Melodiya refused to record his music. Government officials reviewed the songs and rejected them on the grounds that they were not patriotic enough. And the famous violin virtuoso Konstantin Verstakov playing the electric guitar?"

Zaslavsky shook his head. "Back then? No way. I remember. Young people loved Konstantin Verstakov The Soviet government certainly could not have him up there playing the electric guitar."

Vladimir spotted another crooked framed and moved to it. "The symphony threatened to take away his nice apartment in Moscow if he didn't stay with them. The tax bureau was pounding on his door. And prosecutors started to look into his drug use. He got overwhelmed by it all, so he decided to give up on the rock band and stay with the symphony. He lasted until 1980."

Zaslavsky looked up from the file, rubbed his beard. "1980? What happened in 1980?"

Vlad shuddered at the thick layer of dust atop the frame. He ran one finger through the dust, wiped it on his jeans. "I didn't actually witness it. But it happened in Moscow; what would be Konstantin's final performance."

Dr. Zaslavsky held up his pen. "I remember hearing something about this. Konstantin played the Soviet national anthem on his electric guitar that night, didn't he?"

Vlad looked at Zaslavsky and smiled. "Oh, I think it's safe to say he blasted that ode to Communism right out of the auditorium."

Dr. Zaslavsky laughed heartily. But abruptly stopped, his face going very serious. "Oh, yes, I do remember now. Go on."

Vlad looked at the dust layer again. "Well, after the anthem was over, the audience was crazy. Konstantin smashed his guitar to pieces. There he was on stage, got to play the guitar like he wanted. You know, doc, I bet that was the greatest moment of his life. The guitar was his Iskra."

"But it did not end well, did it?" Zaslavsky added.

"Nyet." Vlad blew the dust away. Thousands of tiny particles shimmered in the single ray of sunlight coming through the window. "He blew his head off. Suicide, right there on the stage."

Dr. Zaslavsky said nothing.

Vladimir meandered over and sat down. "A few months after the suicide, Dad received Uncle Konstantin's effects. Some nice watches, two violins, a notebook with hand-written lyrics in it, and an envelope full of snapshots of me. A notice came by relating to the Makarov. Dad went down to the courthouse and filled out the necessary paperwork to have it legally registered in his name."

"And what happened?" asked Zaslavsky.

"Well, Mom was flipping through the notebook. She got really upset. That evening was the first time I ever saw her pour a real drink. Actually, she poured drink after drink all evening. At supper, she barely touched her food."

"And what happened?" asked Zaslavsky, again.

"Dad asked her why she was so upset. She kept hesitating, but eventually, she passed the notebook over. Said she was tired of keeping secrets."

Vlad twisted around, placed down his mug. "Dad read the lyrics out loud." He turned back around. "Halfway through, he started biting his lip, trying not to cry. He really tried to hold back, probably for my sake."

"What about the song?" asked Zaslavsky.

Vlad exhaled. "The song was dated 19 April 1973, my tenth birthday. It's about a man who sees his own green eyes in a sweet boy across the table. The boy is happily eating birthday cake, opening gifts, surrounded by two loving parents. The pain the man feels knowing he will never be a father to his son because of the turmoil it would cause. But how the situation is for the best; the boy is in better, more capable hands."

"I see," said the doctor. "Konstantin was your natural father."

"Yeah," replied Vlad, shaking his head.

Vladimir took a breath and shifted his weight within the chair. "Mom said that after seven years of marriage, she had been desperate to hold a warm, cooing baby. Getting pregnant was a problem; she never had as much as a missed period." He paused, and then went on. "So, she went to Konstantin one night. Nine months later, I came along, cooing and warm."

He looked away and exhaled. "By eighteen months, I was sporting Konstantin's green eyes, unruly hair, and left-hand dominance. No one said a word."

"And Stepan?" prodded Zaslavsky. "How did he take the news?'

Vlad held his hands out. "Well, after Mom's confession, he left. Didn't go far, though. He was back the next morning, clearing away Mom's empty bottles, as if nothing happened."

"For fear of losing you and your mom," Zaslavsky stated.

Vladimir nodded. "Yeah. He's a good man."

Zaslavsky cleared his throat. "And your parents now?"

Vlad shook the hair from his face. "Mom has written three books of poetry and gives public readings all the time. Still drinks like a fish. Little sips out of dainty flasks. Dad cleans up her messes and keeps her going."

He leaned back and crossed his legs. "After I got married, I asked Dad for the Makarov. Morbid, I know, but I wanted something of Konstantin's. The violins were too fancy. Besides, I never had any musical talent."

Zaslavsky nodded. "And what did you do with the gun, Mr. Verstakov?"

Vlad shook his head. "Tried to blow my head off with it, then turned it on my wife," He leaned back and exhaled. "Fuck. I hate myself."

Dr. Zaslavsky shifted within his chair but said nothing.

Vlad exhaled. "After I found out Konstantin was really my father, I was mad for a while. Figured he never cared enough to tell me. But now that I've talked about it, I see he did care. That song was his way of showing it, wasn't it? And allowing me to be raised by Stepan really was for the best. Konstantin cared enough to let me be."

Vladimir stood up, rubbed his stubbly chin. "Huh. Didn't think I'd say this, but you're right doc, it is good to talk things through." He left the doctor's office feeling better than he had in years.

53.

"The Taliban? Never heard of 'em," I say, looking at Asef. "What kind of Stone Age religious freaks are they? You know, this is exactly why Afghanistan needs us here. Nothing personal, but come on! Cutting off an ear? A nose?" I place both hands on the wheel, make a left.

Asef starts to laugh. "My father would agree with that!"

He pushes up his glasses. "The Taliban has always been the subject of ridicule for us city kids. The men are still virgins at thirty, and we used to joke that the woman must be so ugly, they have to stay covered up."

Now, that makes me laugh.

***

The memory faded as hearty laughter nearby filled the boxing gym. Vladimir looked over. It was coming from Roman. He stood next to the boxing ring telling old stories from his glory days as a middleweight champ to a group of teenage boys who had recently been in trouble with the law. It was Roman's latest idea; work with the local police department to get these kids into the gym as part of their sentences. Most of the kids listened intently; they looked pumped up, ready to get into the ring.

Vlad patched a tear in the weight bench, added a bit of lubricant to the stationary bike to stop the squeaking, and dusted off the rack of free weights. Next, a pile of towels on the front desk awaited folding.

With his back to the desk stood an extremely well dressed man holding a briefcase. The man turned around. "Hello, V.V."

Vladimir stopped. "Pasha," he said, more than a little exasperated. "What are you doing here?"

Pasha took a look around the gym. "Just came to see what you've been up to. So, what are you making here, about fifty, sixty rubles per hour?" Vlad paused. "I'm not risking my life or hurting anyone else, Pasha. That is worth a lot to me." He picked up a towel, started folding.

Pasha set down his briefcase. "Here's a bonus," he said. "One more job? Then I will leave you to your new... whatever this is called...career. I promise."

Vlad folded three more towels in silence. Over at the ring, Roman had his back to the whole scene. "What is it?" Vlad whispered.

Pasha handed over a sheet of paper. "This is the original business agreement between myself and the two partners. As you can see, all of our signatures are on here."

Vlad took the paper. "Yeah. So?"

Pasha handed over another sheet titled *Request to Delay Tax Payment*. Pasha's signature was on that one, as well as Grigory's. But it wasn't really Grigory's signature, Pasha said; he had forged it. "I have my eye on an oil and gas deal near Irkutsk," he said. "The equipment is already set up. It's a sure thing." His plan was to use money from the café to invest in the deal. "I'll pay the taxes, don't worry. Just as soon as the money comes through."

Vlad looked the form over. "Why can't you do it?"

Pasha pointed to Fyodor's signature on the business agreement. "See the slant? And the way the ink is smeared along the paper? He's left-handed. You are the only person I could think of who could copy that."

Vlad looked over to the boxing ring. The rowdy boys were jabbing and sparring, Roman excitedly coaching them on from the side.

Then he looked down to the briefcase. Some cash would help. American money helped at the bread lines, and it afforded better items through the street vendors. He folded the two sheets of paper, slid them in his back pocket. "I'll have it done for you tonight."

54.

3 December

Zhanna put her broom away and took a look around the empty salon, letting out a sigh of relief. Another long day, finally over. The place had been booked solid all day, no time to sit down, let alone eat a proper dinner. Between appointments, around two o'clock, she had darted to the alley outside and quickly devoured a slice of *syr* and an apple, trying to breathe in a little fresh air in the process. Now, with the cleaning done, she looked at the door leading to the backroom. The towels still needed to be transferred from the washing machine to the dryer. She yawned, making her way to the backroom. *Oy, the realities of a free market economy*.

With the towels tumbling in the dryer, Zhanna grabbed her little black coat from a hook and pulled it on. She pulled the salon keys out of the pocket and looked down to button her coat. Five orders for Karina Baby Totes awaited completion at home. Perhaps then, a little supper, sleep a few hours, and show up early tomorrow for another fully booked day. She sighed, and opened the door.

Zhanna froze in her tracks. She dropped the keys. "What in the hell is going on?"

Pasha's disgruntled business partners stood near the cash register. "Good evening, Mrs. Verstakova," said the fat one, tipping his hat. The other one stood at the door, puffing away on a stinky cigar. "My dear, we have come for our money."

Zhanna snapped. "So, what, the two of you don't believe in calling ahead or anything?" To her right, a Chechen man took hold of her arm.

"Hey!" she yelled, looking at the fat one. "I have your money, but I'm not about to leave that kind of cash lying around here. You'll have to meet me at the bank in the morning."

The fat one straightened out his coat. "We have come for our money, yes. But we got to thinking."

"We can do much better than just the down payment, as you so dutifully promised us," said the smoking one. "We think your husband can get us a lot more cash than that."

The fat one laughed. "We've been watching you. You are coming with us, and writing a letter to your husband. You need to arrange for another one of your little dates. Now, let's go."

The Chechen thug tightened his grip on Zhanna's arm and pulled her through the back door where a van waited in the alley.

55.

Vladimir shivered inside his fur-lined coat. He pulled his hat tighter around his ears and hopped up and down in an effort to stay warm. Odd, Zhanna had sent a letter setting up another date. But she wanted to meet in October Park, at seven-thirty in the evening. Strange, she didn't send it by regular post; the letter had been slipped under the door. Didn't even use her regular stationary. Even more strange, she wanted to meet on the east side, off the main path.

He continued to hop, a trail of icy breath before him.

"Viva?" came a shaky voice from out of the darkness. "It's me."

Vlad stopped. Zhanna was standing beneath a dim, overhead light, shivering in her flimsy black coat, thin gloves, no hat.

"Zhanna!" he called out, striding toward her. "Hey, what are you doing? It's not safe out here."

Behind Zhanna, a dark man with a pistol in his hand stepped out of the shadows. He grabbed her arm and pointed the pistol straight ahead. "Stay right there," he barked in a thick Chechen accent.

Vlad skidded to a stop. "Zhanna."

Two men emerged from the darkness, one obese, the other in a wrinkled brown suit beneath a fur-lined coat.

"This is Doku," said the brown suit guy, puffing on a cigar. "I think you two have met once before, at a certain apartment fire back in January." He tapped his ash. "You fucking idiot."

Vlad made a fist and went for the smoking one. "Who the fuck are y—" Then he got a better look at both men and backed down. "Grigory. Fyodor." He stepped back and exhaled. "What do you want?"

Zhanna shivered in her stance. "Viva, they've been watching us."

Fyodor crossed his arms. "Yeah, we knew Pasha was buying land with our money. We couldn't kill him since our money was tied up in his investments, so we followed him. Once he hired you to do his dirty work, we sent Doku to put an end to it. More importantly, to put an end to you. Figured it would send a message; scare Pasha away from his misdeeds."

Grigory stepped forward and chuckled. "But you survived, didn't you? After that, we waited, figured you'd hit rock bottom, end up on the streets with a needle in your arm like all of Pasha's other hired hands. But I have to say, we really underestimated you and your ability to survive."

***

How many Soviet bodies have they removed? Must be all thirty-two of them. I'm the only one alive.

***

Vlad shook his head. "I've survived much worse. I will survive this, and so will Zhanna. Now, what the hell do you want?"

Fyodor looked at Grigory, then back again. "What we signed over to Pasha from our retirement funds. Plus another million rubles each. That should be enough to equal our rightful profits from the café."

Vlad held out his hands. "Hey, I was just Pasha's hired security. I don't have that kind of money, but he does. Your fight is with Pasha, not with me, and certainly not with my wife."

"Oh, but she's involved, isn't she?" said Grigory. "Yeah, we've watched you on those cute little dates of yours. A bit too sweet for my taste, if you ask me. After your date at the art museum you gave her some money, didn't you? To purchase the salon from the government? Those were co-mingled funds you gave her."

Vladimir remained still. "Co-what funds?" he asked, completely exasperated.

"Co-mingled," interjected Fyodor. "Meaning the money you gave her was not wholly yours to give. Some of it was ours. We are coming for our money."

"I told you, I don't have that kind of money!' Vlad yelled. "But Pasha does."

"Pasha manages to stay one step ahead of us," said Fyodor. "Keeps himself insulated with people like you. We know you can get it."

Grigory slowly adjusted his gloves. "You did a professional job on that arson, I'll give you that much. But breaking into my apartment? Not such a good idea. You left all kinds of fingerprints, and sticky footprints up the stairs led right to my door." He looked up. "What did you do, step in a puddle of soda or something? That was the work of an amateur if I ever saw one."

Fyodor pointed a finger. "And you know what? I should shoot you right now for what you did to our wives' Garden for the Children project. Strictly uncalled for. She's still upset about that. You know how much I have to hear her bitch and moan about it? It's making me crazy."

Grigory nodded in agreement. "Oh, and let us not forget about your latest little deed, the forgery on the tax document, Mr. Verstakov. Did you really think we wouldn't find out? The KGB may be running on fumes, but we are still the best-trained spies the world has ever seen. That was stupid. Just plain stupid."

Fyodor chimed in. "You've got until morning to get the money, or Doku here, throws your pretty little wife in the Iset. It's pretty cold this time of year."

Zhanna lurched forward against her captor. "Viva!" she cried. But Doku yanked her back like a doll.

Fyodor tossed his cigar. "She'll be in the basement of the old railway station until morning."

"I'll get you your fuckin' money!" Vlad barked. Then he looked at Zhanna. "I will fix this, Zhanna. I promise."

"I know you will, Viva. I know you will." Her lips were turning blue and she shivered uncontrollably.

"Here, give her this," Vlad said, pulling off his coat. "She's freezing." He tossed the coat on the ground. Grigory picked it up. Doku kept the gun pointed, but it was shaking in his grasp. This hired thug did not look a day over twenty, and even though he had been the taller one of the two at the apartment fire, he was not all that big.

"You sent teenagers to do away with me?" Vlad snipped. "They didn't stand a chance, you know. I fought that smaller one easily before he fell through the floor. And Doku here, he was coughing up a storm."

Doku stood up straighter and got a better grip on the gun, his commitment to his employers all but cemented. "That was my cousin who fell through the burning floor," he said. "My cousin and my friend."

Vlad sneered, hoping to get a charge out of Doku. "You're a Muslim; you must have a thousand goddamn cousins!" He readied himself for the fight that was sure to come. *Just let me get that gun.*

Doku jolted forward. But Grigory quickly pulled him back by the shoulder and demanded, "He's playing you. Calm down."

Grigory pointed a finger. "Our money. By morning."

"Viva, please," cried Zhanna as Doku pulled her backwards.

"I'll be there," Vlad called out. "Stay warm. I'll be there."

They disappeared into the trees. Vlad called out one more time, "I will be there."

56.

Vlad took off, hauling ass back through October Park, toward town. Café Club was still open. Surely, money would be flowing. Pasha should have a briefcase full of the stuff by now.

If he had to borrow the money and pay it back along with sky-high interest, fine. If he had to knock Pasha unconscious to get the money and risk more jail time, fine. Vlad hit the edge of town, leaving a trail of his own icy breath, freezing without a coat, in his jeans and short-sleeved, gray T-shirt.

***

My jacket rests on the seat between Asef and me. I should put it on. The sun is blazing high above and my arms are getting sunburned. Better to be too hot than blistered. I pick up my jacket from the seat. It's heavy. The Koran Asef found on the road tumbles off my jacket and to the floor. Forgot about that damn thing. I lean down and pick it up. What am I going to do with this holy book? Asef shouldn't have this in his backpack; Soviet guards in town don't take kindly to locals possessing the Koran.

I'd better show it to Yurchenko, tell him we found it on the road into the village, but I'd rather be the one to present it to him. Don't want him to discover it here amongst Asef's books.

For now, I toss the Koran on the seat and reach around to pull on my jacket. I roll down the sleeves to protect my arms.

I grab the book again, hold it up, turn it around in my hand. What am I going to do with this? I don't know, but for now, I stuff it in the waistband of my trousers. The book is partly resting on my pelvis, half of it sticking up to the right of my navel, not real comfortable, but it'll be okay until we stop again.

Asef glances over. He pulls his glasses down to his nose and smirks. "Uh, Vlad-ee-meer, I'm pretty sure what you are doing with that Muslim holy book violates Sharia law in every way imaginable!" He looks away, chuckling to himself.

***

Lights were still on at Café Club. Young women in miniskirts congregated outside, laughing, smoking. Vlad flew passed them and up the steps. In one smooth motion, he tore open the double doors and burst inside yelling, "Pasha!"

57.

Guns and Roses blared through the speakers like cats on fire. Vlad ran in, scanned the bar. "Pasha!" Pasha was neither behind the bar, nor sitting at it, chatting up one of his sloshed honey traps as usual. A tall waitress in a miniskirt was striding his way with a tray of drinks balanced on one hand. "Haven't seen him," she said, and veered off.

The spiky-haired DJ lifted the Guns and Roses vinyl off the turntable and replaced it with something closer to home, Gorky Park. More screeching vocals, wailing guitar, and heavy bass. The DJ threw a fist in the air and jumped in circles. The crowd followed suit.

Vladimir pushed his way through the crowd into the kitchen. "Pasha!" A man washing dishes pointed next door. Vlad nodded and turned, headed outside.

"Pasha!" he yelled, franticly turning the doorknob of the apartment. As precious seconds ticked by, so did Zhanna's life. "Pasha!" He stepped back and kicked open the door. Pasha was inside, sitting on the couch, his head back. Red lipstick smeared on his neck; his shirt was unbuttoned to his chest, pants undone. A bleached blonde, wearing nothing but a black miniskirt and black heels, knelt in front of him. The woman turned around and shrieked as Vlad bolted into the room. "They know everything!" he yelled. "And they have Zhanna!"

Pasha abruptly stood, pulling up his pants, adjusting his belt. "V.V! What the hell?"

Vlad paid no attention. "Fyodor and Grigory. They have Zhanna, and they want their money. Now!"

Pasha stopped with his belt. "Huh, thought it would take them longer to track me down." He pulled out a wad of bills from his shirt pocket, and threw it down to the blonde. "Here. Go," he barked. "Now!"

The blonde frantically swiped her sweater off the couch and scrambled for the cash. She stuffed it in her purse and hurried out over the flattened door.

Pasha bolted to the coat rack, tore off a duffel bag, and tossed it on top of his desk. He ripped open the file cabinet and started taking out secured piles of cash and stuffing them into the bag.

Vladimir breathed a sigh of relief. "They want their retirement funds back, plus one million each."

Pasha said nothing, kept stuffing cash.

"They are holding her at the old railway station. I have to show up with the money by sunrise," Vlad said, moving toward the desk.

Pasha kept stuffing cash into the duffel bag. "That's close to a million right there," he said. Next, he pulled a briefcase from under the desk, laid it out. "Now, for insurance."

He placed several piles of cash into the briefcase and latched it shut. In one final push, he opened a drawer and tossed a toothbrush and tube of toothpaste into the duffel bag. He zipped it shut. At the coat rack, he pulled on his long black coat. "Time for me to go," he winked.

"Wait!" Vlad shouted. He lurched forward but didn't get far.

Pasha already had his hand in his coat pocket. "Sorry V.V.," he said, and brought out a gun. This time it was not wrapped in a towel. "Gotta feed the Iskra, you know." He pulled the trigger. A blast, a hit to the shoulder, and Vlad flew back against the wall.

Vlad hunched forward, cupping his shoulder. "Damn it!" Blood spotted his palm, but did not gush. He could stand. The pain was not so bad. But Pasha was gone. So was the duffel bag and so was the briefcase. He stumbled out of the office. Guarding his shoulder, he headed outside.

A black-and-red cab was pulling away from the curb. Vlad stumbled over and slammed his bloody palm against the window to no avail. Pasha turned and gave him nothing more than a smug little smirk as the cab entered the flow of traffic.

He took off in a sprint down the busy street, keeping the cab in his sights for maybe two blocks. The cab gradually morphed into the traffic, disappearing, nothing but yellow tail lights and red brake lights.

***

Yurchenko's brake lights all of a sudden light up. I almost hit him. He's holding the two-way radio up to his ear as he steps out of the truck. He looks to the gunners in front of him, barks an order. He looks back, points up to the mountain, and yells, "Vlad, Red, Danil. Fire! All men, fire!"

I see four. Men dressed in flowing white. Faces covered, situated way up the road. They move about the mountain with ease. They've got rifles and are coming toward us. I grab my rifle and exit the vehicle. Before I close the door, I yell to Asef, "Stay in the truck and get down!"

***

58.

Huddled in the corner of the makeshift prison cell, Zhanna hugged her knees to her chest, stretching Vladimir's coat down to cover her shins. Her captors were treating her well enough; even let her keep her own clothes on, right down to her fifteen-centimeter high, pointy black heels. Doku even delivered a warm mug of tea. The cell was nothing more than a cramped little square, made of cement, lit only by the fluorescent light poking through a small portal on the hulking metal door.

Even if Doku went away, she'd never be able to push open that door. Even if she could get out, more KGB thugs patrolled the place. She rested her head against the cold wall.

Zhanna's brain spun into overdrive thinking of all the horrible things that could possibly happen to her and to Vladimir before they were finally thrown in the icy river. They could be tortured first, locked up and forgotten down here for months, starved. She shook her head, cursing herself for letting her mind wander. Things were bad enough already. Persistent thoughts of certain misery ending in a horrible death would not help matters.

As she tried to focus her mind, the excess worries fell away, leaving just one thought. Less of an actual thought, but more of an overall feeling. A presence. The presence gave her hope despite the dismal situation. "That's it," she mumbled in disbelief. "My Iskra."

There came a commotion outside the cell. Zhanna stood up and grabbed the mug. The bright light out in the hall flickered; someone had run by, interrupting the light to her small portal. She jumped up to look out, but couldn't get close enough to the portal.

A door, maybe two doors, opened and slammed shut. Doku, her Chechen captor, yelled out, "Hey!" Heavy footfalls came down the stairs, scuffling. There were hurried voices. A cry of pain. Silence. The lock rattled.

Zhanna backed up in the corner ready to pounce as soon as the door opened.

The hinges creaked. The heavy metal door swung open. Bright light poured into the cell, all but blinding her. On the floor lay a body, she couldn't tell whose, but someone was down.

Before her, standing in the doorway, was the silhouette of a tall, muscular man in a T-shirt, with a wide chest, bulging biceps, and horribly unruly hair.

She dropped the mug and held out one arm. With the other she shielded her eyes, crying, "Viva!"

59.

Vladimir shot into the cell. "Zhanna, are you okay? Did they hurt you?"

Zhanna brought her hand down and looked up, squinting. "No. I'm fine."

Vlad glanced outside the cell. "Pasha and his money are gone. We will have to bust out of here," he said looking around for anything useful.

Zhanna threw her arms around Vlad's neck but he recoiled in pain.

"Oh my God, what happened?" she asked, placing her hand over his shoulder. Blood was seeping through his T-shirt.

"Pasha shot me while I was trying to get the money. Luckily, he has terrible aim. It's not that bad." He took her hand. "Come on, we have to go."

"What about the guards?" she asked, pulling him back inside.

"I've subdued two of them, one at the entrance, and the Chechen, right here. I laid into them with a triple combination followed by an elbow jab to the neck. They are out cold. Come on, let's go."

Zhanna didn't move. "Huh?"

"I've learned to box," he explained, looking out to the hall. "Come on, let's go." But he hesitated and nudged

Zhanna back inside. "Wait. Better take off your shoes," he whispered. "They will be too loud."

Zhanna kicked off the shoes. She also threw off the coat and hiked her skirt above her waist to peel off her nylons. "They will just slow me down," she said.

Vlad kept watch, his body halfway out the door. "We have to go, now. Come on," he whispered, motioning with one arm.

Zhanna grabbed his hand, but abruptly pulled him back inside the cell. "Wait, baby, I have to tell you something, in case we don't make it out of here tonight."

Vlad hurriedly looked at her, only partly listening. "What? What is it?"

"Remember you told me I needed an Iskra to get through the bad times? Well, I found my Iskra tonight. It's the only reason I am not going completely crazy right now."

Vladimir took a deep breath. There was no time for this. "Yeah, yeah, an Iskra, what about it?" He turned away to look out in the corridor.

"It's you, Vladimir. You are my Iskra," Zhanna said, speaking louder than she should have. "With you, I feel I can do anything. It may be pathetic and horribly self-destructive, but I can't control it."

Vlad swiftly turned to face his wife, the perilous situation forgotten. He looked down into her eyes and said, "We are going to make it out of here, I promise you," He glanced outside the cell once again, then turned to her. "And I will be your Iskra for as long as you will allow me to be." For a brief moment, standing there in the KGB secret prison cell with government-trained assassins looking to kill him, nothing mattered. He could die right here, right now, with her, and it would all be worth it. Maybe they would die together in a haunting type of tragic love story that would be told throughout the ages; Vladimir and Zhanna, star-crossed lovers flowing throughout the universe forevermore.

"Okay, Viva. That's all I had to say," Zhanna quipped, not about to entertain any sort of tragic death scenario. "Now let's go!" She brought both hands to his chest and pushed him out the door. He took her hand, and pulled her into the bright corridor.

At the last second, Zhanna leaned down and swiped one of the pointy black heels off the pile of clothing on the floor.

60.

Just outside the cell, Vlad dropped to his knees and patted down the unconscious guard for weapons. Maybe he had a gun hidden on him somewhere.

***

I take aim. Red is already shooting. Danil is loading. The gunners have engaged their weapons, set on automatic fire. They shoot one rebel and he falls down the mountainside. Yurchenko is barking orders. "Return fire! Repeat, all men return fire!"

Now three rebels are running along the mountainous road, darting in and out of the shallow caves, shooting at us whenever they can. They move along this rocky mountain with ease, born and raised in this rough terrain. One skids to a halt and ducks behind a boulder. I quit firing and keep watch above my rifle at that boulder. I am not taking my eyes off that damn boulder.

Another muj goes down. Red got that one. "Hell, yeah!" he shouts. Red is out of bullets, he slinks down and hustles back to the truck. Danil is beside me, firing away. He hits one in the shoulder. The rebel stumbles backwards but keeps shooting.

Yurchenko sees this. He drops his radio, aims, and takes out the rebel with a single bullet to the head. I am holding out, still got my eyes on that boulder.

The chopper crests the mountaintop. The pilot squawks over Yurchenko's radio, which is lying on the sand. "Captain, approximately seventy muj coming over the mountain. We can do what we can from here but we are running low on fuel." The chopper turns, sweeps over the mountain.

Danil brings his gun down and looks at the radio. "Seventy muj! Captain, this is a goddamn ambush!" He moves to the right, taking a small step toward the radio as if he's going to pick it up.

"Danil, stop!" I yell, without taking my sights off the boulder. "The boulder!"

The rebel peeks out from behind the rock. I see his leather boot first, then half his body, clad in white, leaning out. He takes aim at Danil, and shoots.

I know this is not possible, but I see the bullet traveling toward Danil. I can see it. Right toward his head. It's not possible, but it's true. Quickly, I dart right, covering Danil, and return fire. Just one shot.

All of a sudden, I'm dizzy, seeing spots. My forehead touches my knees. I'm hunched over. What the hell just happened? Yurchenko is at my side, supporting me, keeping me from falling over. "You've been hit, Verstakov." He sounds so far away, like he's underwater. Carefully he guides me down to the sand. I'm on one knee; think I'm going to vomit. Yurchenko steps away, yelling into the radio. "I have men down, we need support down here!" The radio is squawking in and out of existence.

How bad is it? I wonder. I clutch my belly, bring my hand to my face.

No blood anywhere. The spots disappear. As soon as I catch my breath, I look up and shout, "Captain, I'm okay!"

I stand up. Yurchenko lurches toward me. He doesn't want me to stand up, but I'm fine. Perfectly fine. "Did I get him?" I shout.

Danil yells from behind me, "Fuck yeah, you got him, Verstakov! Right in the head. Nice shot, man!"

Now I know why I am not hurt. I reach to my waist, pull out the Koran. There is a bullet-sized hole going through at least two-thirds of it.

The Muslim holy book saved my life. How bizarre.

***

"Nothing," Vlad mumbled, defeated. "No gun."

He stood up. "Stay behind me," he said, taking Zhanna's hand.

They skirted the cinderblock wall and reached the end of the corridor where it made a T. "Which way?" whispered Zhanna.

Vlad poked his head around the corner; saw a flight of metal stairs at the other end. It led up to a door. "That way," he said. "Stay with me." They slunk around the corner, staying close to the wall. Zhanna's heavy breathing filled the air.

"There they are!" came a sharp voice from the left. Vladimir whipped around. Zhanna startled. Two guards were running towards them. Vlad grabbed Zhanna by the shoulders and pulled her behind him. "I'll take these two," he said. "Run to the stairs. Don't stop. Get out!"

She bolted down the hall.

Vlad sprinted toward the guards. He landed a good, solid punch to one guard's face. The guy fell backwards, hitting the concrete floor.

A hurried jab to the other guard's temple, but he stayed upright and countered with a mighty blow to the gut. Vlad stumbled backwards into the wall but pushed away. The guard pivoted around, ready to kick, but Vlad tripped him up by grabbing his ankle mid-swing. The guard stumbled, fighting to keep his balance.

Vlad rushed in, steadied the guard, and delivered a fierce triple combination followed by a sharp elbow jab to the neck. The guard went down quickly. "Wow, Roman was right, works every time," Vlad said, standing over the unconscious body.

The first guard was no longer on the floor. Vlad frantically looked around. No guard. No Zhanna. "Shit!" he yelled, taking off in a run toward the door.

A high-pitched scream came from somewhere near the stairs. Zhanna's voice called out, "Viva! Help!" Vlad darted down the hall. He reached the metal stairs in time to see Zhanna backing slowly out of a storage room at the base of the stairs. "He pulled me in," she said, pointing into the room.

Vlad rushed into the storage room but skidded to a clumsy halt. "Whoa! Damn, Zha-Zha!" On the floor, among the mop buckets and rags, laid a man folded up in the fetal position, moaning in pain. A ladies' black pump firmly embedded in one eye; fifteen centimeters of sharp, pointy heel had made his face nothing more than a mash of blood and syrupy goop.

Vlad turned, grasping Zhanna's shoulders. "As long I live, Zha-Zha, I will never, ever complain about you buying too many shoes!"

They flew up the metal stairs together, Vlad leading the way. A solid kick to the wooden door and he busted it open. They emerged outside, running through the icy, starless night. "No matter what happens, keep running!" Vlad commanded. "About six blocks and we'll hit downtown. We should be okay there."

But it didn't take long for two other guards to find them. At the edge of the building Vlad heard lightning-quick footsteps pounding the pavement behind them.

He tightened his grip on Zhanna's hand. "Come on, you can do it!"

Zhanna's body, curvy and soft and stylish, built for so many things. She looked great in whatever she wore, could dance the night away, could glide across a room. She could climb three flights of stairs in the highest of heels, effortlessly balancing keys and two bags of groceries. Zhanna's body perfectly suited her life. But there was one thing she was not built for. Running. It really didn't matter that she was barefoot, in a knee-length skirt and freezing. Even in the best of conditions, the woman could not run.

"I can't keep running!" Zhanna huffed, slowing down rapidly. "I can't do it!"

Vlad released Zhanna's hand, wrapped his arm around her waist and pushed her along. "Almost there, Zhan, I see city lights. Keep running. You can do it." He played up the optimism, hoping she wouldn't discover that two KGB guards were gaining on them.

A thankful sight, city lights. Even better, a city bus. Down two blocks, and off to the right, maybe three blocks, if they ran straight ahead, with enough speed and luck, they could catch that bus. "Keep running, Zha-Zha. There's a bus."

They hit the edge of town. At busy Lenina Prospekt, Vlad glanced around to see the guards two blocks behind, but coming in fast. Vlad turned back toward town. "We have to cross the street, and flag down that bus!"

They wove through four lanes of traffic causing a cacophony of honks, screeches, and profanity. *Blast. Gunfire. Commands. Blast. Gunfire. Commands.* The noise grew, but Vlad held it together, made it to the curb just as the bus pulled up. Zhanna bolted up the steps, and then turned around, motioning with her arms. "Viva, get on!"

Vlad remained still with his hands on either side of the buses' door. "No, Zha-Zha, I caused this whole ordeal, I need to end it. Otherwise you will never be safe."

Zhanna stepped down, tried to exit the bus. "I'm not leaving you!"

Vlad pushed her back in. "Yes you are! Stay on the bus. Don't worry. I'll be fine."

Apparently, Zhanna had little faith in that claim. She brought her hands to her hips. "It's Wednesday night. Two KGB agents are after you. You need help! Where exactly are you going to find help on a Wednesday night?"

Vlad released his hands from the doorway, took a step back and smiled. "It's Wednesday! Hell, yeah, it's Wednesday! Stay on the bus. I'll meet you back here at this stop. It's Wednesday!" The doors folded to a close. Zhanna stood in the stairwell looking horribly confused as the bus pulled out and rumbled away. Traffic became snarled with another barrage of honks, screeches, and profanities as the two KGB agents crossed Lenina Prospekt.

Vladimir looked left then right. His pursuers were almost through traffic. He darted right, running straight for the Red Torch Pub.

61.

Oleg Maksimev stood a yard from the dartboard, a dart in one hand, his other arm wrapped around the tight waist of a petite, well-stacked cocktail waitress he had just met. "Now, what you gotta do is place your thumb on the side, like this, see? Aim just to the right of center." He positioned the dart in the woman's hand. "Yeah, just like that, give it a little toss, not too much power, now."

The waitress tossed the dart. It promptly landed on the floor. She giggled and said that was fun but she'd better get back to work.

Oleg pulled her toward him and nuzzled close to her ear. "How about after your shift, my place?"

She giggled again, tossing her big scarlet curls back. "Maybe. I don't know."

There came a deep, hurried voice from the pub entrance. "Oleg! Oleg! Where are you? Are you here? It's Vladimir! Oleg where are you?"

Oleg abruptly turned away from the giggling waitress. "Hey, I'll be right back." His friend was here. He elbowed his way through a crowd of rowdy construction workers, disgruntled factory employees, and career drunks.

Near the entrance, he held his arms out wide and exclaimed, "Vlad-O!"

62.

Oleg looked fairly drunk, but stable enough, his body solid from hockey and years of construction work. With his dark, scraggly hair, crooked nose, and two missing teeth, no matter how intoxicated, Oleg could kick some rookie KGB ass, for sure.

"Vlad-O! Hey, we are all here. The whole crew," exclaimed Oleg. "We just started a new game, and, uh, my friend, sorry to tell you, but you look like bloody hell. What happened? Are you okay?"

***

"Vlad-ee-meer? Are you okay? What happened? Did you get shot?"

It's Asef. He's out of the truck, running across the sand toward me. I hold up the Koran with the bullet hole and then toss it to the ground. "Yeah. Asef, just give me a minute."

Yurchenko quits tending to me. However concerned he was for my well-being, he's over that now. He's pissed. He nearly snaps my head off with those steely blue eyes of his. "What is Asef still doing here? Why the fuck is he here?"

I have nothing to say. I don't understand.

Asef slides to a halt. He holds his hands up, looks to Yurchenko. "Uh, sorry cap-teen. I couldn't go back home. I just couldn't go back."

I manage to stand up. "Captain, what's going on?"

Asef pleads. "Please don't blame Vlad-ee-meer. He did nothing wrong. I didn't tell him you arranged for me to stay back with the Pashtuns."

So that's it. Earlier, as we left the Pashtun village, Yurchenko must have arranged for Asef to stay with the Pastuns until we came through again.

Now I am pissed, too. I walk toward him. "Asef, you should have listened to Yurchenko. This isn't a game, kid."

He looks sheepish. "I like being out here. You hear me."

Whatever the hell that is supposed to mean. I look back at Yurchenko. "Captain, if I had known you didn't want him to go farther with us, I never would have let him come along."

He's cursing himself for not telling me. But he recovers quickly. You have to around here. "Hell with it," he barks. "We've got muj descending upon us any second now. I've called for backup. Give the kid a rifle. He may bloody well need it." He holds the radio up to his mouth, orders Mikhail Astafurov and crew into position. I run to the truck to get another rifle.

***

Vlad looked at Oleg. "Long story. I'll explain later." He scanned the door. "But listen, I got two guys chasing me." He looked back at the bustling dart area, and back at Oleg. "Can you get some of those guys up here? Create a distraction? I just need time to get Zhanna to safety."

"Don't start shittin' me now, man." Oleg sneered. "You're being chased? What the hell is wrong with you?"

"I just need your help," Vlad said, turning back to the door. "Buy me some time."

Oleg crossed his arms. "Yeah? Well, maybe I'm done helping you. You lash out at work, don't show up for darts, now here you are, needing my help."

Vlad quickly reached out, grabbed Oleg by his flannel-covered arm. "Okay, look. I'm sorry I haven't been a good friend lately. I'm sick. But I'll get better, gotta find an Iskra."

The front door swung open. Vlad ducked and turned away. "Shit. There they are." He started to push through the crowd.

Oleg yanked Vlad back by the shoulder. "Huh? Iskra? Vlad-O, just what in the fuck are you—"

Vlad grabbed Oleg by the collar. "That's them. Come on!" He pulled Oleg through the crowd. "Just create a distraction. I need them off my trail."

He stopped near the dartboard and released Oleg. "And an Iskra," he said out of breath. "An Iskra is something to believe in. I don't know, it makes you feel more complete or something. That's all. It doesn't really matter anymore."

Vlad headed to the back exit. He pushed open the door.

"Vlad-O!"

Vladimir turned. Oleg was standing tall, his eyes brighter than usual. He punched his fist repeatedly into his open palm. "I ain't going to distract them!"

Vlad let go of the door. "What?"

"I gotta fight!"

The two agents came around the corner. Oleg motioned to the guys playing darts. "Come on boys, our friend is in trouble. We've got some ass to kick!"

Oleg and the guys rushed the corner, barreling into the two men, shoving them to the floor in a frenzy of fists and sneakers. From somewhere in the mix, Oleg, already with a bloody lip, popped his head up and shouted, "I don't know about you, Vlad-O, but I just found my Iskra!"

63.

Vlad lurched toward the scuffle. "Oleg, no. I didn't mean…oh, crap."

Too late. The agents were getting their butts kicked and Oleg was in utter heaven.

He turned away, pushed the metal handle on the door. *Blast.* He released, stepped back, and tried it again. *Blast.* He ran outside accompanied by the noise. *Blast. Blast. Blast.*

***

At the truck, I take out a rifle, look it over. I respect Yurchenko, but this is not a good idea. Asef can barely stay upright and now we are arming him with a rif—

A deafening blast. I stop, turn around.

Mikhail Astafurov and his crew have been moving up the road in their armored vehicle, getting into position to fight off the invading muj. And now. Shit. They've hit a land mine.

The armored vehicle is on its side. A fat plume of smoke rises, engulfing the vehicle. Nothing but black wheels, still turning, and gray smoke. That's all. Yurchenko is running, yelling into the radio, "Men down, we have men down!"

Two rifles in my hands, I stay low and sprint toward Yurchenko. "Captain! I'm here!"

Through the smoke, figures emerge. Six of them, standing, coughing, slinging their weapons. Mikhail waves his arms overhead to signal they are all okay. They start to move around, away from the smoke and the downed vehicle.

They are stumbling, coughing, and a few are hunched over, but seem to be moving all right.

Then, another high-pitched whine. No one seems to hear it but me.

"There's another one!" I scream. The sound only goes for maybe ten seconds, but in my head it goes on for hours. I take off toward the downed vehicle. "Get out of there now! Get out!"

Yurchenko yanks me back. But I fight to get over there. "Captain, there's another land mine. It's gonna blow. I can hear it!"

Mikhail steps toward us. The gold wedding band around his neck catches the sun. A sharp golden flash, so brilliantly bright, and then it's gone. The second land mine blows. Mikhail Astafurov is ripped apart.

***

Stifling hot from the memory, Vlad stopped running. The street was a mountainous road, the cobblestone had given way to sand, the people were gun-toting mujahideen rebels.

He took a deep breath and imagined himself boxing in the ring, throwing jabs, uppercuts, kicking ass with a series of one-two combos. Feeling his heart race, beads of sweat flying. *Left. 1,2,3. Right. 1,2,3. Left. 1,2,3. Right. 1,2,3.* But nothing changed. The agitation remained as did the noise.

Boxing would not be his Iskra.

64.

Vlad quickened his pace with each passing second, as if to keep a step ahead of the noise. His head throbbed with each foot strike. *Blast. Gunfire. Commands. Blast. Gunfire. Commands.* The noise would not die. He leaned against the covered bus stop, hopelessly certain that there was no Iskra, nothing to dampen the noise or take away the memories. "Bloody hell," he muttered beneath his breath. "Bloody fucking hell." No wonder Konstantin blew his head off. It did not seem like a bad idea at this point.

The city bus was stopped three blocks up the street. Vlad sat down on the bench, took a deep breath, and cupped his hands over his ears.

***

Asef is behind me, screaming my name. He's on his knees, covering his ears. Blood and other liquids are leaking out from between his fingers. The impact from the two blasts has ruptured his eardrums.

The remaining men in Mikhail Astafurov's crew are making their way over to us. One is missing an arm. Another falls down. He doesn't get up. One man is carrying another, draped over his shoulders. A second soldier drops. Yurchenko is running toward them.

I slide to my knees in front of Asef, peel his hands away from his ears.

"I can't hear, Vlad-ee-meer, I can't hear!" I tell him it will pass, even though he doesn't know what I am saying.

"Asef! Hey, you will be all right." I know he can't hear me, but seeing me helps him calm down. He nods. I take the rifles and sling them over my right shoulder, and then I take his arm, drape it over my left. "I'm taking you back to the truck!"

Together we hobble toward the truck. His head is down. I know he's scared, but he's holding together quite well. "Almost there, you are doing great."

He acknowledges me, only that I am speaking. As we stumble over rocks, his glasses fall off. "My glasses, Vlad-ee-meer, my glasses!"

Mujahideen are closing in. Maybe fifteen of them. Several of our men are severely wounded. Red and Danil are out there, shooting. Yurchenko is fighting, too. "I'll get your glasses later, Asef, right now, I need to get back out there!" He doesn't protest.

"I got ya, it's going to be all right." I yell over the constant rat-tat-tat of rifle fire.

The truck is close. I'm going to stuff him in the passenger side, make sure he's out of sight, and get back out here.

But out of nowhere comes muj. They must have been looting the trucks because they have the rifles that we are transporting. Three are coming toward us. Five more are loading.

"Shit!" I yell and push Asef down so he is out of range. I bring my weapon over my shoulder. I fire two shots. Two go down right away. More are coming. They are yelling something. I can't make it out. It's the same word over and over. I just keep shooting.

"They are saying traitor! They are calling me a traitor," Asef yells from the ground.

I run, quickly slide the other rifle off my shoulder and toss it to Asef. "Just point and shoot!"

I run to get atop a little mound near Yurchenko's vehicle. Better vantage point. Another muj goes down from my bullet.

Asef is screaming. I don't see him anymore but the rifle I tossed to him is still on the ground. Damn it.

I leave the mound. "Asef! Where are you?"

Staying low to the ground, I kneel behind my truck, looking for Asef. I peek around the bed of the truck and find him sitting on the ground, outside the passenger door. He's shrieking in fear, covering his face.

A muj has a rifle to Asef's face. Another one stands, laughing, flicking cigarette ash on Asef's head. I shoot the first one from my kneeling position. He falls and I dart around the truck again.

Quickly, I rise to full height, step around, and shoot the other guy, too.

***

A cold, wet nose and a furry little head brought Vladimir back to reality. A fat black paw plunked down on his knee. A feminine voice called out. "Maksem. No! Bad dog! Down. Down, Maksem!"

The paw immediately slid off Vlad's knee to the ground. Vlad pulled his hands away from his ears, reached out to touch the dog's head. Even with the horrid noise and violent images in his head, he couldn't help but smile. "Hi there, boy." Before him sat the most friendly dog, a black Labrador retriever with a bright red collar about his neck.

The dog's owner, a stout woman in her sixties with short, curly hair, sat down on the bench. "I apologize for my dog. Maksem is normally very well behaved."

"No, that's all right, ma'am," Vlad replied. "He's a nice dog."

The woman shuddered. "Don't call me 'ma'am.' Makes me feel older than I already am. My name is Galina. This here is Maksem, but obviously you two have already met."

"Okay, Galina. And Maksem." The dog perked to attention at the mention of his name. Vlad breathed easier with this happy dog sitting in front of him. He scratched Maksem behind the ears. Maksem's tail swatted the ground repeatedly, his furry chin tilted upwards. "I think he likes me."

Galina agreed. "My husband and I train dogs for hunters. We teach them to focus on the task and never leave the hunter's side, even with all kinds of commotion." She pulled her wool coat more tightly around herself. "So, occasionally I bring a dog into the city to test his ability to focus. Maksem has not veered from me all evening—that is, until he saw you. He practically dragged me over here!" She laughed. "You know, dogs have a special sense. They know when someone needs extra love."

Vlad brought his face down to Maksem's. "Do I seem like I need extra love, boy, huh? Do I?" Maksem popped both paws up on Vlad's knees and gave him a lick on the face.

Galina glanced down the street and pointed "Well, young man, looks like your bus is coming." She lumbered to her feet. "Maksem and I are headed home, got the old truck parked around the block. Maksem likes to ride in the front seat with his head out the window." She gave the leash a slight tug. Maksem promptly sat at attention.

Galina looked Vladimir up and down. "Young man, you must be freezing! Don't you have a mother or a wife to dress you properly?" She shook her head while Maksem looked up with soft puppy eyes and gave a little whine.

Vlad looked down to his jeans and bare arms and shrugged. "I'm not that cold, really. I spent nearly a year in Afghanistan. A real Russian winter feels great after that stifling hell hole."

Galina's stern look grew even harder. "Oy. The bloody Afghan war. Useless, if you ask me! Our stagnant economy. Perestroika. Restructuring. The bread lines. I don't need any of that shit. That's why we live outside of town. No television. No newspapers. Only nature and the company of dogs."

Vladimir looked down to Maksem, who had his tongue dangling from his mouth. "To live in the company of dogs, that sounds nice. That would be a good Iskra."

"Huh? Iskra?" Galina quipped, not at all impressed. "Is that a new rock band or television show or something?"

Vlad stood up, put his hands in his pockets, and looked for the bus. "No. An Iskra is something to believe in. That's all.

Galina made a sweeping motion with her hand. "Young man, you don't need any New Age Iskra bullshit. Get out of town and live in the company of dogs, that'll make you right in the head!" Maksem perked up, gave a little bark. Both Vlad and Galina laughed.

The bus rumbled up to the sidewalk. The top of Zhanna's head bounced along. Vlad waved to her and said to Galina, "That's my wife. We've had quite a night."

Galina started to leave but stopped. "Young man, you tell that little wifey of yours to knit you some warm sweaters. Maybe a hat or two."

Just then, Zhanna sprang out of the bus in her thin blouse, short skirt, wearing neither stockings nor shoes. "Viva!" she exclaimed. "You're all right!"

Galina turned and rolled her eyes. "What is it with you young people today? You can't bother to dress for the weather? Come on, Maksem, let's get out of here. You be my Iskra, I'll be yours." Maksem looked at Vlad and tilted his head to the side. Galina gave a little whistle and she and Maksem walked away, off to live in the company of dogs.

So happy and relieved to see her husband still alive, Zhanna was barely listening. She wrapped her arms around her shivering body. "It's over! This dreadful night is finally over! Let's go home. It's freezing."

Vlad pulled her in and looked around. "This game ain't over. Fyodor and Grigory are still out there. Come dawn, they are going to find out we've escaped and the money hasn't been delivered. They will come looking." He pulled back. "We can't go to either of our apartments. Should probably stay away from family, too. If the KGB finds out where we are, we will just attract trouble for everyone."

Zhanna looked down and sighed. "Okay, makes sense. So, where should we go?"

65.

Gray concrete walls, equally gray floor. Metal toilet in the corner. A moth-eaten blanket thrown on a concrete slab for a bed. The jail cell was freezing, and gray, much too gray for Zhanna's taste.

"Tell me again, Vladimir, why are we staying the night in jail?"

The way she used his full name, *Vladimir*, with such disdain; the manner in which she said *jail*, too sharp, too quick. So harsh. Zhanna was pissed off. Vlad couldn't fault her, but there was no other choice.

"I know it's bad," he said, trying to rub her shoulder. "But this really is the safest place for us to be right now. Tomorrow it will all be over. We just have to get through tonight." Maybe she would come around. Doubtful.

They both sat on the concrete slab. She was having nothing of the shoulder rub as she scooted to the end of the slab and crossed her arms around her body to keep warm. "I'll tell you one thing, Vladimir, I am not using that toilet!"

Vlad chuckled. "You don't have to, Zha-Zha. Look, our cell isn't even locked. You can get out if you need to. There's a bathroom by the front desk." He slid the metal bars halfway to the side to show her that they really were not prisoners. "Officer Rogusskii has gone out of his way to let us stay here."

"I know," she sighed. "But, still." They sat in cold silence for a moment. Vlad grabbed the moth-eaten green blanket, wrapped it around his wife's shoulders and moved back to his end of the concrete slab, sensing she needed space.

After a few moments of silence, Zhanna laughed. "This is clearly, without a doubt, the most bizarre night I've ever had, Viva."

He nodded. Good. She was back to calling him Viva.

Vlad shrugged. "We will always remember this, that's for sure. Maybe in ten years we'll be telling this story to our kids. They will think we are some kind of special agents or super heroes."

Zhanna burst into laughter and covered her mouth. "Oy! They will never believe us! Maybe we should just wait and tell it to our grandkids." Gradually, centimeter, by centimeter, she moved to the center of the slab. Vlad quickly did the same. He put his arm around her and kissed her temple. She laid her head on his shoulder.

"Special delivery!" came a hefty voice from outside the cell. Officer Rogusskii was there, holding two cups of steaming hot tea. He used his foot to slide the gate open. "I found some thicker blankets in the back. I'll bring those, and I may be able to fit a couple of cots in here. They are more comfortable than the concrete slab."

Zhanna shot up and took the tea. "Oh, thank you so much!" She turned sideways to leave, said she needed to use the restroom. Vlad stood up and gratefully took the hot mug.

With his hands free, Rogusskii immediately found a cigarette in his chest pocket and lit it. After one drag, he pulled a little notebook from his chest pocket. "Okay, so this is what's happening." He had dispatched a team of police officers to stake out the railway station. "We got absolutely no jurisdiction over the KGB," he said. "But we can slow them down for a while." He also alerted the transit authority to be on the lookout for one Pavel Grachov, who was traveling with a duffel bag and briefcase full of ill-gotten cash. "I'll come back with the first aid kit, too," he said. "That shoulder needs a bandage."

Rogusskii stuffed the notebook back into his chest pocket. "So, son, besides doing the dirty deeds of a co-op millionaire, and getting wrapped up with the KGB in the process, I trust you have been staying out of trouble." He took a long drag off his cigarette.

Vladimir laughed nervously, ran his fingers through his hair. "Yeah, yeah. Don't worry, you won't see me here again."

Rogusskii exhaled a stream of smoke. "I should hope not."

But the past year came crashing back. The arson job, destroying the Garden for the Children, forging the tax document, all for piles of cash. "Uh, listen," he said, "I've done some bad things this past year. I'm not proud of them and I need to turn myself in."

Rogusskii stuck the cigarette back in his mouth and crossed his arms, shaking his head. "All right, then. Come talk to me before the weekend, and we'll work something out. I've got a big hike scheduled Saturday way out into the Urals to take photographs of snow in trees, and I sure as hell don't want to be worrying about this."

Vladimir quickly nodded. "Okay. I'll be here. Thank you for everything."

Rogusskii brushed him aside, making his way out of the cell. "Eh, whatever."

But Vlad stood up taller. "Hey, that cigarette ain't going to help you on your big hike Saturday. You know that, don't you?"

Rogusskii paused and let out a strained breath. He slowly turned, leaning one hand on the gray concrete, and pulled the cigarette out of his mouth. "My wife hates it. My daughter is coughing. I've been trying so hard to quit again. Man, I just can't. I just don't think I can do it this time."

Vladimir held his palm out. "Yes, you can. You survived the war, even overcame your demons with an Iskra. You can do anything. Now hand 'em over."

Rogusskii narrowed his eyes, deeply annoyed, but he dug into his chest pocket anyway. "Here." He handed over a full pack of cigarettes.

Vlad stayed put.

Rogusskii rolled his eyes. "Oh, all right." He dug in the pocket of his trousers and handed over another pack. "Here."

Vlad nodded in acceptance and turned away to put the two packs down on the concrete slab.

"Wait, wait. There's one more." Rogusskii grudgingly brought another pack out from the other pocket. He took one more drag from the lit cigarette, and threw it to the floor, snuffed it beneath his boot. "There, that's all of 'em. Thanks. I needed that, you dirty, rotten son of a bitch."

66.

With Rogusskii's help, Vlad managed to fit two cots in the cell. Rogusskii brought in two thicker blankets and a decent pillow, which he handed to Zhanna. "You'll be safe here tonight. Don't worry," he said, tipping his hat.

Zhanna lay down on the cot and brought the blanket over her head in complete and utter denial of the entire night. Vlad smoothed the second blanket over her and took the moth-eaten one for himself. Soon, he heard Zhanna's heavy breathing. She was fast asleep.

One row of industrial lights shut off. *Gunfire.* Another row shut off. *Gunfire. Gunfire.* As the last row shut off, the sound of gunfire filled the cell. *Gunfire. Gunfire. Gunfire.*

***

Gunfire. It's all around me, echoing. Rat-tat-tat, rat-tat-tat. Bullets whizz by, men scream, men fall. Soviet men, Afghan men.

I step around the truck. Asef is attempting to stand up. He has to crawl over the two dead muj who had been taunting him. He can't see very well without his glasses.

"Get down and cover your head!" I snap. I have to get him out of here. They are going to kill him.

He hunkers down, brings his arms around his head. "Vlad-ee-meer! Help!" he cries like a child. Hell, he is a child.

"I'm trying!" I yell back. I kick the dead muj out of the way and open the truck door. Asef starts to crawl in. I help the process along by shoving him down on the seat. "Stay down, and don't come out!" He nods in return, looking more like a lost puppy than ever before.

I slam the door shut and run to help my men.

Red is staying low, moving backwards toward the truck. "Vlad, I'm out!"

I run past. "I've got ya," I say, motioning to a big rock. "Reload behind that rock!"

Red slips around the rock. I lay flat down on my belly and start shooting.

So this is what it's like to kill men. I don't panic. I don't hesitate. I don't run. I shoot. The sharp rat-tat-tat sound fills my head. It's a rhythm I can follow. I keep up with it. I am creating it. My mind has never been this clear, I have never been this focused. This one moment is everything. It is my life, and the lives of my men. Time slows, even stands still so I can peel off the best shots possible. I aim and shoot; muj fall.

A bullet flies by; I duck my head. "Red!" I shout over my shoulder. "I need backup!" He doesn't show up. Shit. Where the hell is Red?

I peel off three more shots. Three rebels go down, and then I slink backwards to the rock.

The soles of two combat boots are sliding away along the sand. Two muj are dragging Red away. His body is limp, leaving a thin trail of blood through the sand. I shoulder my rifle. "Hey, motherfuckers!"

They barely have time to turn around before I peel off two single shots. One hits the guy on the right in the head, the second hits the other guy in the neck. They fall.

Red's limp body slumps to the ground. He's been shot. A bloody wound to the stomach. I place my hand over it to try to stop the bleeding. He's breathing and coughing. That's good.

He tries to stand up. "I'm all right," he says, but he falls back to the ground clutching his belly.

I grab Red's rifle, toss it away. He never had time to reload. Mine is almost out, as well. I swipe the AK-47s off the dead muj, and then hoist Red over my shoulders.

The wounded are being placed near the gun-mounted truck, so I head over there, running as fast as I can. Bullets are flying by, but I keep low.

We make it. Two platoon medics are here with the wounded. They are doing as much as possible; placing tourniquets, applying pressure, cutting open uniforms to get to the wounds. So many men are here, several missing at least one limb. It smells of blood and rotted flesh.

I place Red down on the ground. He's lost all color, but he's moaning. Still alive. "Bullet to the abdomen!" I yell, and run back out.

Blood is everywhere, splattered on our faces, pooling in the sand. Blood is on my chest, soaking through my shirt. I try to stop the bleeding, but can't. I can't save anyone.

***

Vladimir jolted up to a sitting position, wide awake. His skin slick and clammy, body shivering with the cold. The cell closed in like a vice. "Red," he muttered, barely able to breathe. "Shouldn't have told him to go behind that rock." He kicked the blanket away and dropped his head in his hands.

Zhanna poked her head out from under the two blankets. "Viva? What's wrong?"

Vlad shook his head and lay back down on the cot.

He turned to face Zhanna. "There are so many victims. Not the soldiers who died, but all the people who love and depend on those men, they are victims, too. They suffer as much, if not more."

Zhanna brought up one hand and laid it on Vlad's clammy cheek. "Baby, you're burning up. Breathe, try to relax."

But Vlad shook his head. "Captain Yurchenko's son, Luka, started stuttering as Yurchenko left for his fifth tour of duty. The kid is a nervous wreck, all because of the war."

He looked up to the ceiling. "And Asef, our interpreter, was just a kid looking to break out of his privileged life for a while. His parents didn't even know he was with us." He looked back to Zhanna. "Officer Rogusskii told me his own story. As he was drinking himself nearly to death, his eldest daughter was starving herself. It all came from the war. I met a guy over at the lumber yard. Both of his legs were blown off and he only had one arm. Amazingly, he appeared to be handling it all right, but his mother's spirit was all but dead."

He took her hand, held it to his chest. "And you, Zha-Zha. You've suffered the most because of my demons. You and our baby." He exhaled and went on. "Countries send their men to the front lines to fight the wars, and that's how it should be. We are disposable. But as soon as we return home, it's the mothers, wives, and children who suffer the most. It's not right."

Zhanna sniffed and touched his hair. She was sitting up. "Viva, you are not disposable. I have never thought of you that way." She sniffed again. "Your mother loves you dearly, even risked her marriage to have you." She moved around, the blankets rustled. "And that mother at the lumberyard probably feels her son's pain more than he does, because that's what women do; we feel all of the pain. Now don't say you are disposable; we need our men." She unwrapped the two blankets from around her body and pulled them over to cover them both.

67.

DOMODEDOVO AIRPORT, MOSCOW

3 December

Pasha stepped into the gate, placed the briefcase on the carpeted floor, and made the two-hour time adjustment on his watch. He picked up the briefcase and quickly moved on. His in-laws had a vacation *dacha* an hour outside Moscow; that would be a good place to hide out while things cooled over in Sverdlovsk. Fyodor and Grigory had probably done away with Vladimir and his wife by now, but they would come after their money with a vengeance. The KGB's reach would surely be long, swift, and state-sanctioned. Maybe the dacha for a few days, then a series of hotels. He looked up, saw an arrow pointing to the right accompanied by the word TAKSI in bold, capital letters, and headed that direction.

Up ahead, a tired-looking, graying cop stood with a radio to his mouth. He was talking into it and looking around. Pasha slowed his pace and slunk down to the water fountain to get a drink. He stood up, wiped his mouth, and made his way in the other direction. Another cop was heading toward him, this one young and muscle-bound. He, too, was on a radio, but brought it down it as soon as his eyes fixed upon Pasha. Pasha turned around. The first cop was closing in, as well.

"Mr. Grachov? Are you Pavel Grachov?" the muscle-bound cop asked. He had his hand on his holstered gun.

The first cop came to a stop. "We need to see your papers."

Pasha placed the briefcase down and looked up to the graying cop. "I've my papers right here in my coat, officer. If you would allow me to reach inside."

The cop nodded.

Pasha brought out his state identification as well as his passport and handed them over. After checking, the cop gave them back and pulled out a sheet of paper from his chest pocket. "Mr. Grachov, we've been given an order for your arrest for crimes stemming out of Sverdlovsk. Says here embezzlement and fraud. You better come with us."

The first cop put the warrant back in his pocket and went for his handcuffs while the second one kept his hand on his gun.

"Listen," Pasha said with a little smirk. "I know what the warrant says, but it's all a big misunderstanding. I'm sorry you had to be dragged into it."

Not amused, the graying cop barked an order. "Mr. Grachov, please place your hands behind your back."

Pasha looked around, and then tapped the briefcase with his toe. "Officers, there are approximately five thousand things in this case that say you never saw me here tonight."

The two cops looked at each other. The older one nodded to the younger one, who picked up the case and looked around. The older one motioned to a custodial closet across the way. He grabbed Pasha by the elbow and all together, they stuffed themselves into the tiny closet.

"Let me go, and it's all yours," said Pasha, brushing off the sleeve of his coat.

The younger one unlatched the case. His eyes widened. The older one looked upon its contents with subtle approval. He reached into his chest pocket and handed over the arrest warrant. "We never saw you."

Pasha smiled as he took the sheet of paper and shoved it in his coat pocket. "Bye-bye," he said, turning to open the door.

A warm feeling of calm rushed over him as he hefted the duffle bag full of cash over his shoulder. He headed out the automatic sliding doors, into bustling Moscow, with a smile on his face. Another hurdle to the acquisition of wealth, overcome.

68.

SVERDLOVSK

4 December

Left. 1,2,3.

Right. 1,2,3.

Left. 1,2,3.

Right. 1,2,3.

Left. 1,2,3.

Right. 1,2,3.

Left. 1,2,3.

Right. 1,2,3.

After spending the previous night in jail, Vlad's neck was stiff and his lower back ached, but the speed bag exercise helped loosen his tight muscles. The left shoulder was tight and weak from the bullet grazing, but still, it felt good to move.

Left. 1,2,3.

Right. 1,2,3.

Left. 1,2,3.

Right. 1,2,3.

Vlad had spent much of the morning convincing Zhanna to go stay with a cousin out of town for a few days. Fyodor and Grigory been arrested early in the morning at the old train station, but city police did not hold much, if any, power over the KGB; the judge would most likely let them loose after a bribe. Vlad needed a few days to figure things out. The salon would be fine. He'd check on it himself, he assured her, just go. Eventually, she relented.

Left. 1,2,3.

Right. 1,2,3.

Left. 1,2,3.

Right. 1,2,3.

Vlad spent the early afternoon in the hospital, checking on Oleg. Police officers had broken up the fight in the Red Torch pub and threw everyone in jail for the night. But paramedics were called in when Oleg started hyperventilating and clutching his chest. His lips turned blue and he passed out on the Red Torch floor. At the hospital, doctors hooked him up to various machines and told him no more extreme exertion; his heart just could not take it.

Oleg looked pale and weak in his little hospital bed with electrodes on his chest, but he remained in good spirits. He retold the story of the bar fight with such fascinating detail and enthusiasm that the machine started beeping out of control until he took a moment to calm down. Vladimir did not want to test Oleg's heart further by telling him those were KGB agents-in-training he beat up.

Vlad listened intently, nodding and saying things such as "wow," and "no way." He shook his head and laughed, knowing he was going to hear this story over and over again for many years to come.

Left. 1,2,3.

Right. 1,2,3.

Left. 1,2,3.

Right. 1,2,3.

After the hospital, it was time to go to work at the boxing academy where he stayed busy maintaining the equipment and keeping the towels folded and in adequate supply.

Left. 1,2,3.

Right. 1,2,3.

Left. 1,2,3.

Right. 1,2,3.

The Soviet Boxing Academy had emptied out hours ago. Just before closing, Roman left to attend his son's high school wrestling tournament, leaving Vlad to close the place down. He had locked up and turned off all the lights except for the bank of fluorescents above the speed bag.

Too restless to go home, not in the mood to go out, Vlad wrapped his hands with tape. The time was his alone; time to sweat, time to move, time to hit the bag.

Left. 1,2,3.

Right. 1,2,3.

Left. 1,2,3.

Right. 1,2,3.

Left. 1,2,3. Beads of sweat formed along his brow.

Right. 1,2,3.

Left. 1,2,3. Heavy breath. Cleansing.

Right. 1,2,3.

Left. 1,2,3. His feet shuffled side to side.

Right. 1,2,3.

Left. 1,2,3. His pulse quickened. Centering.

Right. 1,2,3.

Left. 1,2,3 Boxing was not his Iskra;
Right. 1,2,3.
Left. 1,2,3. But, man, it felt damn good.
Right. 1,2,3.
Left. 1,2,3. Nothing but the fist.
Right. 1,2,3. Nothing but the bag.
Left 1,2,3. Nothing but the fist.
Right. 1,2,3. Nothing but the bag.
Left. 12,3. Nothing but the fist
Right. 1,2,3. Nothing but the bag.
Left. 1,2,3. Nothing but the fist.
Right. 1,2,3. Nothing but the bag.

Commands. With each hit, Yurchenko's voice cut through the focus. *Commands. Commands*. Vlad hit harder, moved faster, but only heard *Commands. Commands. Commands.*

***

Yurchenko's commands are rising above the gunfire. "Verstakov, Danil, everyone, get up closer, get higher. Go. Go. Go!" He's making a sweeping motion with one arm and holding the radio with the other, calling for more air support. I run forward and skid onto my belly, taking pot shots at the coming muj. I look to my right. Danil is standing atop a truck, a cigarette dangling from his mouth. His AK-47 is on automatic fire. If this were a movie, Danil would be the action star, without a doubt. Shit, I wish we were acting.

I rise up to one knee so I can shoot higher. The sand before me is strewn with bodies. Afghan and Soviet. Mostly Soviet. But more Afghans are coming. Cavernous hiding places mark the mountainside; muj are coming out of those caves. Most of them are barefoot, or in sandals, gliding about the mountain.

I stop shooting and peer over my rifle. Yurchenko calls out, "To the west! Head west!" I duck and run to the right, passing behind Danil.

Yurchenko was correct, muj are all over here. Danil has shot several, but more are right behind them. I hear Danil's automatic fire and I am firing, as well. Two go down. Another four go down. We are getting them.

The chopper is coming in from the north. Can't see it, but I hear it. Good, we need backup.

Two muj left over here, from what I can tell. Danil and I can take them. I get up a little higher, take a shot. One goes down. The other muj go down at the same time. Not my shot; that bullet came from Danil. Danil's rifle abruptly goes silent. I don't look because I'm too focused on looking for more muj.

"Vlad-ee-meer! Vlad-ee-meer!" It's Asef. Shit, what now?

Things are under control here, so I stand up to go to the truck.

But I don't get far. I trip over something lying on the sand. My ankle twists within my boot and I fall. It's a body. Russian. Wearing a blue-and-white-striped shirt, a smoldering cigarette lies next to his head. "Danil," I say quietly. I flip him over. He's dead. One shot between the eyes.

"Vlad-ee-meer! Vlad-ee-meer!" Asef is crying now. I stand up and run.

Asef is on his knees, hands behind his head. Tears streaming down his face, his eyes are closed tightly; he's screaming my name, "Vlad-ee-meer! Vlad-ee-meer!"

Behind him stands a muj with a bandana covering his nose and mouth. Two other men flank him. The man with the bandana holds a pistol to the back of Asef's head.

I need to get a little closer in order to get a good shot at the guy.

"Vlad-ee-meer! Vlad-ee-meer!" Asef cries. I run to where I can get a shot. I bring my rifle to my left shoulder. "I hear you, Asef!" I yell. "I hear you!"

He opens his eyes and sees me. I must be blurry because he doesn't have his glasses on, but he knows I'm here. All the tension melts from his face. He's confident I will take care of this.

One of the men takes a shot at me. I quickly dart away. I aim for the bandana man's eyes and fire. Get him. He falls.

But for the first time today, I have not been fast enough. Just as the man falls, so does Asef. He falls forward, flat on his face. A pool of crimson blood slowly forms a puddle in the sand beneath his head.

***

Left. 1,2,3.

Right. 1,2,3.

Left. 1,2,3.

Right. 1,2,3.

Vlad took one final punch to the speed bag with his left hand. The sheer force knocked the bag off its hinge. It dropped to the floor.

Vlad bent forward, "Asef," he said, resting his hands on his knees, chest heaving, trying to catch his breath. "Kid, I heard you. I really did."

69.

A sweaty, stinky mess, Vlad tore the tape from his hands, tossed it in the trash. He secured the speed bag back where it belonged, and left the boxing academy to catch the bus home.

Once the bus hit downtown, Vlad hopped off, still too restless to go home. Perhaps a walk would burn off some energy and calm his mind. As he stepped off the bus, a light snow began to fall from the street-lit sky. He zipped up his coat, tucked his chin, and walked on.

Traffic was moderate, but not a whole lot of people were out. A rowdy group of teenagers ran past, and darted left, down into a sunken stairwell. Vlad approached the crowded stairwell to see more young people coming and going from the abandoned old tea room. Heavy metal music blared from the door each time it opened.

Five or six teenage boys lined the railing of the steps, smoking cigarettes, laughing, talking. With Soviet rules waning, police were hardly enforcing the strict nine o'clock curfew for young people anymore. It must be after ten. So what was going on in that old tearoom now? A party? A fight? A drug deal? He walked on, not wanting to get involved with any of it.

The teenage boys glanced over, flicked their heads up. Vlad only saw a mob of hair, heavy eyeliner, and multiple ear piercings. He nodded in return but remained highly amused by the spectacle. Teenagers. Nothing more awkward than teenagers.

***

He's just a teenager. Was just a teenager. I stand frozen, staring at the body that used to be Asef. His blood pools in the sand. Some sinks in. How long have I been standing here? Shit, I don't know.

The chopper has arrived. I turn around as it crests the mountain. Not much gunfire happening anymore, a few bullets still cut through the air, Yurchenko is calling out commands, but the battle has died down considerably. Actually, most of the people have died, that's why it's so quiet. The medics are standing up, waving their arms for the chopper pilot. I head in that direction, too. Maybe I can help. Red is there, is he still alive?

Someone grabs me, throws me to the ground. It's Captain Yurchenko. "Stinger!" he yells. "Stay down!" For a split second, I see a muj, clad in flowing white, up in the mountain far above us. He's got something big and cylindrical on his shoulder. A stinger missile. He lets it fly.

The missile hits the chopper. The chopper is sputtering, jerking around in the air like a child's toy. It explodes. Fire. Shrapnel flying.

Yurchenko covers my head with his arms. His body jerks. "Goddammit!" he yells. I think he's been hit with shrapnel, but he keeps covering my head.

Yurchenko scrambles to his feet. "Those are my men," he says, and takes off toward the devastation.

Medics are picking up soldiers by the arms, the ones who have arms, and dragging them away. One soldier stands up. I don't know his name. He has a bandage around his head. He's hobbling toward Yurchenko. But just as Yurchenko gets a hold of the soldier's arm, a sharp hunk of metal from the chopper hits the soldier in the back, tearing him in two.

But my captain doesn't give up. He runs directly into the smoke and fire.

***

Tears came out of nowhere. Gushing down his face. Vlad couldn't control them. Neither could he control the noise. *Blast. Gunfire. Commands. Blast. Gunfire. Commands.* The tearoom behind him, Vlad quickly turned down the alley on his left.

Lined with a few industrial-sized trash receptacles, the alley was littered with garbage and stunk of urine. Snow fell harder now. It slanted sideways in the dim light cast by the three lamps that had bulbs.

For the first time in two years, Vladimir couldn't wipe away the tears and move along with his life. The tears would not let him do that anymore; they paralyzed him, as did the noise. *Blast. Gunfire. Commands. Blast. Gunfire. Commands.*

Maybe another appointment with Dr. Zaslavsky was in order. They could sit in his ramshackle office and talk things through. Just talk, over and over again, talk, talk, talk. Dr. Zaslavsky would ask him how he felt and Vlad would keep talking. Maybe go on like that for years. But the idea of talking things through did nothing to dampen the noise. It may work for some things, but not for this.

Talking things through would not be his Iskra.

Vlad stumbled down the alley, tears distorting his vision. He steadied himself against the brick, trying to breathe.

***

I stand, grab my rifle, walk toward the smoke and fire. Except for some moaning and random gunfire, it's quiet. Bodies are strewn across the rocks and sand.

"Yurchenko!" I call out. My voice is gravel. "Captain!" I don't see him. I move in closer. "Captain!" Still don't see him.

***

Stumbling a couple more steps, he reached an orange metal door lit from above by a dim bulb. He stopped, leaned one shoulder against the door and took a breath. *Blast. Gunfire. Commands. Blast. Gunfire. Commands.*

Nothing would take away the noise. Not pills, not vodka, not a life of crime. Not life as a sharp-dressed man, not an endless parade of cheap and easy pussy. Not money, not business, not the acquisition of wealth. Talking things through would never cut it. Even boxing couldn't calm the chaos.

Perhaps getting out of the hustle and bustle of city life would help. It was too loud in the city. Everything was a potential trigger. Living out in the country might do the trick. Surrounded with joyful dogs and nature. No television, no newspapers. No bullshit about the fall of Communism or the rise of a New Russia.

But living so far away would mean be no more boxing academy, no friends nearby, no Wednesday night darts. Zhanna would give it a good try, maybe start a dog-grooming business, but she wouldn't be happy living so far from town with a bunch of dogs. Not much opportunity to wear high heels. Resentment would surely set in. To live in the company of dogs would not be his Iskra.

With tears flowing down his face and noise echoing in his head, Vlad slid down the door, buried his head, and cried.

70.

A long, dim shadow formed at the end of the alley to Vlad's left. It was accompanied by slow, light foot strikes. Someone walking down the alley. Whoever it was had a sense of grace and wore a nice pair of boots. Vlad tried his best to wipe the tears away, but couldn't.

***

Two shadowy figures are moving about the smoke. The medics. They are hurt but standing and moving about. I start to move in. "Hey, I'm coming in. I can help!" But all of a sudden, two sharp gunshots ring out. The medics go down. Both shot in the abdomen. I halt in my tracks, grip my rifle.

***

A figure emerged from the darkness. Somewhat tall, slight build, delicate, but masculine nonetheless. A small plume of smoke rose above him, releasing a faint hint of cloves into the icy air. He held something in his left hand.

The figure came to a stop, but shuffled around nervously. Through teary eyes, Vlad saw only sleek, knee-high, black leather boots and a guitar case.

The figure spoke hesitantly. "Um, sir. I need to get in there. I'm, uh, on in thirty minutes."

Vlad looked back over his shoulder and scooted away from the door. "Oh, right. Sorry."

The dark figure said, "*Spasiba*," with much relief and went inside.

Hard rock music blared out as he opened the door. The metal door came to a close and the alley went quiet again.

***

It's quiet. Too quiet now. I have my rifle aimed into the smoke, waiting. Someone has just killed the medics and I don't know where the hell Yurchenko is. The smoke clears a bit. I kick some rocks out of the way.

Three figures emerge. Two muj, their faces covered by scarves. They flank another figure. They have a firm grip on his arms. The man in the middle is short, compact, and platinum blond. It's Captain Yurchenko. The mujahideen have captured Captain Yurchenko.

***

The orange metal door swung open again. Uncontrolled electric guitar, overshadowed by a most high-pitched, piercing voice, filled the alley.

The same dark figure with the guitar case stepped out; silence returned once the door closed again.

"Oy, they are terrible indeed! We really need to screen our warm-up bands better," he sighed. The dark figure stood still for a moment. He placed his guitar case down on the cobblestones and lit a clove cigarette. His feet shuffled around a bit, and then he kneeled down and asked, "Hey, man, are you okay?"

Vladimir brought his head up, finally got a good look at the guy. Early twenties, flawless skin, delicate facial features. His dark hair was shaved into a Mohawk, but it had been combed down. His grayish blue eyes were defined by heavy black eyeliner and long, soft eyelashes. Two small hoops pierced his right ear. The guy looked like he could have been sketched on paper, or rather, chiseled out of pure marble. This young man was downright beautiful, even Vladimir had to admit that much.

Vladimir ran his hands down his own ruddy face and shook his wet hair away, didn't bother wiping away the tears. "No, I haven't been okay since the war. Don't think I ever will be." For the first time, he didn't attempt to cover his pain, didn't try to stay strong. For some reason he felt safe and comforted in this dark, snowy alley sitting across from a perfect specimen of humanity. No need to hide anything.

"We were on a routine supply mission," he said, through waning tears. "When the mujahideen ambushed us. So many good men died that day. I am the only one left. I don't deserve it."

The beautiful young man settled down into a cross-legged position next to his guitar case. He smiled a bit and nodded. "Wow. A sole survivor. Out of the ashes, one man rising," he said wistfully, looking to the sky. "He is above it all. He is flesh. He is stone." He brought his head back down. "That is you, soldier. Truly stoic." Then he pulled a pack of clove cigarettes out of his coat pocket.

"Soldier, you are the stuff of legend," he said, tapping the pack on his lap. "But yes, I can imagine that in the bland routine of day-to-day existence, being a legend could get lonely. The things we get upset over, what we find disturbing, they would be so far beneath you." He offered up the clove. "We mortals. You know. We forget that our fighting men are only human. They, too, bleed. They, too, cry."

Vlad declined the smoke, but asked, "So what's going on here tonight, anyway?"

The beautiful young man chuckled and shoved the cigarette back in its pack, took a drag off his own. "Well, nothing as dramatic as what you have been through, that's for sure. I play lead guitar for Stingray, that's my band. We are playing tonight in the old tearoom."

Vlad nodded. "Oh, yeah, I saw the teenagers lined up. Looks like a big crowd."

The beautiful young man threw his head back and laughed. "Oy! Wish you hadn't told me that. I get so nervous in front of people. That's why I always come in the back way. I'm too shy to talk to fans. Our singer handles all that. He lives for it, actually." He tossed his cigarette to the ground and unlatched his guitar case; brought out an acoustic guitar.

"We play heavy metal mostly; try to model ourselves after the American bands, Poison and Motley Crue. It's all rather silly, really. More of a Depeche Mode fan, myself, but Western-style heavy metal is what pays the bills these days. And really, as long as I'm playing music, I'm perfectly fine. Don't know what I'd do without music." He strummed a few chords.

Then he thrust out one hand and smiled. "So, my name is Demyon."

Vlad took Demyon's thin hand and gave it a hearty shake. "My name is Vladimir." His shake was almost too powerful for such a delicate person, as evidence by the way Demyon grimaced, then laughed. "Whoa. Soldier!"

Demyon struck a few more chords, then paused, looked at Vlad. "Here, why don't you give it a try?" He handed the guitar over and promptly started giving instructions. "See those rectangles on the neck? Those are called frets. Now I'll show you an easy chord. Place your index finger on the second string, second fret, forefinger on the third string, first fret. Strum all but the first string."

Vlad did as he was told. "Like that?" he asked.

Demyon nodded in approval. "That's a B chord. B chord is green, like the trees in spring, rather hopeful and happy, don't you think?"

Vlad stopped, looked up. "Oh, uh. I didn't see any green trees."

He strummed the B chord several more times. Still no green. But yes, it was a little spring-like. Full of energy, rowdy, but restrained.

Demyon smiled. "Okay soldier, now move your third finger down, third fret, first string. Slide the second finger to the second fret, second string. Bring in your pinky on the last string, third fret. Strum all six strings."

Vlad did just that.

Demyon nodded. "Good. That's a G chord. It's yellow, like the sun. It sparkles."

Vladimir scratched his head. "Um. Sparkles? I don't think so." He chuckled, almost embarrassed to even utter the word *sparkles*. He strummed the G chord a few more times. The finger placement felt awkward, and the blend of notes should not have complemented each other, but they did. Strange notes combining to create a unique, brilliant sound.

But Demyon was already moving on. "Okay, soldier, now move your first finger to the fifth string, first fret. Index finger to the second fret on the third string and the third finger goes on the third fret, second string. Strum only strings two through five."

Vlad performed that task, his fingers moving with ease. But before he strummed, he looked up from the strings. "I suppose you are going to say this one sounds like a little fluffy bunny hopping through the forest or something."

Demyon laughed. "No way! You've got a C chord right there, soldier. C is the deepest of blue, like the middle of the ocean at night, right before a storm, extremely serious. C does not joke around and C would most definitely not hop."

Vlad strummed the C several times. He nodded in agreement, not about the color blue, but the C chord did sound awfully serious.

Vlad played through the chords several more times. B, G, C. Each time his fingers moved faster; the music flowed together. B, G, C. It felt easy and natural, B, G, C, as if he'd been playing for years.

Vladimir kept strumming B, G, C, B, G, C, while Demyon looked on, smiling. "Soldier, you are a natural. Do you come from a musical family?"

Vlad handed back the guitar. "Um. Well. Have you ever heard of Konstantin Verstakov? He was a violinist with the Moscow symphony."

Demyon's eyes perked up. "Have I heard of him? Are you kidding me? The man is a god among musicians." He placed the guitar back in its case.

"He was also my father," Vlad said. "Didn't know him that well, but we obviously share some demons."

Demyon nodded as he latched the guitar case shut. "You know, everyone credits Viktor Tsoi and his band KINO with bringing rock music to the mainstream during the late eighties. But just listen to Tsoi's voice, you'll hear Konstantin Verstakov's deep, rich baritone in there." He grabbed the handle and picked up the case. "I'd venture to say that just about every rock musician playing in Russia today was influenced by Konstantin Verstakov and what he did in Moscow that night. He was the ultimate rock star, born in a time when Russians were not allowed to have rock stars. Luckily, his music lives on through all of us."

The door opened again. Another blare of wailing guitar accompanied by a high-pitched scream. Out stepped an older man in jeans and a dirty, white T-shirt. He was scruffy, with a wayward beard and a huge belly. He motioned with both hands. "Demyon, there you are! Come on! You are on in five minutes, kid! We still have to spike up your Mohawk and get you into your spandex suit." He went back inside. The alley went quiet again.

Demyon looked at Vlad and laughed. Vlad laughed, too.

Demyon gave a little salute. "Gotta go, soldier. Take care of yourself." They both stood up. Demyon moved toward the door.

Vlad turned down the alley. "Have a good show, and thanks for the guitar lesson."

Demyon stood with his foot in the door. "You're welcome. Hey, are you sure you're going to be okay?"

Vladimir put his hands in his pockets and nodded. "Yeah, I will be. I have to find something called an Iskra. Something to believe in, calm the demons." He sighed. "I know, it sounds silly, but—"

Demyon stopped Vlad's words with a smile. "No, that does not sound silly. An Iskra, what a beautiful concept. I do hope you find your Iskra." Demyon gave another smile and disappeared behind the door.

71.

The tea room started to shake; reverb tore through the alley like a freight train. With that, Demyon's electric guitar wailed into existence. Vlad laughed to himself as he turned the corner.

On the edge of downtown, traffic was light. Not many people were out. Vlad broke into a jog to keep warm. The few people he passed looked at him as if he'd just robbed a bank. Home was four kilometers away, but he kept running as snow thickened on the ground.

***

"I want you to run, Vlad," calls out Yurchenko. He's weak but he still has the fighting spirit. "Run like hell!"

One of the muj stops. He steps back and bashes Yurchenko in the head with his rifle. Yurchenko stumbles. He's limping badly; they resort to dragging him at times. Looks like he's been shot in the leg.

I recognize these muj. They are the same ones who stood by bandana man as he shot Asef.

I bring my rifle up, so steady and focused. "I'm not going anywhere, Captain. I am going to shoot these motherfuckers and you and I are getting out of here together!"

They throw Yurchenko to the ground. He falls in a heap. One muj takes a shot at me, but misses. I aim my rifle, prepare to fire. But the other muj brings out a knife. He pulls Yurchenko up to his knees and holds the knife to his neck. I bring the rifle down.

The muj with the knife says something in Pashto. Instinctively I turn, as if Asef is by my side, I am so used to him translating. But all I see is a body slumped over by the truck. The muj says it again. He's telling me to drop my weapon, I'm sure of it.

"Don't drop it, Vlad," says Yurchenko. "I'm the one they want. Just run. Run like hell."

I assess the situation. Muj on the left has Yurchenko's rifle. Muj on the right has a knife to Yurchenko's neck. Yurchenko himself is injured. I can't run and leave him behind. Ultimately, I toss the rifle in the sand, in front of my feet. Yurchenko looks at it, heartbroken.

The muj with the knife hoists Yurchenko up to his feet, keeps the knife to his throat. The other guy has his rifle set on me. I keep my hands in the air. "Let him go. Take me instead." They know exactly what I'm saying but they don't budge. A captain as a hostage is better than a foot soldier any day.

Captain Yurchenko and I make eye contact. "Don't tell him it was a knife," he mutters. "My son, Luka, don't let him know it was a knife that killed me. Tell him it was easy."

I shake my head. "I ain't telling him anything, Captain, because you are going home to see him."

He doesn't look as hopeful as I am trying to sound, but he keeps talking. "I sent him a letter before we left, like you suggested. Told him I love him very much, that he is everything to me."

The knife wielding muj wants Yurchenko to shut up, so he knees him in the kidneys.

Yurchenko falls to his knees. The muj leans forward, yanks Yurchenko's head back. He takes the knife to the left side of Yurchenko's neck, slides it sharply to the right. Yurchenko gags and sputters as blood runs down his shirt. Blood is everywhere. All I see is blood.

"Captain!" I lurch forward in an attempt to catch him.

The muj steps toward me with his rifle. He barks out something in Pashto.

This rag head has no idea how fast I am, or how good of a shot I am, or how extremely pissed off I am right now. At the last second, I swipe my rifle off the ground. Without even standing all the way up, or seeing exactly what I am doing, I take two shots. One hits the gut, one hits the head. The muj falls.

The other muj is coming for me, knife in hand.

I can shoot him easily, but I don't. Instead, I take the rifle by the barrel and bash the handle into the side of his head. "We were sent to keep you safe!" I yell.

Blood shoots out his ear. He stumbles sideways. I can't stop. "We were sent to show you Socialist freedoms!" I bash him in the center of his face. He nearly falls. "And this is how you thank us? Huh? By waging war on us! My whole platoon is dead! Asef is dead! He was just a kid. My captain is dead!"

He clumsily makes a move toward me, stabbing the air with the knife. I can't stop. "Get away from me, fuckin' rag head!" I yell.

I bash the other side of his head. His nose, then his gut. He doesn't stand a chance with that knife. Finally, he hits the ground. His face looks like raw meat. I aim my rifle; take a shot. It hits him in the heart. His whole body jerks. I think I hear a moan.

Quickly, I kneel, pat him down, looking for a weapon or a radio. I don't feel confident with a knife, so I toss it.

From the inside of his jacket, I pull a small stack of documents and papers. His identification papers, all typed in swirly Pashto, and a few black and white snapshots. One photo shows an Afghan woman, pretty, with long hair, in her early twenties, smiling, holding a sleeping infant girl. A small boy stands at her side, smiling, and holding a stuffed elephant. He has chubby arms.

I stand up, take a step back. The papers and photos litter the sand one by one from my hand. This guy was the muj. The rag head. The enemy. A father. A husband. A son. Maybe he was a teacher or a policeman before joining up with the rebel forces. His wife will wait up; worried. That chubby-armed little boy will clutch his stuffed elephant tonight and cry.

I fall to my knees, clutch my stomach, and vomit. Yurchenko is beside me. His eyes are open, forever fixed on the battlefield, still a steely blue. I touch his chest, his blood is still warm. I reach over and close his eyes.

Again, I vomit on the sand, all the tea and olives the Taliban served to us. As I start to stand up, I hear a distinct crack of glass. Something is under my heel, buried partially in the sand. I brush the sand away and reach down. It's Asef's glasses. They are bent and have a bloody smudge on the right lens, a slight crack, too.

I fold Asef's glasses, slide them in my pocket, and grab Yurchenko's rifle. I take off.

I am running like hell.

72.

SVERDLOVSK, RUSSIA, SOVIET UNION AND YEKATERINBURG, RUSSIAN FEDERATION

31 December 1991-1 January 1992

Ten minutes to midnight on New Year's Eve, but the gathering in October Park was hardly the festive party of years past. Grumblings about bread lines, complaints of empty shelves, sky-high inflation, a nation's currency in the toilet was all Vladimir heard as he walked into the park from the north entrance.

He pulled his stocking cap down below his ears. Zhanna had given him a decent haircut the other day, no more unruly locks. It looked much better short and neatly clipped about the sides, but he couldn't go without a hat these days, or his ears froze.

Zhanna was heading west, coming from a New Year's party with her employees, clicking along in high-heeled black boots, dressed in a black skirt and black tights. Her flimsy black coat was tied at the waist, no zipper. The plum-colored beret perched on the side of her head looked stylish against her long, blonde hair, but not at all practical.

Vladimir met up with her near the flagpole. "Hey, Zha-Zha." He gave her a kiss. And as if on automatic pilot, he took off his own coat and wrapped it around her.

"Hey," she smiled. Together they looked up in silence.

Lit from below by a large spotlight, the Soviet flag, in brilliant red with its golden hammer and sickle in the top, right-hand corner, billowed overhead in the icy wind. A solidly built soldier close to retirement age stood at the base of the flagpole. Five more uniformed soldiers stood at attention behind him, red berets atop their heads, rifles held diagonally across their chests.

"Guess we won't be seeing that flag again," Zhanna said.

"You're right," Vlad replied, lighting a cigarette. "In ten minutes we won't even be the Soviet Union anymore."

Vladimir took a drag and exhaled. He put an arm around Zhanna. "So what is the status of Salon Americana?"

Zhanna looked up at him with a glossy red smile. "It's still mine. The judge ruled I had no knowledge that the funds used to buy the building were co-mingled, so I retain ownership." She tightened Vlad's coat around her and crossed her arms. "To top it all off, the KGB is fuming. They fired Fyodor and Grigory for using agency recruits and agency time to conduct their own personal business. They are also pressing criminal charges against them. Fyodor and Grigory each face eighteen months in prison and one year of community service."

Vladimir nodded. "Good. They won't be a problem anymore."

"Oh, and this is interesting," perked Zhanna, grabbing at Vlad's arm. "The Café Club building was just bought by Grigory and Fyodor's wives in a state auction, since Pasha abandoned it. They are turning it into a flower shop, with 20 percent of the proceeds going to area orphanages."

Again, Vlad nodded. "That's a good use for the place." He made a mental note to purchase flowers from that place every single day.

The entire park went quiet. No more grumbling, no more complaints, just an entire country about to change. The solidly built soldier reached up and pulled on the rope. The Soviet flag, still proud and billowing, slowly crept down the pole. A few quiet minutes passed while the soldier properly folded the expired flag.

A young boy walked by wearing a red scarf around his neck, a stack of newspapers in his arms. He held up a single newspaper. "*Sverdlovsk Times*! Get your last *Sverdlovsk Times* newspaper right here! Hurry, there will be no more!"

Vlad checked his watch. The kid was right, in two minutes, the city of Sverdlovsk would cease to exist, right along with the rest of the country. At midnight, the city would return to its original name, Yekaterinburg.

The soldier reached up again, this time pulling one hand over the other. A new flag with three horizontal stripes—white, blue, and red, started to rise. It billowed just as proudly as the old one.

Zhanna and a few other people clapped as the flag rose. Some people looked relieved, some nervous, others turned and left the park altogether. Vladimir glanced at his watch again. "Midnight. It's official. We are no longer the Soviet Union."

Zhanna smiled. "Russian Federation. I like the sound of that."

The flag rippled overhead. A collective *click* of five soldiers, each with a rifle, broke the silence. It came just as the solidly built soldier finished his task. The resulting bang of five rifles shooting to the sky in unison made Vladimir jump. There came another bang. And another.

Vladimir's throat constricted. He dropped his chin to his chest to catch a breath. *Blast. Gunfire. Commands. Blast. Gunfire. Commands.* Beads of sweat formed along his forehead. His tongue immediately went dry; his head ached with each inhalation. The soldiers fired again. There would be twelve altogether. The noise hung in the air and echoed throughout Vlad's head.

***

The sun is not yet high, but it is already stifling hot as I step outside the mess hall. I have to squint. I walk across base to my truck. My entire platoon is out here, busy, getting ready to move out on our supply mission. I can see the platoon so clearly. My men. These are my guys. They are alive. Right here, right now, everyone is alive.

***

"They're dead," Vladimir muttered into his hands. "They're all dead." Another loud bang from the rifles, battle mode. He looked around for a place to hide from the enemy.

Zhanna placed a hand on Vlad's shoulder, snapping him back to reality. "Are you all right, baby? I didn't know it would be so loud, let's go some place quiet." She pulled on his shirt as she started to walk away.

Another loud pop from the rifles. *Blast. Gunfire. Commands. Blast. Gunfire. Commands.* Vladimir remained still. He took Zhanna's hand, pulling her back. "No. I need to stay. Can't keep drowning my demons like my father did. You said once that you wanted to live life. Well, so do I."

Zhanna's face brightened. "You remember me saying that? Viva, I don't even remember saying that!"

Vlad nodded. "Yeah, you said it the night we met. And it's what got me out of that damn desert."

Another bang of the rifles. *Blast. Gunfire. Commands. Blast. Gunfire. Commands.*

Blast. Blast. Blast. Blas. Blas. Bl. Bl. B. B. B. The B chord. Index finger on the second string, second fret. Forefinger on first fret, third string. Full of energy, a little rowdy, but restrained. *Red and Danil, two soldiers, highly amused as they pull up alongside my truck that has a flat tire. Danil is leaning out his window with his middle finger in the air, a huge smile on his face. He's shouting, "What the hell happened, getting a blow job from the towel head or something?" Red is hunched over the steering wheel, laughing his ass off.*

Vlad chuckled at the memory. His breath regulated. He stood a bit straighter.

He took a breath. "Hey, Zha-Zha, you know I did some bad things when I worked with Pasha. Basically, I was a thug for hire. I'm not proud of it, and I need to make amends as much as possible. So I have already confessed everything to Rogusskii. And as my punishment, he decided that he and I are going to start a discussion group for war veterans. We'll meet once a week to talk things through. Dr. Zaslavsky is on board to facilitate the group."

Zhanna smiled. "I think that is a wonderful idea! There is a beautiful studio downtown next door to the salon. It has new windows with beautiful, flowing curtains. I can make tea and snacks and...and...and you could have guest speakers and, oh, there are so many things you could do!"

Vlad shook his head and laughed. "Are you nuts? We are men! We don't want snacks and flowing curtains. No one will talk with all that prissy crap going on. We are going to smoke and swear and drink cheap, bitter tea. I'm eyeing an abandoned tire factory south of town. It's more our style."

He nudged her arm. "But you should rent the studio, expand the salon, or sell your Karina Baby Tote bags there."

Zhanna raised her eyebrows. "Hmmm, that's not a bad idea. I've been thinking about a line of baby blankets and bibs to match the tote bags." She smiled and touched his nose. "See? There you go again. You are always infusing me with ideas and inspiration."

Another pop of the rifles. The noise returned. *Blast. Gunfire. Commands. Blast. Gunfire. Commands.*

Gunfire. Gunfire. Gun. Gun. G. G. G. The G chord. First string, third fret. Second fret, second string. Bring pinky to last string, third fret. Strum string two through five. An awkward mixture of sounds. It works, but you wouldn't think it would. Like Asef, an Afghan teen. Brilliant, yet stunted in maturity, needing more than anything to be heard. Constantly smiling, pushing up his glasses. *"Vlad-ee-meer, this is so great! Working with you has been the best summer of my life. I will always remember this summer!"*

Vlad smiled at the memory. His stomach settled. His heart rate slowed. He tossed his cigarette aside. "Hey, I found a new apartment. Had to use the rest of my cash to bribe the caretaker, but I got it."

Zhanna bit her lower lip and looked down. "Hmmm."

Vlad folded his hands. "And it's within walking distance of the salon."

Zhanna smiled but otherwise ignored him.

He looked up to the sky. "Did I mention there's space for an extra closet?"

Zhanna finally relented. "Okay, tell me more," she said with a laugh.

"There's space to build a closet just for your shoes. I've already bought the materials. Four shelves. Nothing but shoes. Just think of it. If you don't use it, I'll just fill it up with my tools."

Zhanna shuddered. "Well, in that case," she brushed her hair aside as she reached into her purse. She brought out the envelope with the divorce papers and handed them over. "I don't think these have a spot in the new place," she said with a smile.

He took the envelope and stuffed it in his back pocket. "We can make a fresh start."

Zhanna smiled, leaning in closer. "A fresh start. I like that."

Another pop of the rifles. *Blast. Gunfire. Commands. Blast. Gunfire. Commands.*

Commands. Commands. Commands. Comm. Comm. Com. C. C. C. The C chord. Deadly serious; the deepest ocean, calm and still in the eyes of a storm. Captain Yurchenko standing with a clipboard in hand, ordering all brave Russian troops to move out. *"Listen to me, Verstakov, you are an old soul; far smarter and stronger than you give yourself credit for."*

Vlad felt a sense of warm calm sweep from head to gut. He looked at Zhanna. "I've been thinking about completing my degree. I've got forty credits of math and science already and I think I would be a good engineer. What do you think?"

Zhanna laughed and threw her head back. "Engineering sounds perfect for you. Now will you please just kiss me? We are about to enter a whole new country. A whole new city. A whole new year!" She held her arms out. "And you and me are making a fresh start!"

Vladimir leaned in and planted his lips on hers as the final four shots blasted into the sky. The noise did not abate entirely, probably never would, but it died down enough for the fog to lift, allowing for the positive experiences of war to shine through. Vladimir had found his Iskra. He pulled away. "The guitar, that makes sense. Konstantin is still around, after all."

Zhanna looked at him completely blank. "What do you mean by that, Viva?" Vladimir shrugged. "It's nothing." He kissed her again, feeling himself becoming a better man.

ACKNOWLEDGEMENTS

Thank you: Diana Garrett, Mark Harbert, Gail Cleary, Jason Ulven, Sally Mallicoat, Angela Norse, Leslie Ulven, for endless reading; Bridget Laird and CreateSpace for endless editing; and Mark for endless everything else.

A Better Man playlist

The following songs, for one reason or another, provided an Iskra for *A Better Man*.

"One"	(Metallica)
"Fell on Black Days"	(Soundgarden)
"It's Not My Time"	(Three Doors Down)
"Hey Man Nice Shot"	(Filter)
"Shadow of the Day"	(Linkin' Park)
"It's Been Awhile"	(Staind)

Further Reading

The occupation of Afghanistan, Soviet or otherwise, is superbly documented by Steve Coll in *Ghost Wars: The Secret History of the CIA, Afghanistan and Bin Laden from the Soviet Invasion to September 10, 2001.* (Penguin, 2004)

If interested in the technical aspects of the war, please read *The Soviet-Afghan War: How a Superpower Fought and Lost* (Kansas, 2002)

For a mujahideen point of view, see Jalali and Grau, *Afghan Guerilla Warfare: In the Words of the Mujahideen Fighters.* (MBI Publishing, 1995)

A wonderful look at Russian life, post-Soviet. Service, Robert. *Russia, Experiment with a People (*Harvard, 2003)

A great book with a fantastic title: *Everything Was Forever, Until It Was No More*; *The Last Soviet Generation.* Alexei Yurchak. (Princeton, 2006)

For a very interesting, and at times, hilarious look back in time, try to find a copy of *Lonely Planet USSR–A Travel Survival Guide* by John King and John Noble (Lonely Planet Pub. 1991)

Numerous Web sites, newspaper and magazine articles went into making *A Better Man* hopefully, all the better.

Spasiba for reading. A. Lynn

Audrey Lynn lives in Missoula, Montana, with her husband and two children. *A Better Man* is her first novel. Running is her Iskra.

Read more Vladimir Verstakov in,

Vital Presence

Second in the Better Man series.
Coming soon.

GROZNY, REPUBLIC OF CHECHNYA. 1050 KM. SOUTHEAST OF MOSCOW

October 1993

A flashlight balanced perilously atop the makeshift saw-horse. The light from it eclipsed each time the police officer came forward to deliver another swift kick to the temple, but it came back into view as he stepped aside. The light was a constant, and in a strange way, an anchor. Doku was relieved to see it again each time. The light meant he was still alive, however little his life was worth at this moment.

Doku sat slumped, handcuffed, against a dilapidated barn far from his bustling downtown apartment. Heavy, wet snow dropped from the night sky like lumpy wads of paste; no one around but drunken Russian cops who were having a great time hurling punches, throwing kicks throughout the night.

But there was the flashlight. At least there was the light.

The cop lording above lit a cigarette, then pulled out a small notepad from his knee-length, fur-lined coat. "I will ask you again," he barked. "Where did you get the drugs and alcohol? I need names." He nudged Doku in the ribs with his bulky leather boot as he spoke.

Doku could only groan as he had few teeth remaining after the endless night of beatings. Thick droplets of blood fell onto his lips from the gash on his forehead. The blood seeped into his mouth, coating his tongue, but he could no longer taste it, no longer had the strength to swallow.

The cop squatted down, took a slow drag, and exhaled a plume of smoke in Doku's face. "I asked you a question." He said. "We know you did not orchestrate all of this because you are a stupid, little fuck. So, I will ask you one more time." He tapped his cigarette; ashes flickered down upon Doku's jeans. "Who is your supplier?"

Doku struggled to shove the cop, but only managed a weak head butt. He strained to form his words. "You think...you're better...than me?..Fuck...you." He tried to spit on the guy, but gagged on the blood pooling at the back of his throat.

The cop shot up with another swift kick to the temple, sending Doku to his side. With no strength left, he flopped over onto his belly. The cop stomped down between his shoulder blades, mashing his face into the gravel.

Gingerly, Doku turned his head, spitting out blood and bits of rock in the process. "Nuura. Where...is... she? Where's...Nuura?" No response from above, just a chuckle. Doku struggled to breathe as the light grew brighter, the edges fuzzier.

Just days ago, Doku had been flush with cash, showering his new bride with gifts. Nuura was so happy; laughing, her eyes lit up like stars, until the black van pulled up and the cops jumped out. Now, he was trying to survive by staring at a light, his only solace.

And Nuura was inside the barn. The cops dragged her in. She had fought hard, even drew blood with her fingernails, but they easily overpowered her. For half the night, he heard her muffled screams, now all was quiet.

Heavy, smoke-laden breath filled the air. The cop was now at his ear. "Possession of alcohol, dealing drugs. Not a very good Muslim now, are you?" The few cops lingering about all laughed as they shot back more vodka. The cop snuffed the cigarette butt into Doku's neck. He screamed with all the strength he had left, which wasn't much. His head abruptly yanked backwards.

"Get up, goddammit!" said the cop and Doku at once was forced to his knees. Another belligerent cop stood near the sawhorse, one thigh eclipsing half the light. He brought his arm up and took aim.

Doku glanced over his shoulder. "Nuura...I'm... sorry...Nuura." He could only mumble as blood leaked from his mouth down his chin. He looked ahead, wavering back and forth. The rays of light blurred into one giant mass. Doku gave into it, allowed the light to take over his entire being.

The cop next to him laughed as he lit another cigarette. "Nuura. Sweet Nuura. Oh, yes, we've been enjoying Nuura."

A blast of the gun, and Doku dropped to the ground like stone, choking on the last breath he would ever take in his twenty-three years of life. Lights out.

EIGHT
MONTHS
LATER...

1.

MOSCOW, RUSSIA

Friday, 4 June 1994. 4:48 p.m.

The meeting of ALFA brigade's counter-terrorism department was coming to a close, but Special Agent Alexei Danchenko stood up and cleared his throat. "Sir, if there is time, I have one more item to discuss," he said. A collective groan flowed around the table. It was Friday afternoon after all and Alexei was known for his painfully exhaustive presentations. But today he would be concise, it was that important.

From across the table, gray-haired Commander Pavovich leaned forward as he pulled the cigarette from his craggy lips. "What is it, Lex?

Alexei took a breath. "Recruitment, sir. I would like to discuss recruitment."

His Commander's deadpan look was not encouraging but Alexei went on. "Sir, in these days of post-Soviet restructuring, I think we can all agree, ALFA brigade is hanging by a thread. We've lost half of our senior agents for better jobs overseas, and Russia has become a target for terrorist activity."

He looked down at his clipboard. "Since the Soviet Union dissolved, Moscow alone has witnessed the torching of two government buildings, there have been nine brutal beatings of journalists, and—" He tossed the clipboard aside because the facts seemed too cold now, too sterile. "And, sir, that suicide bombing last week at the post office went down completely undetected. Five innocent Russians are now dead, including a twelve year-old kid. We had no idea anything was even in the works."

He took a breath and pinched the space between his eyes. "Sir, my department can't work like this anymore. I...I can't work like this anymore."

Commander Pavovich nodded. He laid his cigarette down and folded his hands beneath his chin. "What do you suggest we do, Lex?"

Alexei pushed his glasses up. "Sir, intelligence shows that all of these acts have been committed by Islamic radicals from Chechnya. As head of Chechen Intelligence, I am telling you, I need more resources and more men."

Commander Pavovich nodded, motioned for Alexei to go on.

"Okay." Alexei said, with his hands out to his sides. "This is what we know. There is someone in Grozny, most likely a religious scholar on the fringe, he's sending his minions east to Kazakhstan where they slip over the border into Russia. That way they enter our largest cities from the east where security is not as tight."

Alexei leaned forward. "Now, I've already alerted border patrol, but bottom line, we need to boost our anti-terrorism division out east. Yekaterinburg is our biggest division over there, I suggest we recruit more agents in Yekaterinburg."

Alexei sat down and exhaled for the first time during the past five minutes. At least he had said what he needed to say.

Commander Pavovich went quiet as he rifled through his notes, took another drag off his cigarette. "Our funds are tight, but Lex, if you are right and the Chechens are sending Martyrs to blow themselves up on Russian soil, this sounds like something we need to do." He looked up at Alexi, pressing down on his reading glasses. "We can take on one, maybe two men. Go ahead and call the Yekaterinburg division. Have them search the military archives, police departments, security agencies, whatever they need to do to find some good candidates. Tell them the Chechens are winning and we need more manpower right away."

Alexei nodded, finally able to relax. "Yes sir. I will call the Yekaterinburg office. *Spasiba*, sir."

CPSIA information can be obtained at www.ICGtesting.com
Printed in the USA
LVOW041624310112

266405LV00001B/104/P

9 780615 449685